"I want the twins to dream whatever they want to dream." Cassie truly meant those words.

"You'd probably make a good talent agent for kids," said Adam.

"Me?" Cassie snickered. "Hardly. I like my orderly career in web programming. It makes the rest of life's messiness easier to face."

"You're great with computers, but you also have solid instincts for people."

The compliment was sincere, but it was the look in his eyes that made her pulse jump. When Adam leaned closer and kissed her, it was everything it should have been. His lips were firm, his arms strong and gentle. But the moment was so brief, it left her aching for more.

Dear Reader,

I'm so excited to have my next Emerald City story published with Harlequin Heartwarming.

My hero, Adam Wilding, is a special guy who became a famous model more or less by accident. Now he's embarked on a second career as a talent agent, and he has his hands full with Cassie Bryant, the aunt and guardian of his two newest clients. Cassie can be a little prickly, but she's fiercely protective of her niece and nephew.

The two cats in my household have an odd relationship—the female dislikes all other felines, and the male just wants to play. There's a great deal of spitting, but not the all-out war that we expected. Over time it's become clear that a certain amount of affection has grown between the two.

Relationships aren't easy, but the fun part of writing is that I don't have to just wait and watch. Adam and Cassie have a number of hurdles to overcome before they find their way together... but I enjoyed showing how they got there.

I love hearing from readers and can be contacted at: c/o Harlequin Books, 22 Adelaide Street West, 40th Floor, Toronto, Ontario, Canada M5H 4E3. Please also check out my Facebook page at Facebook.com/callie.endicott.author.

Best wishes,

Callie

HEARTWARMING

A Father for the Twins

—

Callie Endicott

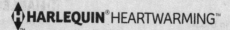

Recycling programs
for this product may
not exist in your area.

ISBN-13: 978-1-335-63368-2

A Father for the Twins

Printed in U.S.A.

www.Harlequin.com

As a kid, **Callie Endicott** had her nose stuck in a book so often it frequently got her in trouble. The trouble hasn't stopped—she keeps having to buy new bookshelves. Luckily ebooks don't take up much space. Writing has been another help, since she's usually on the computer creating stories instead of buying them. Callie loves bringing characters to life and never knows what will prompt an idea. So she still travels, hikes, explores and pursues her other passions, knowing a novel may be just around the corner.

Books by Callie Endicott

Harlequin Heartwarming

Emerald City Stories

Moonlight Over Seattle

Montana Skies

The Rancher's Prospect
At Wild Rose Cottage
Kayla's Cowboy

That Summer at the Shore
Until She Met Daniel

Visit the Author Profile page at Harlequin.com for more titles.

To Ruby and Albert

PROLOGUE

ADAM WILDING WANTED to turn the car around and drive away from his parents' house, but that didn't seem very mature for a college student. He had to face telling them the truth.

The golden late afternoon light played on the Sandia Mountains in the background. Dried red chile ristras hung on the porches and thousands of luminarias lined the yards and walkways of homes, ready to be lit once it was dark.

He'd grown up in New Mexico and the sights and scents of Albuquerque brought back an avalanche of memories. Especially at Christmastime.

His nerves tightened even more as he turned into the driveway. Three months had passed since his mother's emergency heart surgery, but it was never far from his thoughts.

Elizabeth Wilding must have been watching, because she met him at the door. He looked at her closely. She *seemed* healthy. There was good color in her cheeks and her eyes were bright and lively.

"Hey, Mom." Adam stepped inside and kissed her cheek. "Merry Christmas."

"Merry Christmas, dear. Are you well?" she asked anxiously. That was his mom—always concerned about everyone else's health.

"I'm great."

Dermott Wilding appeared from the back of the house. He was thinner than when Adam had seen him a couple of months earlier. "Merry Christmas, son. Did you have a good trip?"

"Not too bad. There was snow in Flagstaff, but I got through it okay." When time wasn't an issue, he preferred driving over flying when traveling from Los Angeles to Albuquerque.

"Are your classes for next term lined up?" Dermott asked. "You can't take anything frivolous, you know, it might look bad on your application to law school," he added without waiting for an answer.

Adam managed a tight nod. Ever since he could remember, his parents had expected him to grow up and become an attorney. It had been the same with Sophie. How often had they heard their father say, "My children are going to be respected lawyers instead of working stiffs like me"? Along with, "Before you know it, Adam and Sophie will be on the Supreme Court." To Dermott Wilding, being appointed to the US Supreme Court was the ultimate success.

"Is Sophie here?" Adam asked.

"Right behind you."

He turned and gave her a hug. "Hey, sis, where's the ponytail?"

"Gave it up, along with my tricycle."

"Sophie is such wonderful help around the house," Elizabeth declared, yet sounded anxious again. "But she hasn't been able to enjoy her new school."

"It's okay, Mom," Sophie told her quickly.

Adam had wanted to take the fall term off at UCLA to help take care of his mother, but the idea of him interrupting his life had upset his parents so much, he'd decided it would do more harm than good. As a result, too much responsibility had dropped onto his sister's shoulders.

"I hope you're hungry," Elizabeth said.

"Starved."

They went into the kitchen for pozole, a traditional Christmas Eve soup in New Mexico made of hominy and meat and seasoned with various toppings.

"Fantastic as always," he said after the first spoonful. "It wouldn't be Christmas without your pozole, Mom."

"Thank you, but Sophie made it."

"Great job, kiddo."

Sophie just shrugged.

An awkward silence fell and Adam decided to give his parents his news. "Mom, Dad, you know how much I've wanted to do something to help out?"

They nodded.

"Well, I saw a notice about this company wanting new faces for a marketing campaign. I sent my picture in, and after a several interviews and stuff, they picked me to act in their commercial. And now I've got a bunch of other modeling work scheduled. The money is really good, so I'll be able to contribute toward paying the bills. I have a check for you."

Dermott's face grew tight. "You're a pre-law junior. You have to focus on grades, not add another job. Especially modeling. It's vain and superficial."

Adam let out a breath. "There's nothing wrong with modeling and it earns a heck of a lot more than minimum wage, which is what my other job at the college paid."

"Paid?" his father repeated. "That means you've quit."

"Yeah. Like I said, modeling pays more." Actually, Adam had been shocked at the fees his new talent agent had negotiated for him. If it kept up, he'd be able to cover the rest of his mother's medical bills and all of his college expenses.

"How will you be taken seriously as an attorney if people know you've paraded around, selling some product?" Dermott demanded. "I want my children to have respect, not be laughed at."

"I'm not parading, I'm modeling, and nobody is laughing."

Adam decided not to add that he'd switched from pre-law to another major. Being a lawyer was his parents' goal for him, but he'd become convinced over the past year that he wasn't cut out for a legal career.

In all honesty, he'd never been that interested. As for modeling? It was fun and there was a lot of money that could be made. If he hit it really big, he could save enough to retire early and start a whole new career. He wasn't sure what that career might be, but he knew it would be something he wanted, rather than a dream of his parents'.

"No," Dermott barked. "That isn't—"

"Would you quit it? You're upsetting Mom," Sophie suddenly yelled.

Shocked, they all looked at Elizabeth, who was pale and had her hand to her throat.

"I'm...okay," she gasped. Yet her face lost even more color and Adam saw beads of perspiration dotting her forehead.

He barely managed to catch her as she pitched forward in the chair.

TWO HOURS LATER at the hospital, Elizabeth Wilding's heart specialist glared at Adam and his father equally.

"Mrs. Wilding is going to be all right. She hyperventilated due to anxiety and passed out. But how many times have I said that she requires rest and calm? She worries far too much, and I'm convinced she feels guilty for getting sick in the first place. Regardless, having the two most important men in her life squabbling like boys in a school yard is unacceptable."

"How can she feel guilty for needing heart surgery?" Adam asked, bewildered.

"Because that's how patients with a major illness often feel. It's human nature."

"It isn't logical."

"Agreed, but the emotions are real. I've seen it over and over again. Now, as to the argument between you and your father, that's the last thing she needs to hear at this point in her recovery." Dr. Chu crossed her arms over her chest and her glare became even more severe, except this time it was specifically directed at Adam's father. "So your son is modeling to help pay the bills and you don't approve. *Deal with it.* One of Elizabeth's concerns is about money."

Dermott, who was at least ten inches taller than the surgeon, flushed and looked abashed. "I'm sorry, ma'am. It's just that Adam won't be respected in the legal—"

"Frankly, I don't care how you feel about it," Dr. Chu interrupted. "My concern is Mrs. Wilding. She has a full, happy life ahead *if* her family resists putting undue stress on her. Now, I've said a whole lot more than I'd intended, but I don't appreciate a patient's recovery being hindered this way. I trust that I won't have to say any of this again in the future?"

"No, Doctor," Dermott and Adam declared in unison.

"Good."

Dr. Chu gave Sophie a reassuring smile, then turned and marched down the hallway.

Adam and his father glanced at each other.

"Are you going to keep modeling?" Dermott asked.

"Who cares?" Sophie hissed. "Adam can do whatever he wants. Just give his check to the hospital. I have to keep hiding the bills from Mom because she gets upset and I'm sick of it." With that, she burst into tears.

Feeling awful, Adam fished the certified check from his wallet and handed it to his dad before putting an arm around Sophie's shoulders. At twelve, she'd had too much put on her the past few months.

"Fine. For now," Dermott muttered. He turned and headed down the hallway. Clearly he hadn't given up, just temporarily retreated.

Adam ground his teeth, knowing a part of him blamed his father for Mom's illness. Okay, maybe that wasn't fair. But Dermott was her husband and he'd been there, every day. Why hadn't he noticed his wife losing energy and the other slow, insidious signs of declining health? She might have gotten treatment earlier, before it came to a crisis.

Adam squirmed at the thought, knowing he could have returned to Albuquerque for the summer and gotten a construction job. Then he would have been at home, too. Instead he'd stayed in Los Angeles, helping build swimming pools for the Hollywood elite and hanging out with his friends.

So if he wanted to blame anyone, he didn't need to look any further than his own mirror.

CHAPTER ONE

Fourteen years later...

A KNOCK SOUNDED on Adam's office door and he looked up to see Nicole George, one of his three business partners.

"Hey, Nicole, you seem excited."

She grinned. "I just learned that a new TV movie is going to be shot here in the Seattle area. They're hoping the network will like it enough to turn it into a series. The casting director saw Doria Atchison in the clip we posted online and was impressed enough that he's emailing a list of what they're looking for. Auditions won't be for a little while, but it sounds promising."

"Excellent."

When he and his friends had bought the Moonlight Ventures talent agency, one of their concerns had been that Seattle wasn't at the heart of the fashion or entertainment industry.

Local business was fine, but they also wanted broader exposure for their clients.

Their concerns had proved unfounded, though. Several of their models had already gotten television ads for national campaigns and they'd placed actors with two movies being filmed locally, as well as guest and extras spots with a network series based in the region.

"I'll forward the list as soon as I get it," Nicole assured. She was an exceptionally beautiful woman, but ever since she'd gotten engaged, her face possessed a special glow. If she hadn't quit modeling, it would be easy to pick up the phone and get her a dozen top contracts.

Adam almost chuckled at the thought; after just a few weeks on the job, he was already thinking more like an agent than a model. Nicole had run Moonlight Ventures by herself for months, though he and their other partners, Logan Kensington and Rachel Clarion, had flown in regularly and teleconferenced with her. Now that his own modeling contracts had been satisfied, he'd started working at the agency full time.

"How is the writing going?" he asked. The previous owner of the agency had put out a quarterly trade newsletter, but they were working toward converting it to a general circulation publication. For the launch issue Adam wanted a feature piece by Nicole about "lessons learned" from her years as a supermodel.

She scrunched her nose at him. "Slowly."

"Anything I can do to help?" he asked.

"You can tell me you've changed your mind about having me write it."

"Afraid I can't."

Actually, Adam felt bad that they'd asked her to be "the story" again, as Nicole put it. Ironically, it was when *PostModern* magazine had asked to do a series of articles about her transition from supermodel to agent that she'd met her fiancé.

Technically she'd simply met Jordan *again*, having known him as a kid. Jordan had still written the articles, telling readers that while he was now engaged to the subject of his interviews, he'd tried to be unbiased—but might have failed. In response, the articles had been well received, which had been good for the agency.

In turn, Nicole had penned a piece for the agency's blog about Jordan and the process of being interviewed. The popularity of the blog site had convinced them it was worth giving their own magazine a shot.

"I had to try," she said. With another grin and a flip of her hand, she rushed out again.

Adam rubbed the back of his neck, thinking about the years he'd known Nicole. He'd watched her go from being hopeful about falling in love to being convinced it could never happen for her. Now she'd come full circle, deeply in love and full of plans for a future with Jordan.

He was glad she was happy.

He'd like to find that kind of happiness himself again, but it wasn't easy. He'd been engaged for a brief, wonderful time to a woman he'd met while still at UCLA and wouldn't settle for second best.

Isabelle had charged at life with enthusiasm and laughter, unconcerned by his growing success as a model. He'd always known where he was with her—first when they were just friends, and later when they were falling in love and deciding to get married. But a brain aneurism had changed everything in the blink of an eye.

Renewed grief went through Adam at the memory. One minute Isabelle had been there, the next she was gone.

It had taken a long time to be ready for another serious relationship, and then the frequent travel and the less-than-kind scrutiny of the press had played havoc with his dating life—lots of first and second dates, few beyond that. Maybe it would be different now. He'd like to find someone confident and outgoing, who shared his interests and could be a real partner.

Not like his parents.

Adam sighed, knowing he was being unfair. His parents had a good marriage, but it had always seemed as if his mother's needs came second, at least until her heart problems developed. As for shared interests? Hardly. Dad was interested in construction, period. Mom was a science fiction and fantasy buff. She loved to write and had wanted to earn a place among authors like Arthur C. Clarke and J.R.R. Tolkien. Instead she'd slogged away at a dull teleservice job because it was secure and helped earn money for her children's educations.

Adam got up and moved restlessly around his office, pausing to look out the window at the trees that softened his view of the street.

He felt bad that his parents hadn't pursued their own dreams instead of ones for their children. It wasn't just his mother—his father's plan to become a contractor had been deemed too great a risk to the family's financial security, so Dermott had done construction for someone else and taken jobs as a handyman in his spare hours.

Just then Adam's personal line rang, breaking into his musings. The caller ID displayed his sister's number.

"Hey, Sophie." He could hear his nephew and niece in the background, shrieking and giggling. Bobby and Lila were great, but like most kids they could be loud. "What's up?"

"The twins had friends over this weekend and now I want to speak with someone closer to my own age."

He grinned. "How bad was it?"

"We had a serious outbreak of video games, *Star Wars* battles and *The Lone Ranger*."

"The Lone Ranger?"

"I made the mistake of bringing out my classic TV DVDs and the next thing I knew they were all running around with pretend six-shooters, trying to catch pretend bank robbers and cattle rustlers. Mom retreated to my bedroom along with the cat."

Adam sat back in his chair. He was proud of his kid sister for making a tough situation work. She'd gotten pregnant at seventeen and married her boyfriend, only to have him leave before the twins were born.

Now Sophie had a brisk mail-order business selling New Mexico–themed Christmas ornaments and decorations she made herself. That way she'd avoided childcare costs for the twins—which would have outstripped any income from a minimum-wage job—and was still able to make a decent living using her artistic talents. To Adam's frustration, she'd even insisted on repaying the checks he'd sent after her brief marriage fell apart, though they'd been a gift.

"How is Mom adjusting to them both being retired?" he asked.

"Pretty good. But I should warn you, I think the folks are planning a trip to Seattle this summer to see you."

Gripping the phone, Adam counted to ten. "Any special reason? I was home two months ago and expect to come for Christmas as usual."

"I don't think so."

"Surely they don't think I'm going to change my mind about becoming a lawyer. They must know it isn't in the cards." Even when he and his friends were buying Moonlight Ventures, his father had suggested it wasn't too late for graduate school, unable to resist trying to resurrect the remnants of his old ambition.

"I think they're getting resigned to your new career, especially since it means you won't be gazing back at them from magazine covers in the grocery checkout line. You know how stuffy Dad can be. Seeing you in those swimsuit editions used to really get him going."

Adam rubbed the back of his neck. He was sorry it bothered his parents that he didn't have the career they'd chosen for him, but he had the right to live as he saw fit. Nevertheless, maybe the agency's success would alleviate their vague sense of failure since "our son is a businessman" must sound more respectable to them. While he didn't crave their approval, he wanted them to be happy.

"But get this," Sophie added, "remember when Dad cut his hand and Lila kept helping change the bandage?"

"Yeah."

"Now he thinks she should become a doctor."

Adam instinctively tensed. "But she's only eight years old." He understood where his worry came from. It had taken him long enough to shake off family expectations.

"I know." A crash reverberated through the

phone and she sighed. "Sorry, I'd better go see what happened."

"Tell the little terrors 'hi' for me."

They said goodbye and Adam started going through the seemingly bottomless stack of photographs and videos received each day at Moonlight Ventures. Few of the submissions possessed the special something they wanted as a signature aspect of the agency, but occasionally they found someone in the pile who stood out.

A couple of the pictures were interesting and he put them aside to ask Nicole's opinion. It might have been useful to have his other partners take a look as well, but it wasn't practical. Rachel wouldn't be on board for several weeks, and Logan still had a few months left on his photography contracts. They didn't have time to agree on every decision.

At length, Adam turned to the picture of the prospective client he was meeting with at 1:00 p.m. Her aunt would be there as well. Tiffany Bryant was thirteen, with an engaging smile and energy that seemed to leap out of her photograph.

Standing, he decided to go for a walk to clear his head. He had been thinking a lot about the past, probably because he'd made another big change in his life. It wasn't that he had to work any longer—with his savings and investments he could have a life of leisure, doing whatever suited his fancy. That might be fine for some people, but he wanted to accomplish something, not just play. A talent agency had seemed the right place to use his experience and find a new way to succeed.

CASSIE BRYANT DROVE toward the Moonlight Ventures talent agency with her niece and nephew, still filled with doubts. She wasn't convinced that a modeling career was the right thing for her niece, but it also didn't seem fair to discourage Tiffany's dreams.

Hopefully this agency wasn't like the one where a friend of hers had first gone. They'd required Phoebe to take expensive modeling and acting classes conducted by the agency and then charged costly fees to create a formal portfolio. But they never called her for a job and she'd learned they made most of their income from such practices. After a while, Phoebe had tried other agencies, who'd said that they didn't think it would be worthwhile for her to pursue modeling.

Cassie figured genuine talent agencies were the most common, but she still wanted to be wary.

Sighing, she pushed the thought away.

From what she'd been able to determine, Moonlight Ventures operated on the straight and level. So the immediate concern was not wanting Tiffany to get her hopes too high only to have them dashed.

Glancing in the rearview mirror, Cassie saw her nephew, Glen, playing a video game. In the front passenger seat, Tiffany finished the milk Cassie had insisted she drink. Nervous about the interview and worried about her weight, she hadn't wanted to eat anything, but Cassie couldn't let her niece abandon proper nutrition to reach a size zero. She'd also argued that being hungry wouldn't help her make a good impression, so Tiffany had agreed on low-fat milk. Now she was anxiously tidying her hair again.

"Don't you think I should wear makeup?" she asked. "Just a little?"

"The instructions said everyday clothes and no makeup."

"I want them to see me at my best."

"Then they'll have to wait, like, years or something," Glen told her with typical brotherly boredom. He'd eaten his sister's chicken sandwich and french fries, along with his own, and was probably wondering what came after the hors d'oeuvres. He was an insatiable eating machine...called a teenager.

Twisting around, Tiffany stuck out her tongue at him.

"Yeah, nice look," he told her. "That's the face they want on a magazine."

Deciding not to intervene in the minor dispute, Cassie pulled into the talent agency lot and parked the car. "We're here," she announced.

Glen unbuckled his seat belt, but Tiffany sat frozen.

"Come on, Tiff," Cassie urged.

"I—I can't."

Cassie understood her fear, the sense that when it came down to it, you'd almost rather not try than fail. But she didn't want her niece's life to be full of regrets about what she'd missed because she hadn't been willing to take a risk.

"Sure you can," Cassie urged. "You're just nervous. That's natural. You'll get over it."

"Good grief, Tiff-Niff," Glen muttered, "you dragged us here, at least you can go inside."

"Will you go with me?"

He rolled his eyes but slid from the car.

Swallowing a lump of emotion in her throat, Cassie opened her door. For all the sniping between her niece and nephew, they shared a special bond, born from the struggle to survive once their mother had become an alcoholic.

The previous summer, Marie had been declared unfit. With her parents unable to take the twins due to her father's health problems, Cassie had filed for custody. Even after nearly a year, she still felt like a novice when it came to parenting. It was possible anyone raising teens felt that way when they encountered a new challenge—and with the twins, there always seemed to be something new. On the other hand, most parents had all the years between babyhood and adolescence to figure things out—she'd started right in the middle.

The question about Tiffany modeling was a first-class parental conundrum. Tiff had an interest in the sciences, and the same as her brother, she was getting top marks in her classes. She also wanted to be accepted at school, so the modeling interest might be an attempt to prove to her fellow students that she wasn't a nerd. At the same time, Tiffany enjoyed clothes and performing, so maybe she truly wanted to be a model.

Moonlight Ventures was located in an interesting building—probably converted industrial space—with several shops and other businesses in the center atrium section. The agency fronted on the parking lot.

Inside they were greeted by a receptionist who seemed close to Cassie's age. "Hello, I'm Chelsea Masters. May I help you?"

"We have an appointment with Adam Wilding," Cassie explained. "I'm Cassie Bryant and this is my niece, Tiffany, along with her brother, Glen."

"It's nice to meet you. I'll let Mr. Wilding know you're here."

Cassie sat in one of the comfortable chairs with Tiffany perched edgily at her side. A few feet away, Glen slumped in a seat and started playing his video game again. He was a brilliant kid who already had big plans for the future, though most of the time he did his best to fly under the radar, disliking attention.

"Hello," a low-timbre voice greeted them after a couple of minutes.

It was Adam Wilding. Cassie had seen him in dozens of magazines and TV ads. She'd always thought he was good-looking, but had figured it was partly airbrushing, hype and makeup.

It wasn't. No wonder he'd been one of the hottest male models in the business. With his black hair, blue eyes and commanding presence, he was alarmingly handsome and possessed a magnetism that practically took her breath away.

"Good afternoon, Mr. Wilding," she answered.

"Please call me Adam."

"Hi," Tiffany said in a shy voice.

"Hi," he replied. "I've seen your picture, so I know you're Tiffany. It's great to meet you."

"Me, um, too. That is, I'm glad to meet you, too. I really, *really* want to be a model and maybe an actress."

"Then let's go back to the small set we have. With your aunt, of course. We'll take pictures and see how it goes. The nice part is that whether or not you become our client, you get to keep the photos at no charge. We give them to you on a flash drive."

Cassie had been prepared to question if there was a fee for the photography, but his promise of no charge sounded different from what her friend had encountered.

Tiffany hesitated when Adam gestured to the hallway, and looked back at Glen. "Can my brother come? His name is Glen."

Adam seemed to be assessing Glen, then he nodded. "Of course. Come along, Glen."

In a small room, there was an area with sand

and an ocean backdrop and on the other side was a city street scene.

Another man was there, working with a camera. "Hey," he said. "I'm Logan Kensington and I'll be taking the pictures. Sorry we're cramped in here, but this is the only space we have."

"Logan is one of my partners and was able to be here for a few days," Adam explained. "He's done photo shoots for some of the best-known models in the world, so you're in great hands."

The two men conferred quietly in a corner and Cassie did her best not to listen.

The world of fashion and advertising was completely outside her experience. She was a website designer and manager, for heaven's sake. At home, she had a high-tech office with three computers, each with dual monitors. *That* was the world where she was comfortable. Taking responsibility for her niece and nephew had forced her out of that world to some extent; now she was being pushed into more unfamiliar territory.

For the next hour, she simply stayed out of the way. It wasn't hard, though Adam wouldn't let Glen remain buried in his video game, instead pulling him onto the set for "action" shots with his sister.

"That's great, Tiffany," Logan announced finally. "We have a small lounge stocked with snacks. Would you and your brother like something to eat while Adam talks to your aunt?"

"Sure," Glen said enthusiastically, though Tiffany looked instantly worried.

Cassie gave her niece a hug. It would be tough if she had to explain Moonlight Ventures wasn't interested, but they could always send her pictures to other agencies. After all, it was encouraging that the first one had asked to interview her... Cassie had already rehearsed several supportive speeches. In fact, she'd spent a sleepless night trying to find the right words.

The spacious office that Adam Wilding showed her to was quietly elegant, with a mahogany desk, comfortable chairs and a large flat-screen television on one wall.

"Please be seated," he urged.

She sank into a padded leather seat. "If it's bad news for Tiffany, please say it straight out, Mr. Wilding. You don't have to let me down easily."

His eyebrows lifted. "What makes you think it's bad news?"

"I love Tiff with all my heart, but I don't know what advertisers are looking for. She doesn't seem to fit the pictures I've seen in magazines."

"No," he agreed, and Cassie's heart sank. Though she might not be entirely comfortable with Tiffany's desire to become a model, her niece had experienced enough hard knocks and disappointments. The practical side of Cassie's brain said that was real life, but it didn't keep her from wanting to keep real life from intruding again for a while.

Adam had been punching buttons on his computer, then gestured at the TV where photos of Tiffany began appearing.

"Tiffany wouldn't be a typical teen model," Adam said, "but that's okay. She has something special, a uniqueness that we like and these confirm what we saw in the picture you submitted. She's also cooperative, is highly photogenic and able to follow directions, which was the main reason we wanted to do a practice photo shoot. Once Logan is in Seattle full time, we plan to do this with all prospective clients."

"R-really?" Cassie managed to choke out. Having prepared herself for bad news, she wasn't sure how to react to the opposite.

"Absolutely. Naturally Tiffany's bio didn't contain much information, so now I need to ask a few questions. Who is her legal guardian?"

"I am. My sister has, uh…problems. I've had custody of the kids since last August."

"What kind of problems?"

Cassie gave him a narrow look. She had a passion for privacy and it wasn't easy to talk about Marie being an alcoholic at the best of times. "Why do you want to know?"

"You don't have to answer, but all sorts of things affect a model's career and his or her agent can function best by knowing the gritty details. I'm sorry if it seems intrusive. Frankly, I already know something is going on. While Tiffany is young in many ways, there's a look in her face that suggests she's been through quite a bit."

"I guess I understand." Becoming a model was so important to her niece, Cassie knew she would have to explain. "Marie, my sister, started drinking after the twins were born and it became progressively worse."

"They're twins?"

"Yes."

Adam smiled a high wattage smile that practically knocked the sandals off Cassie's feet.

"My niece and nephew are twins, too. Is

your sister likely to sue to regain custody if control of income becomes an issue?"

Nausea threatened at the idea. Cassie honestly couldn't say what Marie might do. The court had declared her unfit, but she could be very convincing when she wanted to be.

"I'm sorry," he said quietly. "I can see it's upsetting to talk about, but for Tiffany's sake, it needs to be considered."

ADAM HAD SEEN Cassie Bryant's face turn pale and wondered if he should consider not moving forward. Presumably Tiffany had a decent home with her aunt since she appeared to be a well-adjusted kid. Having a career as a model wasn't worth taking a chance on upsetting her stability.

Still, if she was determined, they would simply find another agency. At least Cassie didn't seem to have stage-mother instincts. He hadn't told her, but the practice photo shoot had also served in finding out if she would try to interfere or coach Tiffany.

"My sister would have the fight of her life if she tried to get her daughter's money, but regardless, I'd want it put in a trust so it couldn't be touched until Tiff is eighteen or older. With a third-party trustee or something."

The comment told Adam that Cassie wasn't interested in having access to the money herself.

"The contract can specify how the fees will be paid," he said. "You should have a lawyer set the account up."

"My godfather is an attorney and he helped with the custody arrangements, so I'm sure he'll be able to protect any earnings Tiffany might have until she's no longer a minor."

Adam nodded. "Good."

"Then this means you want Tiff as a client?"

"Yes, but there's something else I want to discuss." He clicked forward to the close-up shots of Glen that Logan had taken as unobtrusively as possible. "I believe your nephew would also make an excellent model."

Cassie sat up straight as an arrow. "He isn't interested."

"You haven't asked him yet."

"He's going to medical school."

At her adamant statement, Adam's gut tightened. No kid should have his or her life laid out by the adults in their lives, no matter how well-intentioned the plan. He'd been through it with his father, and just that morning, his sister had mentioned how Dermott was encouraging his eight-year-old granddaughter to become a doctor.

Perhaps this was Cassie Bryant's attempt to salvage Glen's future after life with a difficult mother, but he was only thirteen and should grow up to make his own choices.

"I see." Adam controlled the impulse to say she shouldn't put such rigid expectations on any kid; it wasn't his place, even if he disagreed with her. Besides, he knew little about the situation. "College and medical school cost a great deal."

His comment may have hit home since Cassie began digging her fingernails into the palm of her hand. He realized she was pretty in an understated way, though she'd made no attempt to jazz herself up. To him, a huge part of a woman's beauty came from attitude—an inner something that made him sit up and take notice. He didn't know about Cassie—it was as if she was concealing herself behind a carefully constructed mask.

"I know it's expensive," she said at length. "I've started a savings account for both their educations."

"They might not need it if they become successful as models. By the time Tiffany and Glen graduate high school, they could have enough in their trust funds to pursue a career of *their* choosing." Adam hadn't been able to keep the emphasis off *their*, but Cassie didn't seem to notice. "And this is one of the few options they have at this age to work," he added.

"I don't know if he'll be interested," she said, "but I'll discuss it with him."

At least that was more than Adam's parents would have been willing to consider.

"Why don't you talk to Glen right now?" he suggested.

Cassie's mouth tightened and he wondered how she'd present the idea to her nephew. Positively or in a way that would make it appear unattractive? Glen was an engaging adolescent who might have an opportunity to make a decent amount of money; Adam hoped his aunt would play fair.

Half an hour later, she returned. "Tiffany is excited, which is no surprise, and Glen wants to think about it."

Adam had an impulse to speak with Glen himself, to ensure the youngster had been adequately informed about the possibilities. But that was a knee-jerk reaction to his parents' plan for his life. Having this particular problem with objectivity wasn't something he'd anticipated in his decision to become an agent. He and his partners had weekly bull sessions where they discussed issues, so he should bring it up at the next one.

Adam continued questioning Cassie on various details, including the kids' health and whether their father might prove an issue in the future.

Cassie shook her head at the last question about Tiffany and Glen's father. "He's married and doesn't know about the twins. I hate to admit it, but Marie was one of those women who thought he was going to leave his wife for her, when he simply wanted fun on the side."

"You sound cynical," Adam observed.

Cassie stuck out her chin, seeming defiant. "Maybe I am, about love and relationships, at least."

"Then you aren't planning to marry in the near future."

Her eyes opened wide. "Do you need to know *that* to represent my niece and nephew?"

"I'm sorry, of course not," he apologized. "Frankly, I'm still working out exactly how being an agent is supposed to go. You know that I'm fairly new to this side of talent representation?"

"Yes," she acknowledged, relaxing slightly into her chair. "I've done research on Moonlight Ventures. You and your partners might not have a huge amount of experience as agents right now, but you have contacts and name recognition. I imagine it will more than compensate."

"I'm glad you feel that way."

CASSIE HAD ALMOST told Adam Wilding he could take his personal questions and eat them for lunch. His apology and disarming explanation had eased the moment and she was glad she hadn't given in to the temptation.

As much checking as she'd done, she wasn't sure whether a talent agent needed to know a lot about clients and their family. An employer couldn't ask certain details, but an agent obviously needed to have a different connection with a client. And she had to be careful because it was best for Tiffany and Glen if she wasn't antagonistic toward the man who could play a significant role in their immediate future.

However, she shouldn't be overly trusting. Adam Wilding and his partners hoped to make money on Glen and Tiffany. That didn't make them bad people, but money wasn't the only thing that was important; she wanted her niece and nephew to have full, balanced lives.

"From my research, I understand you don't have a family," she ventured.

Adam glanced up from the computer where he'd been entering information. "No. Why?"

"It just means you may also lack experience dealing with kids, but I suppose you don't necessarily need it to be an effective agent."

He gave her another one of the smiles that must have won him plenty of modeling contracts in the past. "I don't believe so. In any case, experience with your own children is completely different than dealing with them in the business world."

"True."

She wondered what Adam's views were on marriage. The research she'd done on Moonlight Ventures and its partners suggested he'd been linked with a number of beautiful women, though no one serious since his fiancée's death years earlier. Her hidden romantic side wanted to speculate that he was still nursing a broken heart, but logic said the truth was probably much more prosaic...not to mention it was none of her business. Did all women turn into hopeless daydreamers when they met Adam Wilding?

"No one is going to release information about us, are they?" she asked, forcing her mind into the moment. "Such as where we live and other details?"

"The agency has strict confidentiality rules. We have security procedures in place to be sure that only legitimate employers can look at photos of our underage clients. Even then, we just post name and age. No other personal data is placed on a computer connected to the internet, so you don't need to be concerned about hackers. Nonetheless, I can't guarantee that someone in the media won't get curious about you as the twins' guardian or want to know more about them beyond their official biography. Especially if they become well known."

Cassie winced involuntarily.

Her carefully cultivated privacy might be at an end. Of course, she could torpedo the whole project, but that didn't seem fair to her niece and nephew. Any money they earned would be a big help toward college expenses.

Glen had become a demon researching which universities to attend and had been talking about top schools in different parts of the country. Out-of-state tuition was high and there were no guarantees he'd get a scholarship. Though Tiffany's ambitions were less established, having a nest egg would help, whether she stayed in modeling or decided to do something else.

Adam leaned forward in his chair. "How

soon do you think Glen will decide if he's interested?"

"Probably by tonight. If so, I'll call the agency in the morning. He doesn't procrastinate, but he's mature for his age and wants to weigh the pros and cons."

"And Tiffany?"

Cassie shrugged. "She already knows what she wants. Tiff is a love. She's also smart and has a good sense of humor. While she was nervous before coming in today, she's over that."

"Then I'll draw up a representation agreement for her and one for Glen, in case he says yes. They should be ready in a few days."

"I'll have my godfather check them over. I don't mean to sound suspicious—"

"You sound careful," Adam returned. "It's nice that you aren't tearing into this like a stereotypical stage, er, *aunt*."

She questioned whether he was telling the truth. Something about his manner made her think he saw her negatively, though it might be her imagination, of which she had plenty. A vivid imagination was how she stayed sane in the midst of complex computer programming issues.

She shook Adam's hand and went back to where the kids were waiting.

Her palm tingled from contact with the dynamic former model and she reminded herself that men like Adam didn't go for geeks like her, which is what she preferred. After all, she'd already tried to be the proverbial square peg in a round hole and she was much happier with her life the way it was now.

CHAPTER TWO

TIFFANY CHATTERED EXCITEDLY all the way back to the small Victorian house that Cassie had bought years ago. It was tight living there with two teenage kids, but they got by. Glen and Tiffany used the bedrooms, converted family room and bath upstairs, while she'd moved down to the ground floor.

Someday she hoped to live in the mountains, but for now she was afraid she'd be ineffective as a website designer if she became too much of a hermit. Her clients wanted someone in touch with modern culture. Yet it was also a question of economics—the kind of mountain home she wanted cost money, her business was relatively new and now she was raising Glen and Tiffany. Her niece and nephew were more important than saving for another house.

Glen was quiet, no doubt processing the Moonlight Ventures offer to represent him, but Tiffany jumped and let out a little squeal of excitement.

"Hey, Aunt Cassie," she declared, "when I make lots of money, we can buy a bigger place."

"Nope," Cassie replied serenely. "Anything you make will go directly into a trust fund. No matter how successful you are, there won't be any sports cars at sixteen and no buying of houses."

"It isn't about me, I want you to have a bigger place and an awesome car like the one you had to get rid of when we moved in here."

Cassie had traded her sporty convertible for a larger sedan before the kids arrived, wanting something safer and more solid. The kids had noticed the change, but she hadn't realized they blamed themselves for the switch to a different model.

"That's really sweet of you, but I prefer the car I have now. It's newer and gets much better gas mileage than the other one."

"Then what do you want?"

Cassie cupped her niece's chin in the palm of her hand. "I don't need anything, except to protect your income so that it's ready to help your dreams come true."

"She wants to make sure Mom can't get her fingers on any dough we make," Glen observed.

Cassie's stomach dropped. She didn't want the kids to feel their mother was a terrible person, though accepting Marie for what she was might be helpful to them.

Tiffany's mouth turned down. "Is that the problem? Because Mom might take our money for booze?"

"I simply want anything you earn to be there for your future," Cassie explained carefully. "This way, nothing can happen that we don't expect."

"Uh, okay." Like Glen, Tiffany internalized and usually didn't say much until she'd thought it through, such as her comment about the car.

LATER THAT EVENING, Glen came in as Cassie finished cleaning the kitchen.

"I'm gonna do that modeling thing," he told her.

"You thought the guys at school might give you a hard time. How will you feel about that?"

He made a face. "Not so hot. But money for medical school sounds terrific, and it might be the best way to earn it. Besides, I hate mowing lawns and yanking weeds and that's the only other kind of job I'm gonna get for a while."

Something Adam had said came back to Cassie...that at the twins' age, they didn't have many work opportunities. It was true. Unless they had a video go viral on social media or came up with a brilliant entrepreneurial scheme, their income-earning potential was limited. In Glen's case, it was largely offering his services as a general garden helper. Even when he turned sixteen, it would mostly be minimum wage.

"We can't know how *much* you'd earn at modeling," she warned, wanting him to be realistic. "It's probable that only a few people make the huge bucks."

"Maybe, but I've been thinking about what Tiff said earlier. If we make some money, it shouldn't all go into a trust fund. We should help around here."

His eyes were serious and Cassie hated knowing he'd needed to grow up faster than other kids.

"That isn't your job. You're thirteen and—"

"Almost fourteen."

"In a few months. But it doesn't make any difference. You're a kid and it isn't your responsibility to provide for yourself."

"That isn't fair to you."

"Right, it isn't fair that I get the pleasure of having my niece and nephew living with me the past year because my sister has a problem.

And it isn't fair that you don't get to have the mom and dad you deserve. But if you're worried about houses and cars, don't. The bedrooms aren't large and you and Tiff have to share a bathroom, but that's no different than any family that has to make do with the space available. Do you dislike this house? I know it's a quiet neighborhood, but there are families with kids your age on the street."

Glen shook his head. "Your place is loads better than our tiny apartment in San Diego, and we really like Seattle. It was so amazing when you told the judge that you wanted us to live with you. I'd figured they'd split us up, and like, you know, all the bad stuff you see on TV about foster homes."

"I'm sure most foster homes are fine, but I thought this would be best and I love having the two of you with me. Okay, in a few days I'll meet with Adam Wilding and get the representation agreements. Uncle Orville will take a look at them and who knows? Next week, you might be posing in front of a camera."

"Uh, yeah."

Cassie studied his expression; he still seemed uncertain. "Are you sure this is what you want?" She didn't want to push him one way or another.

"I'm sure." Glen gave a crooked grin. "I've been looking at how much medical school costs and it could choke a pig, the way Uncle Orville says."

Orville Calloway, her godfather, had become the twins' honorary uncle. "Okay. But if you or Tiff change your minds in the future, we'll deal with it."

"Thanks." Glen reached over and gave her an awkward, boyish hug.

ELIZABETH WILDING FINISHED the dishes and looked at her husband reading a newspaper at the kitchen table. Ever since he'd retired, she could hardly get him out of the house. Part of the time he fussed around "fixing" things that weren't broken, the rest of the time he was just sitting, usually in the room where she was trying to get something done.

She wanted him to enjoy his retirement but not to slow down completely.

"Dear, why don't you call Mr. Villareal and see if he needs help with that clogged drain he mentioned?" Elizabeth suggested.

Mr. Villareal was their neighbor on the corner and he was quite elderly, though he still managed to put out dozens of luminarias every

Christmas in memory of his wife and only child who'd died in a car accident.

"Took care of it yesterday," Dermott said without looking up from the newspaper. "Don't you remember?"

She recalled him being gone for fifteen minutes or so, which hardly seemed long enough to unplug a sink. But Dermott was awfully talented with a pipe wrench.

"I'm sure he would have appreciated having you stay and talk."

"You talk to Hector almost every day."

Oh my, her husband could be dense.

"The women in the neighborhood check on him and bring food, but he enjoys having male company, too."

"I'll go over later. I don't get it, Lizzie. We finally have time to spend together and you keep trying to send me away."

Together?

Elizabeth glared at his bent head—they weren't spending time together, they just happened to be in the same room most of the day. Well, enough was enough. She'd been pushing him to visit Seattle, hoping they could find a way to mend fences with their son. Dermott had agreed to take a trip "sometime," so now she'd have to find the right way to make that happen. It shouldn't take too much…he wanted to go; he just needed the right prodding.

"Why do they have to keep calling Adam a former model and printing a picture of him in a swimsuit?" Dermott said out of the blue, slapping his hand on the table. "Can't they just say he's a businessman?"

Elizabeth tensed. He must be reading one of the Seattle newspapers that Adam had sent. She knew her husband didn't mean to make her feel bad about the direction their son's life had taken, but she did; if it hadn't been for her getting sick, Adam would be a lawyer now.

Or would he?

Thinking back, she couldn't honestly say Adam had been enthusiastic about studying law—not opposed, just unexcited by a legal career. And he'd used his fame as a model in good ways, including helping environmental and wildlife causes…though the videos he'd done interacting with wolves and bears had made her gulp in worry for his safety. Still, who wouldn't take the chance of being that close to such amazing animals?

"No matter how we feel, Adam is famous," she said finally. "I'm sure the agency gets more business when the public is reminded of who owns it."

"Yeah, so we can see more models in bathing suits and other nonsense," Dermott muttered.

Maybe he would have accepted Adam's modeling better if his coworkers at the construction company hadn't kidded him so often about his son, "the swimsuit guy."

Sighing, Elizabeth took an aspirin for the pain starting to throb in her temples. It wasn't just Adam she felt guilty about, it was Sophie, too. She'd been so young when her mother needed major surgery. It was as if Sophie had lost a big chunk of her childhood, taking on responsibilities and worries that a child shouldn't have to face. No wonder she'd turned wild for a period and ended up pregnant at seventeen.

Elizabeth couldn't regret her grandchildren, but her daughter's teen marriage had quickly fallen apart and raising two kids alone was hard. In her own way, Sophie was just as stubborn and proud as her dad and wouldn't accept much help from the family.

"Are you all right, Lizzie?" Dermott asked. "You took something. Is your blood pressure up?"

"It's a headache, that's all."

Her husband's concerned expression eased slightly, but Elizabeth's own tension rose even higher. Sometimes she wanted to scream that she wasn't going to break and for everyone to stop worrying. Okay, the doctor didn't want her getting too stressed and the family knew it, but that didn't mean she was fragile. Her health was pretty good for a woman her age.

She cleared her throat. "Have you thought about when you want to leave for Seattle? We'll get a better price on plane tickets if we don't buy them at the last minute."

"I thought we'd drive. That way we'll have the truck and won't be locked in to a specific time."

Pleasure went through Elizabeth. They'd never traveled outside of New Mexico. Their short vacations had been spent visiting Dermott's grandparents or taking camping trips in the Sandia Mountains or around the Bosque del Apache wildlife preserve, south of Albuquerque. A road trip meant traveling through some of the most beautiful country in the United States.

"I'd love that," she exclaimed. "And maybe we could get a little apartment and spend some real time up there."

"Why not stay with Adam? He mentioned his place has an extra bed."

Elizabeth winced; she couldn't deal with her son and husband in the same enclosed space for more than a few days. Even when they weren't arguing, their colliding expectations were hard to take. "It would be best to get an apartment," she urged. "Not in the city—I'm sure that's too expensive—but in one of the smaller towns."

Dermott brightened. "That way I might be able to pick up odd jobs as a handyman."

Elizabeth almost protested that he didn't need to work, but maybe it wasn't such a bad idea. They could see Adam when he was available—really get to know him again—but Dermott would also have a distraction from driving his wife and son crazy.

"I suppose. I wish we could go right away," she said wistfully. "Summer sounds lovely in Washington."

"Maybe next month."

"How about tomorrow?" she asked firmly. "Packing wouldn't take much time and Sophie can check on the house while we're gone. Please, dear. Adam says it's mostly been cool and pleasant there and I'd love to experience the long days they have farther north in the summer. And what's the good of us both being retired if we can't do what we want?"

Dermott gave her an exasperated look, but he folded the newspaper and got up. "Oh, very well. You pack and I'll do an oil change on the truck. Call Adam and tell him we're coming."

"Maybe it could be a surprise," she suggested. "We'll find a furnished apartment, get settled and then go visit him. Besides, we can't be sure when we'll arrive if we do any sightseeing along the way."

"I suppose." Dermott headed out the door and she knew he'd probably been looking for a reason to agree to her plan.

Elizabeth happily started a batch of cookies to bring on the trip. Packing was easy, even though they'd also need to bring the basics like bedding, towels and kitchen supplies for an apartment.

She could use her phone to search rental listings on the trip north. They loved Albuquerque, but doing something completely different would be good for them both.

ADAM GLANCED AT the messages Chelsea had given him and satisfaction went through him. Cassie Bryant was coming in at 11:00 a.m. to pick up the representation agreements for both Tiffany and Glen. At least she'd recognized the opportunities available to the twins. He already had several places in mind to send their pictures—photographers and advertisers looking for fresh teen images. He had a feeling both of them would be in demand.

A few hours later, Chelsea escorted Cassie to his office. This morning she wore jeans and a green T-shirt. *Nice*, he couldn't help thinking, noting that she also moved gracefully, a quality he'd always found particularly attractive.

Yet Adam frowned. Her eyes were striking, but he could have sworn they were a different color.

"Is something wrong?" Cassie asked.

"No, but when we met, I thought your eyes were golden brown, now they're almost green. You must have colored contacts."

"I don't wear contacts, but my eye color appears to change depending on what I wear. My old boyf—someone I used to know complained that it was confusing."

Adam noted the cut-off reference to what must be a previous relationship, *and* her reluctance to refer to him that way. Perhaps while she was caring for her niece and nephew, she'd chosen to put off the idea of romance or had found the man in question wasn't interested in sharing her responsibilities.

Not that it made any difference to Adam, but they had to establish an effective working relationship. While he and his partners didn't want to perpetuate the way the prior owner had dealt with his clients—Kevin McClaskey had held their hands through everything—they *did* want to help clients learn professionalism. It was one of the reasons they'd shifted the focus of their careers to talent management; each of them had benefited from someone helping them in the past, and now they could do the same for other people in a field they understood.

"Sorry for the detour," Adam apologized. "But I notice eye color and details relating to appearance. It's a professional hazard."

"I suppose it's useful in your work."

Unlike some women upon realizing how closely he recalled details of their appearance, Cassie didn't seem uncomfortable under his scrutiny.

"Here are the agreements." He handed her the two manila envelopes from his desk. "I know you're taking them to your godfather for review. Space has been left to enter information for a trust fund account and data such as social security numbers. I've also included pamphlets for Tiffany and Glen, explaining the basics of how this works. It might be beneficial for the two of us to meet and discuss the details after you've read everything."

"Wouldn't you prefer the kids to be here as well?"

"With clients who are minors, I think it's best to meet first with the parents or guardians. That way you can ask questions or raise concerns that aren't appropriate in front of them."

A faint smile crossed her lips. "You talk as if you were a seasoned professional, but you said yourself that you haven't been a talent agent for long."

"True," he acknowledged. "But I was in the modeling business for over fourteen years and it grounded me in what I believe are sound business practices. When I became interested in buying an agency with my friends, I started questioning every agent I met to help learn the ropes. Beyond that, the previous owner of Moonlight Ventures has remained available as a consultant."

"I see."

She pursed her mouth and he didn't think she realized that it came off as provocative. Curiously, she was an increasing mystery to him. Even when she seemed to be revealing something personal, he had trouble interpreting anything in her face. He was accustomed to that in Nicole, who'd learned to conceal her feelings from the paparazzi and had trouble breaking the habit with friends and family. But what had led Cassie to being so reserved?

"Is something wrong?" he asked her.

"No, but to be frank, I'm worried about what I'm doing here."

A weary sensation settled over Adam. The opposite of overanxious parents were the ones who couldn't commit to letting their child try. Neither was a boon to an agent. He hadn't encountered it himself, but Nicole and Kevin McClaskey had told him stories.

In this case, Cassie Bryant's stumbling block might be her vision of how Glen's future *should* be shaped.

A stray thought crossed Adam's mind. Why only Glen? Why was the boy in the family destined for medical school, while apparently it was fine for the girl to consider modeling? Of course, it seemed clear from Tiffany's enthusiasm that modeling was her idea, so that could be the explanation. And a measure of self-honesty also made him acknowledge that he'd done some pushing himself when it came to Glen becoming a model.

"I'm not pressuring you to sign," Adam said, "but I'd appreciate a timely decision. That way the agency doesn't expend hours on something that isn't going anywhere."

Cassie frowned. "You make awfully fast assumptions, don't you?"

"I beg your pardon?"

"The kids want to do this, so that's what we're doing. *I'm* the one in the dark. I'm not Tiffany and Glen's mother. You mentioned parents and guardians asking questions their kids shouldn't hear, but I don't even know which questions I should ask."

"I spoke without thinking," Adam apologized hastily.

Another blunder due to his knee-jerk reactions. Maybe he wouldn't be having as much trouble if Sophie hadn't mentioned their father was now telling his granddaughter she should become a doctor. She was only a little girl. Encouraging her to have dreams was important, but she needed her own dream, not someone else's.

The evening before, he'd had dinner with Nicole and Jordan and suggested she handle the Bryants' representation. She'd just laughed and reminded him that she'd gotten shoved out of her comfort zone when doing the interviews for *PostModern* magazine, so now it was his turn. Knowing she was right hadn't made it easier.

"I should have asked your concerns before jumping to conclusions," he added.

Cassie took a deep breath. "So, what type of questions do experienced parents ask?"

"Especially with girls and young women, they generally want to know how suggestively or appropriately they'll be portrayed."

Her face brightened. "Yes, that's a good one. How do you handle that?"

"At Moonlight Ventures, we aren't interested in putting kids into adult roles before it's suitable. But admittedly, child models tend to be portrayed at least a year or two ahead of their chronological age."

"Will I have veto power if I believe something isn't right?"

Adam nodded. "Absolutely. And I'll tell you immediately if I discover any issues. We're serious about protecting our clients."

"Can I be there while they're working?"

"It's required. No minor can go to a go-see or a booking alone." He knew this part was a turn-off for some parents, and exciting for others.

"I'm glad," Cassie said simply, though her face didn't reveal any sense of how she felt about it.

She really was a puzzle. He couldn't tell whether she wanted to be connected to the modeling world, or if she simply wanted to protect the kids and give them opportunities, even if it meant escorting her niece and nephew to various bookings.

"What's a go-see?" she asked.

"With models, a photographer or advertiser often wants to see them in person before making a commitment. For actors, it would be an audition. Clients don't get paid for either one."

"So basically it's a job interview."

"Exactly."

"I'll research the process some more," she murmured.

"Being well-informed is good protection for a kid in both modeling or acting."

"About the acting… I know Tiff is interested, but is there any real chance?"

"We've placed clients in movies and a television series, and there's always the possibility of others." Adam deliberately didn't mention the new TV movie to be filmed in Seattle or the casting director's offer to audition some of the agency's talent. If Tiffany or Glen seemed right for a role, that would be the time to discuss it with Cassie.

She seemed restless and stood to go look out

the window he'd left open to catch the summer breeze. Her long chestnut hair was fiery in the sunlight. A flash of attraction went through Adam. This was hardly the time or the place for that sort of thought. Even if she wasn't Glen and Tiffany's guardian, he couldn't imagine dating someone who seemed to have so many edges.

"Is this the usual way an agency is run?" Cassie turned to ask. "I checked a number of websites and it's hard to tell what 'business as usual' might be."

"Every agency is different and we've also made changes to the way Moonlight Ventures previously operated. Aside from everything else, the prior owner functioned as a one-man show."

"He must have been busy."

"*Very*, though part of his income came from renting out sections of this building. Changing the subject, will there be any problem getting the kids to go-sees, auditions or bookings? That is, will your work allow for that?"

"It shouldn't be a problem most of the time. I'm self-employed doing website design and maintenance, as well as computer programming, so I have a flexible schedule."

Adam's concentration sharpened. While

their current website was functional, they weren't satisfied with it. Their webmaster simply couldn't grasp their vision, despite numerous tweaks. So far, they'd put up with it because other priorities came first, but priority on the website was moving up fast.

"What sites have you created?" he asked. "We may be overhauling our online presence in the near future and I'd like to see the kind of work you've done."

Cassie dug in her pocket and handed him a card. "I have a site that showcases some of my designs."

"Thanks." Yet he wondered if he should have spoken so impulsively.

Adam recalled the flash of attraction he'd experienced earlier. He didn't think it had influenced him, but it was something he would have to watch in the future to ensure it didn't impact his decisions.

CASSIE SAT DOWN AGAIN. She didn't care for the intense scrutiny Adam Wilding sometimes focused upon her, though it couldn't be unusual. And while his sharp reactions and assumptions when expressing her uncertainty had been disconcerting, his job was to represent the kids, not hand-hold her through parenting issues.

As for his questions about her website designs? Lots of people asked about her work and she handed out dozens of cards for every business that hired her.

"How soon would the kids start getting called for go-sees?" she asked.

"That can't be predicted. We'll put their pictures on our website and send promotional information to a range of approved sources. We also make personal contacts as appropriate."

"So it's possible no one would ever show interest in Glen and Tiff?"

"Possible, but not likely. We're careful about who we represent and to date, our clients have been in demand. Are you disappointed to think they'll be called for work?"

Her lack of enthusiasm must be obvious to him and Cassie warned herself to be careful. She might not be thrilled about the kids going into modeling, but she didn't want them to lose opportunities because of her.

She shrugged. "No, but this is new to me. It was only a few weeks ago that Tiff told me how much she wanted to be a model or actress. Your website said professional studio photos weren't necessary, so I took a bunch of pictures and let her pick the one she liked best. We sent it in and I didn't know what to expect.

Now I have a niece *and* a nephew about to become models. I think I'm dizzy."

Adam smiled. "I can relate. I made some big life changes of my own recently."

"Yeah, I read your profile on the website." She didn't say she had been disappointed to get an appointment with him, rather than with one of the female partners in the agency. It might have been easier to talk with another woman.

Of course, maybe she wouldn't have found common ground with Rachel Clarion or Nicole George, either. The partners in Moonlight Ventures were famous. They had reputations for being stylish, larger-than-life individuals who'd traveled widely and brushed elbows with the elite of the modeling and acting world. They were accustomed to a more glamorous atmosphere than somebody who plunged her shower on a regular basis and fixed spaghetti or baked chicken for dinner at least once a week.

Thinking of which…

Cassie leaned forward. "Will the kids have to eat differently? I mean…well, I don't want Tiff, for example, to half starve herself to be a size zero or something. She's already tried to lose weight the last month and it worries me."

"I won't deny that weight can be an issue in

modeling," Adam acknowledged. "There are terrific plus-size models with solid careers, but generally the demand isn't as high for them."

Cassie made a face. "Sometimes it seems as if you can't pick up a magazine or get on the internet without hearing a scandal about airbrushing, or whether teenaged girls are learning an unrealistic standard of womanhood, or someone slamming an actress or model who's gained a few pounds. Or for being *too* thin, for that matter."

Adam leaned forward. "Moonlight Ventures is concerned about those issues and we've discussed some of them in our quarterly newsletter, *Beneath the Surface*."

"Should I read back editions to catch up on the information in them?"

"You're welcome to copies, but we haven't been in charge of it for very long and it isn't a modeling handbook. We're looking at converting it to a general circulation publication. Naturally the material will involve fashion and the entertainment world, but we want to do thoughtful work on image and how people look at themselves. Also to give opportunities to young writers."

Cassie decided she'd reserve judgment until she read their material. How often had she heard people *say* the right things when their actions showed they believed the opposite?

Good grief, she was getting cynical. It was important to keep an eye on that so Tiffany and Glen didn't get the wrong attitude; raising them was requiring her to do an awful lot of self-examination.

"It sounds as if it could be interesting," she said diplomatically.

"We hope so. Anyhow, about Tiffany, I won't talk to her about weight and I don't approve of extremes. If anyone else says something to her, I want you to let me know. She's fine the way she is at the present time. I agree with one of my partners who tells aspiring models that they should strive first to be healthy and happy. She also says they shouldn't try to be anything except themselves."

"Good advice."

"For everyone, I suppose, not just models."

He had her there. For three years, Cassie had tried to change herself to conform to her boyfriend's world. Michael's requirements had included being attractive without outshining any other woman in the company, being confident and self-effacing at the same time, being well dressed and stylish but not *too* stylish and agreeing with anything management said or wanted.

She'd done it until she couldn't take it any longer, realizing that if Michael had really loved *her*, he'd have loved the woman she was, not the woman he wanted her to become.

"Is there anything else that we need to talk about today?" she asked.

"No, unless you have more questions."

"Not right now."

"If you come up with any, feel free to call. We can talk on the phone or as I mentioned we can meet again. I want the process to be as transparent as possible."

"Thanks. I talked to my godfather and told him I'd bring the representation agreements over today, but I don't know how long he'll need to review them."

"Take the time you need. I don't want to rush you beyond your comfort level."

"I appreciate that." She walked out of the office, smiling politely at the office manager in the reception area.

It was a relief to know the agency's policies seemed to be so positive. Time would tell if Adam Wilding had been telling her the truth or just saying politically correct words. He was extraordinarily handsome and had spent most of his adult life fitting into a limited standard of what the world saw as attractive and successful. So she couldn't help feeling skeptical about both the agency and the man in question.

CHAPTER THREE

GLEN READ A copy of the long agency agreement. At first, he hadn't thought he needed to look at it since Aunt Cassie and Orville were studying the papers and making sure everything was on the level. Then he'd decided if he was going to be a doctor someday, he couldn't leave that kind of stuff to other people.

"What do you think?" he asked his sister, who had avidly studied every word.

She made a face. "Some of it seems weird, but I guess it's okay, only it has all those legal words. The pamphlet thingy is easier because it talked about how stuff actually happens when you're modeling."

"Yeah. I'm just not sure this is fair to Aunt Cassie. She has to go with us to everything."

Tiff nodded. "I didn't think she'd have to do that. She ought to get paid, too."

"That isn't how it works."

"Let's go talk to her."

He followed his sister downstairs to the

small room Aunt Cassie used as her office. Glancing up from her computer screen, she turned off her music and grinned at them.

"Hey, guys. What do you need?"

"We were just… I mean…" Tiffany stopped and wrinkled her nose. "We were just thinking how hard it would be for you to go with us all the time to everything."

"That's the rule, Tiff. I'm okay with it."

"It doesn't seem fair," Glen said. "You aren't going to get paid."

"Hey, kiddo, I don't want to be paid. There might be some modeling jobs you can't take when I have a conflict or if both of you are offered jobs at the same time, but we can work it out. I can even bring my laptop along and stay busy that way."

"But what if someone's website crashes and you aren't available to fix it?"

"No problem. I never promised instant response time anyhow, but in April I hired a friend from college to do backup web maintenance. She works from her house, just like me, so Giselle handles issues that come up when I'm out."

"You're sure?" he asked, remembering how many times his mother had said she couldn't handle what was happening. It had always felt as if she was blaming him and Tiffany for her drinking.

"Absolutely. If there are any problems, the three of us will sit down and decide how to deal with them."

He was still bugged, but he didn't know what to do about it.

Back upstairs again, Tiffany sighed blissfully. "Do you think I might become as famous as Nicole George?"

"Who knows?"

"I want to act, too."

"You wouldn't be bad at that."

She wouldn't, either; Tiff had been acting her entire life. If she banged her knee or felt sad or angry, she'd just pretend everything was okay—anything to keep from upsetting Mom. Tiff was really naive, in a way. She always thought she could fix things for people, including fixing their mother. But Mom didn't want to be fixed; she wanted to keep drinking and that was that.

Suddenly angry, Glen flopped down on his bed and stared at the ceiling where Aunt Cassie had let him put stars that glowed in the dark.

Living with Aunt Cassie was great, much better than with his mom in San Diego, though sometimes he felt bad thinking that. She was his *mom*. Shouldn't he want to live with her, no matter what? But he couldn't forget the smell of booze that had always been in the apartment, and the sour stink in the morning when she got sick from being hungover.

It had gotten even worse when her boyfriends started coming home with her, and then he'd seen one of them looking at Tiffany in a way that hadn't seemed right. His sister was way better off in Seattle, but Tiff might get upset if she knew he'd called the child welfare office and made an anonymous report about Mom's drinking and the other things.

Sometimes he felt like slime for doing it, and other times he knew it was okay. But now that Aunt Cassie's life was going to get messed up even more...well, he wasn't exactly sure what he should feel.

A WEEK AFTER Adam met with Cassie Bryant, he began wondering if he'd ever hear from her again. Of course, her godfather could still be looking at the representation agreements, but she might be dragging her feet, hoping her nephew would change his mind.

Stop, Adam ordered as he ran on a treadmill at the gym over his lunch hour.

He'd explained the opportunities to Cassie. The rest was up to her. Yet he was discovering it was one thing to understand his job as an agent and another to separate personal feelings from the process. That might help explain why the previous owner of Moonlight Ventures had treated his clients as family for whom he needed to take responsibility and protect.

Adam slowed the treadmill to a cool-off pace, still thinking about Cassie. Getting information from her had been like prying an oyster open. Admittedly, he shouldn't have made that remark about her marriage plans. What he could have asked was something like, "Are you expecting any significant changes that could impact Tiffany's and Glen's ability to work?" It would have been far more appropriate.

Pushing the thought away, Adam showered and returned to the agency, endorphins from the exercise still coursing through his system. It would be great if they didn't have to drive somewhere to work out and he wondered if they could convert part of their building into a fitness center or get a professional gym to set up a business there.

He mentally reviewed the layout of the building they'd purchased along with the agency. Several businesses were longtime leasers— apparently Kevin had given his tenants the same intense, personal attention that he had given his clients. Some of them missed the hand-holding, though Kevin probably visited often enough to tide them over.

Adam shook himself. Things were going well for now and while Moonlight Ventures was cramped, they weren't ready to expand quite yet. A fitness center, either private or commercial, could wait.

"Your parents are here, waiting for you," Chelsea said as he came into the reception area.

He stared. His mom and dad had come without letting him know? They'd only mentioned it to his sister in the last couple of weeks.

"What does your 'deer caught in the head-lights' expression mean?" Chelsea asked.

Adam forced himself to concentrate. They'd had trouble finding a good office manager, so it had been a stroke of luck when Chelsea had applied and proven excellent at the job. And now that she'd recovered from a bad relation-ship in Los Angeles, she was even more valu-able, and she had a good sense of humor that helped keep the office balanced.

"Nothing. I'm just surprised they didn't let me know they were on the way."

Sophie must have assumed they'd told him, or she would have warned him.

"Parents, what *would* we do without them?" Chelsea's tone was ironic and Adam recalled that Nicole had mentioned various problems with Jordan's parents, who were also *Chelsea's* parents since she was Jordan's sister. They'd known each other growing up and their respective families didn't get along with each other.

"Right," he agreed.

Chelsea looked at her computer. "By the way, Cassie Bryant called for an appointment. Your 1:00 p.m. had just cancelled, so I told her to come then. I hope that's okay."

"It's fine. Can you ask Nicole if she has time to help answer Ms. Bryant's questions about teen modeling? I'd like to say hi to my parents before she gets here."

"Sure. They're in the lounge. I offered refreshments to them, but they didn't seem interested."

Of course. His mom and dad had never happily accepted anything seen as the fruits of his success, because it came from a career they didn't appreciate. It was time they recognized that he was fine with his life. Even if he had chosen to be a construction worker like his dad, what difference would it make, so long as he was happy and satisfied?

Adam sighed. It would be easier on them if his career path hadn't changed because of Mom's illness; they might have made peace with him becoming a model otherwise. So their visit might turn out to be helpful. They would see that the agency was a solid business, with the potential to become even more.

"Let me know when Cassie arrives," he said.

Putting a smile on his face with the practice of years, he strode down the hallway to the lounge. The door was ajar and he saw his mother and father sitting on one of the couches.

"Hi," he greeted them. "Sophie mentioned you were thinking about a visit."

Elizabeth stood and gave him a hug. "Hello, darling."

His dad had also come to his feet and they shook hands. "Good to see you, son."

"Good to see you both, too. Why didn't you let me know when you were coming? I could have met you at the airport."

"We didn't fly, we drove. We wanted it to be a surprise."

Though surprises weren't his father's long

suit, Adam hung on to his smile. "Terrific. The spare room isn't fancy, but the bed should be comfortable."

"That won't be necessary," Elizabeth said quickly. "We're renting a furnished apartment. It sounded like a nice idea to spend some time up here now that your father has retired."

"Adam?" It was Chelsea. "Sorry to interrupt. Your one o'clock appointment is here. Oh, and Nicole said she'll be free shortly."

"Thanks." He turned to his parents. "Can you wait awhile? I have to see a client."

"Business comes first," his father said.

Adam took the back route to his office, encountering Glen Bryant on the way.

"Hey, Glen, are you meeting with us?"

"No, and Tiff isn't, either. She's got a stomach bug. She's better, but Aunt Cassie said it would be rotten to take a chance of exposing you. We're safe because we got over it already. I thought I'd get something to eat, if that's okay."

"Sure." Privately Adam was uncomfortable at the thought of Glen in the same room as his parents. He preferred keeping his private and professional lives separate, but it couldn't be helped. Besides, when *he'd* been that age, he wouldn't have talked to a stranger over twenty if his life depended on it. Perhaps Glen was the same.

In the office, he found Cassie standing at the window again, the sunlight burnishing her hair the way it had on her last visit. He could see the family resemblance between her and the twins, but the biggest contrast was their outgoing nature and her reserve.

She turned and gestured toward the desk where he saw two large envelopes. "Hello. I brought the signed agreements back. Sorry it took so long."

This time, the black T-shirt she wore made her eyes appear brown again.

"I hear you've been ill."

Cassie made a diffident gesture. "We had the stomach virus that's going around. Glen and I got sick, then poor Tiff came down with it a day and a half later. She still doesn't have much energy and I couldn't be sure she's no longer contagious. But she's so anxious about getting things going on the modeling that I thought it would make her feel better if I called for an appointment."

"It was thoughtful not to share the bug with us."

"I hate exposing someone when I could have stayed home…though since I work out of my house, I suppose it's easier for me than for other people."

"Do you have any questions on the representation agreements?"

Cassie shook her head. "No, but the kids aren't happy because I have to be there for their jobs and go-sees. It especially bothers Glen, so I thought I'd let you know. He doesn't have to worry." She wrinkled her nose. "Though with this added, the kids aren't going to have the normal high school experience I'd hoped for them."

"Normal is highly overrated."

"But it's nice to know what it is, at least."

"Granted. Now, let me show you the promotional materials I've been putting together."

When she sat next to him to look at the large screen, Adam smelled the faint aroma of roses. It reminded him of the time he'd done a commercial for an international florist company in Paris, having to hold an extra large bouquet under the Eiffel Tower for hours, waiting for his "girlfriend."

He made an effort to clear his head, annoyed

that he would associate a romantic image with the guardian of his newest clients.

CASSIE TRIED NOT to be aware of Adam as he clicked through pictures of her niece and nephew. They were the ones taken the first day they'd come to the agency, but cropped to look like the kind of photos she'd seen in magazines. As far as she could tell, nothing had been airbrushed or photoshopped and both Glen and Tiffany were portrayed as wholesome, healthy young teens.

"Satisfied?" he asked finally.

"Yes. It's reassuring to see how they'll be presented."

"We don't want to promote anyone in a way that makes them uncomfortable and that goes double for kids."

"Did you start modeling as a youngster?"

"Nope. I was a junior at UCLA and saw an ad for models, so I gave it a shot. I needed the money. My mom had just gone through major surgery and I wanted to do something to help out."

It was hard for Cassie to picture the sophisticated Adam Wilding as an anxious college student who'd fallen into modeling by accident. Still, it was an engaging image.

"Is your mother all right now?"

His expression seemed guarded. "She's fine. In fact, my parents just arrived from New Mexico for a surprise visit."

At a guess, there was some tension in the relationship with his folks.

"That's nice. They must be proud of your success."

"Actually, they wanted me to be a lawyer, so it's complicated."

Cassie cast another quick, sideways glance at Adam. "I can't picture you in a three-piece suit, arguing a case in front of a judge."

"Me, either," he admitted. "It's hard on kids when grown-ups try to plan their lives for them."

His tone had grown even more intense and Cassie suspected that heavy pressure had been put on him to take a particular route. She couldn't recall whether her own parents had encouraged specific career aspirations in their children beyond wanting them to attend college.

"Instead you happened into modeling and the rest is history," she said to lighten the mood.

Adam's expression changed from intense to cool detachment. "I got lucky. The photographer on that first job sent my picture around to various advertisers he worked with. Before I knew it, I was in demand. But it usually doesn't happen that way. Albeit part of this business is luck and timing."

"I understand. I've told the kids not to think they'll suddenly become rich and famous. Glen doesn't care, but Tiffany has stars in her eyes."

"It's good that you want to keep her grounded. The people who hire models seem to prefer them that way. Just don't try coaching the kids. Let them be natural."

"Of course. I don't want this changing Tiff and Glen."

"You mentioned taking responsibility once your sister was unable to care for them?"

That was a charitable way of describing Marie's condition. She hadn't even been sober for her meeting with the judge, and had refused an alcohol abuse treatment program as a chance of retaining custody.

Cassie cleared her throat. Sometimes she was so furious with her sister, she could hardly stand it. Raising Tiff and Glen was a privilege, but Marie had thrown it away. They had their share of problems, but they were great kids, even after everything their mother had put them through. "Yes. I didn't want them in foster care."

"Your parents couldn't take them? I'm only asking because I'd like to know if a change in custody arrangements might occur."

"It won't. My dad has health issues and my brother's work doesn't lend itself to parenting. Please don't bring this up with Tiff and Glen. They've dealt with enough," Cassie added quickly. "I'd hate for them to get the idea they're unwanted."

"Of course." Adam's expression was hard to read. "Getting back to practicalities, I'll try to drop in on the first booking to see how things are going."

"Is that usual?"

"Every agent is different, but at Moonlight Ventures we want to pass on what we've learned and help our clients to be professional. That way they're more in demand and we all do better. Of course, we're still working out the best way to accomplish that."

Cassie cocked her head. "So you're practicing on your clients?"

"True. Does that bother you?"

"No. I told you that I've done some checking and Moonlight Ventures is earning a good reputation."

"That's good to know." Adam opened the envelopes and glanced through the contents. "What led you here? There are other excellent talent agencies in Seattle and we'd like to know what makes people choose us. By the way, it's all right to say that we were simply the first one that responded."

"Tiffany was researching talent representatives on the internet and was excited when she saw you and Nicole George were involved with Moonlight Ventures. Basically, this is the first place we tried. Now she follows you both on Facebook and Twitter."

He nodded. "Social media is one of our tools. We'll need to discuss the best, safest way for her and Glen to utilize it themselves."

There was a knock at the door and Nicole George came into the office. She smiled at Cassie. "Hi. You must be the aunt of our two newest clients. Adam thought that since I did teen modeling, it might be helpful if I came by to answer any questions."

"Thank you," Cassie said, feeling out of place to be sandwiched between two such glamorous individuals.

ELIZABETH WILDING FELT almost desperate as she looked at her husband. They'd had a pleasant drive north, but the closer they had gotten to Seattle, the more uncommunicative Dermott had become. Her hope of repairing the bond with Adam couldn't happen if either of them refused to really talk.

Good heavens, Dermott was stubborn. Adam took after his father that way, though he was like her in others. Or at least he used to be. Because of everything that had happened through the years, she couldn't honestly say she knew her son any longer. Surely the world of fashion and appearance wouldn't have changed him too much?

"This is such a pleasant building, don't you think?" she asked her husband.

"A whole lot of flash and dash if you ask me. It's good they didn't tear it down, but the place is nothing but an old factory dressed up to look fancy."

Small steps, she reminded herself. It wasn't going to happen quickly. Standing, she went to get a bottle of water from the small refrigerator with a glass door.

The teenager who'd come into the room seemed polite. He'd explained he was waiting for his aunt and hoped they didn't mind him being there. He was a handsome youngster and Elizabeth had wondered if he was a model.

Since Dermott had determinedly buried himself in another newspaper, she decided to get acquainted with the boy.

"I'm Elizabeth Wilding," she said, moving to the table where he was sitting.

"I'm Glen Bryant. Uh, Aunt Cassie is meeting with a guy named Wilding."

"Adam is my son. Are you a model?"

Glen laughed. "Mr. Wilding thinks I am."

In the background, her husband snorted and Elizabeth couldn't be sure if it was from something in the news or because of what Glen had said.

"You don't want to do it?" she asked.

"I guess I don't mind. I'm going to be a doctor and it'll help earn money for college."

"Good luck in getting there now," Dermott muttered.

Elizabeth glared at his bent head. It wasn't his business to criticize, especially a kid that he didn't even know.

"Never mind him," she whispered to Glen with a conspiratorial air. "We need all the doctors we can get and I'm sure you'll be wonderful at it."

Glen's brow had creased at Dermott's statement, but now he relaxed and smiled back.

"Do you live in Seattle?" the boy asked.

"We're visiting from Albuquerque, but we've rented an apartment so we can stay and…and see the area."

"Wow, that's great. We moved here last summer and Aunt Cassie has taken us all over the place. In May, we went to the Gingko Petrified Forest and we've gone to British Columbia twice. We go to baseball games, Mount Rainier and the Seattle Center, along with Mount St. Helens. It's like…*sad*, but also rad seeing what happened when the volcano blasted everything."

What a nice boy, Elizabeth thought. His enthusiasm was endearing.

"Those are good suggestions. I remember when the volcano erupted. It seemed terrible that such a beautiful place got destroyed, but I suppose that's how it formed in the first place."

"That's what Aunt Cassie says. Scientists have done all kinds of studies on how the land is recovering, which is a *bunch* faster than anyone figured. Some of the eruptions were crazy, mostly just super-heated air and rocks that flattened huge trees like toothpicks." He made a gesture with his hands that was probably intended to represent the trees being knocked over.

"I hope the park rangers know as much as you."

"Aunt Cassie tells me a lot and we look things up on the internet and read books. The park rangers are great, too. My uncle works at Mount Rainier. But he's a backcountry ranger, so we don't see him much."

"Your aunt sounds nice."

"She's *awesome*. On Saturday, she's taking us to a science fiction convention. Aunt Cassie likes that stuff just as much as we do."

"It sounds interesting."

"I can't wait, though we aren't dressing up in costumes the way the science nerds do in the *Big Bang Theory*."

Elizabeth's lips twitched. She enjoyed the television comedy, though Dermott wasn't crazy about it. He preferred home improvement shows.

"You probably think I'm too old to appreciate sci-fi, but I love the *Star Wars* and *Star Trek* films along with other science fiction or fantasy," she told Glen.

Once her secret hope had been to get published in science fiction, but while she had written several stories, it had never gone further. She'd been writing since she was a child, but there had never seemed to be enough time or energy to get them ready for submission to a publisher. Now? Well, her stories were probably too dated.

Yet part of her wondered…was there still a chance she could get published? She'd even brought one of her novels with her, thinking she might work on it some more.

"Do you want to go to the convention?" Glen asked. "Aunt Cassie got a bunch of free passes and I think she has some left."

The friendly invitation was appealing and she looked at Dermott. "What do you think, dear? It sounds fun and it's different than the things we usually do."

He let out a small grunt. "Whatever you want, but I thought we came up here to see Adam, not people dressed as Klingons."

Elizabeth was mildly startled that her husband knew about Klingons, which came from the *Star Trek* universe. He'd never shown any interest in sci-fi.

"Mr. Wilding can come, too," Glen said. "Your son, I mean. I think Aunt Cassie has enough passes."

"Adam may already be going. He used to enjoy that kind of thing." It was painful to realize that she was no longer sure where her son's interests lay. He might still enjoy science fiction, but it could be something he'd left behind with his childhood.

"Cool."

They continued chatting and all the while Dermott sat and read his newspaper. Elizabeth felt sorry for him. Guilt and disappointment were terrible burdens. Part of it came from his pride, the rest from his childhood demons of growing up poor. Yet monetary success wasn't what mattered most to him; he wanted respect and dignity for his children.

She only hoped they hadn't given their son his own share of demons.

CHAPTER FOUR

CASSIE'S HEAD WAS spinning when the meeting ended with Adam and Nicole. They'd swiftly covered a huge number of topics and she'd typed notes as fast as possible into her notebook.

"I expect the twins will be popular," Nicole said at the end. "They're photogenic and offer a fresh look. Does Glen have the same interest in acting as his sister?"

"I'm not sure," Cassie confessed. "I think he's primarily concerned that he'll look ridiculous to his friends."

"Modeling has the potential to impact friendships," Nicole acknowledged. "It sounds as if he already understands that."

"Glen is smart. His closest friends are mostly computer-oriented, so he already gets razzed by the general student body about being a nerd."

Adam cleared his throat. "Modeling may help balance his image."

"Maybe."

Cassie kept getting the sensation that Adam was trying to say something without actually coming out with it. Now that she'd met two of the partners, she wished more than ever that Nicole George had been the agent who'd wanted to represent Tiff and Glen. However glamorous Nicole might be, she seemed more approachable. Adam appeared to know what he was doing, but he definitely wasn't approachable.

Or maybe it was just her.

She didn't have experience talking to gorgeous, confident men who knew a thousand times more about men's and women's fashion that she did herself. On the other hand, she'd better get over her discomfort if her niece and nephew were going to be successful models.

With a composure Cassie didn't feel, she tucked her notebook into her computer bag and stood up.

"Thanks for your time," she said. "I'm sure you're both busy, so I won't keep you any longer. We don't have to meet whenever I have a question, Adam. Why don't I plan on mostly using email?"

Both Nicole and Adam looked surprised for some reason.

"That's fine," he agreed. "But we'll need to continue talking periodically."

"If your office manager could let me know when Moonlight Ventures has signed the representation agreements, I'll pick up our copies from her. I'm cautious about identity theft and would rather not have them sent through the mail with the kids' social security numbers and other personal data. In the meantime, I'll find Glen and we'll get out of your way."

"You aren't in the way," Adam said, still looking perplexed. "Glen should be in the snack bar. I'll go with you."

"That isn't necessary," Cassie assured hastily.

"I need to go in that direction, regardless. My parents stopped by for a visit and should be there waiting for me."

"I see."

It was a short distance to the snack bar, which was a casual name for a small, comfortably furnished lounge. Everything about Moonlight Ventures suggested success. They were located in a trending area near Lake Washington. The decor was tasteful and modern, rather than opulent. Their digital setup, from what Cassie had seen of it, was top-notch…all except for their website.

Out of boredom while recovering from the

flu, she'd looked at the Moonlight Ventures site from a web designer's point of view, confirming her original opinion that it had a sophomoric flavor. It certainly wasn't in step with the rest of the operation, but she had no intention of offering an opinion unless consulted for her professional services. People didn't appreciate advice from busybodies, no matter how well intended.

"Hey, Glen," she called to catch her nephew's attention. He was deep in conversation with an older woman.

"Hi, Aunt Cassie. This is Elizabeth Wilding and her husband, Dermott."

He waved his hand at an older gentleman on the far side of room, who lowered his newspaper and nodded courteously.

"I asked if they wanted to see the sci-fi convention with us. Adam, too. Is that okay?" Glen asked, suddenly looking anxious. "You told me you had extra passes."

Cassie had designed a webpage to promote the convention, largely in exchange for passes to the event. They'd sent a bundle, most of which had gone to Glen and Tiffany's friends, but she had several left. But even if no passes had been available, she would have found a way to get more. She didn't want her nephew to second-guess whether he was going to get in trouble just for being a normal, outgoing teenager.

"Sure it's all right," she assured him. "We have plenty. Mrs. Wilding, I hope Glen hasn't been talking your ear off."

The other woman smiled at her. "Not at all, and please, I want everyone to use our first names. Glen is a fine young man. Adam, we don't want to interfere with your plans Saturday, but it would be wonderful to visit the convention with you. Do you…um, still enjoy science fiction?"

"YES," ADAM TOLD his mother, "though I didn't know there was a sci-fi convention being held in the area." It had been a long time since he'd had much time for such events.

"Your father wants to go. How about you?"

Adam heard a faint snort coming from where Dermott Wilding was buried again in a newspaper and figured his mom had stretched the "your father wants to go" part. Dad rarely turned down Mom's requests, so he'd probably agreed to make her happy.

Out of curiosity, Adam glanced toward Cassie and saw a strained look on her face. At a guess, she wasn't excited about him being included in the group. He had concerns as well since it meant further blurring the line between his personal and professional lives. His parents, two clients and their guardian spending a day together? Talk about complicated. Still, it might help establish a more comfortable working rapport with Cassie.

He'd been startled when she suggested emailing additional questions, rather than calling or making an appointment. Not that he objected—overinvested, excitable stage parents could be the bane of an agent's existence—but it added to his concerns about how sincerely she would support the kids as models.

"That's a great idea. I'd love to go," he said.

His mom's eyes brightened while Cassie's expression shuttered to the point he couldn't read anything in her face.

"We'll have to meet at the convention center since I don't have enough room in my sedan for six people," Cassie advised.

"We can all go in my SUV. It's big enough," Adam surprised himself by saying. He'd gotten the second vehicle, partly for business needs since the agency might have a reason to drive a group of models to a booking or to carry equipment. At least that was his excuse. He might be a city guy, but his roots as the son of a construction worker and outdoorsman wanting to be prepared for every contingency were difficult to escape.

"Fine," Cassie said evenly. "We'll meet you at Moonlight Ventures at seven thirty Saturday morning. I have a special VIP pass, so parking won't be a problem and we can go in early."

"How did you get something like that?"

"Aunt Cassie did their website," Glen interjected. "It's *totally* cool."

Cassie's expression softened as she looked at her nephew. "It has more bells and whistles than I normally believe in using, but they work for promoting a science fiction convention."

"Bells and whistles?" Adam lifted an eyebrow. He hadn't found time to visit Cassie's business website and was curious. "Do you have a philosophy when it comes to web design?"

"What web designer doesn't?" she returned in a light tone. "Glen, we should get home and check on your sister. Elizabeth, Dermott, it was nice meeting you both."

"The same here," Elizabeth assured. "We'll see you on Saturday. Do you mind if I bring a picnic? I want to contribute. Just let me know if there are any allergies to watch out for."

"That's thoughtful of you. None of us have allergies. We'll see you then."

Glen followed his aunt out the door with a careless "bye."

Adam's mother looked pleased when she turned to him. "What nice people. Cassie is lovely. Does her niece resemble her?"

"To a certain extent. Both of the kids are engaging and photogenic."

Dermott harrumphed and crumpled his newspaper. "That boy wants to be a doctor and all you can think about is whether he'll take a good picture. You might be ensuring he never gets to medical school. Why don't you worry less about him being a model and more about his future?"

As a rule, Adam tried to brush off his father's attitude, but now anger filled him. "I *am* thinking about Glen's future. Earning money now will give him options. If he decides to be a doctor, fine. If he makes another choice, that's fine, too. It isn't anyone's business but his own. And it certainly isn't any of *yours*, Dad."

A dull red crept up Dermott's throat and Adam instantly regretted being so blunt. He was just tired of the negativity. It was why Adam tried to see his parents in New Mexico, rather than encouraging them to visit him.

Otherwise there were too many reminders that their son wasn't doing what they'd hoped to see him do. He should have had it out with them years ago, but for the sake of his mother's health and family harmony, he'd said little.

It didn't help that Dermott's attitude underscored Adam's own questions about the way he'd pushed for Glen to become a model. It was his job as an agent to spot talent and promote it, but how much was too much? Maybe he'd crossed one of those invisible lines he'd drawn to keep his life in order.

"Maybe all of us going on Saturday is a bad idea," Adam told them wearily. "I'll text Cassie and explain I forgot about a commitment and that you'll meet them at the convention center."

"No," cried his mother. "I want all of us to go. Dermott, tell him you won't say something like that again."

Dermott Wilding visibly set his jaw. "Lizzie, I'm not—"

"Please, darling. I know you don't mean any harm, but our kids are grown now. We can't… well, we can't keep…" She looked ready to cry and Adam glared at his father, angry all over again.

Okay, they might be too protective of Mom.

She complained about it, but it was a hard habit to break. Even with medication, her blood pressure spiked when she got upset and the doctor was adamant about keeping the stress levels down in her life. Tension in the family was what bothered her the most.

"Very well, Lizzie," Dermott conceded, sounding meek. "But that doesn't mean I've changed my mind."

Adam was certain his father hadn't changed one bit in the past thirty-five years. He was like the rock wall of El Morro out in the New Mexico desert, solid, dependable and *immovable*.

"Is that okay with you, son?" Elizabeth asked.

"Fine. But Glen Bryant is off-limits, too, Dad. He's a good kid, who's unusually mature for his age. He doesn't need someone passing judgment on him, any more than I do."

Adam's mother and father exchanged a glance and he hoped it didn't mean Dermott had stuck his foot in it already. Glen hadn't acted upset and had seemed genuine about his invitation to the sci-fi convention. Obviously he didn't have a problem talking to adults, which boded well for his work as a model. Bored, disengaged youngsters didn't make a good impression and the attitude usually came through in photographs.

"I get the message," Dermott said with a scowl. "Maybe we should leave now."

"Yes, Adam must have work to do," Elizabeth added quickly. "Will you come to dinner tonight, son? I'm making chiles rellenos. This is the address of the place we rented. It's an interesting little place—a group of cottages near Snoqualmie that used to be vacation rentals." She handed him a printout about the property.

"I can't turn down your chiles rellenos. What time?"

"Seven." She looked marginally happier as she hustled her husband out of the lounge.

Adam rubbed the back of his neck. His parents' extended visit would complicate the process of getting settled into his new career in ways he could only begin to imagine. Part of him was grateful they'd decided to rent a place rather than stay with him, yet he also wondered if there was more to their decision.

Was his mother sick again?

He thought about the color in her face and the enthusiastic way she'd been talking with Glen Bryant. They'd also driven from Albuquerque, rather than flown. Whichever route they'd taken, it had required traveling through sparsely populated areas, even if they'd taken interstate freeways most of the way. Surely Dad wouldn't have taken the chance of being too far from help if Mom was having health issues.

Or would he?

Adam frowned.

His father was a hardheaded mule who wanted things his own way, but he wasn't stupid or reckless. And he was devoted to his wife.

Making an effort to push personal concerns from his head, Adam strode back to his office. He wanted to review the agreements Cassie had returned to ensure she and her godfather hadn't added or altered anything that required further discussion or action. It happened. Apparently a few people didn't feel the agency should get *any* payment for their work. A few months earlier, Nicole had gone over an agreement where the prospective client had carefully changed the original amount to zero. Nicole had simply told them Moonlight Ventures wouldn't be representing them after all. They wanted clients who were straightforward, not ones who played games.

Adam sat down at his desk and started going through the paperwork, but he didn't expect to find any annoying surprises. Cassie wasn't the sort of person to sneak something into the agreement, hoping it wouldn't be noticed, though he wasn't entirely sure how he'd come to that conclusion.

CASSIE STOPPED AT the store on the drive home to get the makings for dinner.

Truthfully, she wasn't a great cook. She could make the basics, but gourmet was beyond her abilities. The twins didn't seem to mind, though Tiffany's recent desire to cut calories was going to complicate the situation, especially now that her brother had turned into a human vacuum cleaner.

Glen disappeared when Cassie was in the supermarket meat department and appeared a few minutes later wearing a hopeful expression, his arms filled with bags and packages.

Cassie lifted an eyebrow. "What makes you think I'll suddenly approve of you eating that much junk food?"

"*Pleeease*? I don't want soup again."

"We're having chicken." She didn't think Glen's stomach was as fully recovered as he wanted to believe, so baked chicken seemed like a middle-of-the-road alternative.

"With lots of rice and French bread?"

"Uh…sure. Brown rice. Just put that stuff

back where you found it." She didn't bother adding that vegetables and salad would be included on the menu.

The kids had eaten badly while living with their mother—chips, donuts, inexpensive peanut butter, french fries and hamburgers had been the staples of their diet. Cassie shuddered to think about it. Switching them to balanced nutrition had been a challenge, particularly since she mostly ate vegetarian herself and that didn't work well for them.

As a compromise, she made more meat dishes and they ate fast food or pizza once a week. She also kept a good supply of organic peanut butter and whole-grain bread on hand.

Glen left and Cassie pushed her shopping cart toward the produce section, more tired than she'd expected to be. Meeting with Adam and Nicole George had sapped the energy she'd regained after being sick, and now she was going to spend part of the weekend with Adam and his parents.

It was surreal.

Luckily Elizabeth Wilding didn't seem the least bit like her high-voltage son. As for Adam's father? While he'd looked over the top of his newspaper and acknowledged her, it hadn't been enough to tell Cassie anything about him.

Glen returned with an armload of French bread to put it in the cart and she tried not to feel guilty that she hadn't let him have the potato chips and cookies. The kids ate their share of junk food at school and with friends; the least she could do was make sure their diet was relatively okay at home.

The memory of the discussion with Adam about her niece wanting to lose weight returned and Cassie sighed. Tiff was at a healthy size; she'd even taken her niece to the doctor for a confirmation. At least Tiffany was now voluntarily eating more fruits and vegetables, the doctor having advised it was easier to maintain the right weight that way.

"Here," she said to Glen, giving him a pint of milk and a bag of nuts.

"Thanks. I'm starving."

The corners of Cassie's mouth twitched because he'd eaten several peanut butter sandwiches, a bowl of soup and drank three glasses of milk before they'd left the house two hours earlier. She would need to bring a supply of trail mix on Saturday, just in case Mrs. Wilding had forgotten that teenage boys possessed bottomless pits for stomachs.

An image flew into Cassie's mind of a teen-age Adam Wilding, lean, hair a little long, the same intense blue eyes, but not as suave and confident. She would have to hold on to that image when they were dealing with each other—sort of like the trick of imagining an audience in their underwear while trying to give a speech.

She'd have to try, at least. Yet she suspected it would be hard to maintain while actually in his presence.

CHAPTER FIVE

ADAM REMAINED DOUBTFUL about the wisdom of going to the sci-fi convention with his parents and the Bryants, but he pushed the feeling away as he drove to the agency where they were all meeting. The decision was made, so there was no point in chewing over it any longer.

So far, he hadn't seen the city quiet, especially during the high tourist season, but seven on a Saturday morning was calmer than at other times. He inhaled deeply, relishing the distinctive scent of a metropolitan area mixed with pine and sea air—no doubt about it, Seattle was a great city and he was glad they'd ended up buying an agency here.

Adam had expected to arrive before anyone else, but a sedan was in the parking lot and he recognized Cassie as she got out.

"Good morning," she called as he walked in her direction.

"Hello. I've sent the promotional material to a number of sources," he said, deciding he might as well take care of some business, "and posted the kids' photos to the secure section of our website."

It had given him satisfaction to get the ball rolling, so to speak. The twins were the first clients he was representing from the start of the process. With luck and a little persistence, they'd quickly land jobs and their careers would be off and running.

"That's nice. I picked up our copies of the representation agreements yesterday."

Adam glanced into her car and saw both Glen and Tiffany slumped in their seats, asleep. His mouth twitched. "I take it the twins aren't morning people?"

"I wouldn't say that. It only takes an air horn and threats of being doused by the garden hose to get them out of bed. No problem at all."

He chuckled. "Morning wasn't my favorite time of the day at that age, either."

One of Cassie's unfathomable expressions crossed her face. "I suppose it's a teenager thing. Tiff and Glen are better during the week, but Saturday and Sunday are tough for them."

"Were you the early-to-rise type?" Adam asked.

"Afraid so. I used to get up and go for a walk

in the woods around our house the minute the sun started to rise."

"That's interesting. I haven't gotten a chance to look at your website or the designs you've done for customers," he said casually. "Do you commonly use nature themes?"

"Only if it's suitable." Cassie gave him a quizzical look. "Is there a hidden question inside that question?"

So she was both smart *and* perceptive.

"It's just that you're a web designer. Having an interest in the outdoors and choosing a sedentary career seem incongruous. Or maybe you aren't the outdoor type any longer. Not that I'm criticizing. I love big city life."

"I don't think of myself as a type. Someday I want a house in the Cascades with a huge deck, maybe overlooking a lake or river. Away from the city and traffic. I'd like a place where the only things I hear all day are wind through the trees, water lapping and birds singing."

"The Cascade mountain range is volcanically active. Aren't you concerned about eruptions?"

"Not really."

Cassie turned toward Mount Rainier, a giant, snow-shrouded monolith that seemed to float on the horizon. He'd admired the view often since they had bought the agency, but had found little time to explore the area outside of Seattle.

"How could I be afraid of something so beautiful and wild?" she whispered.

A strange sensation went through him. His father had often taken the family camping when he wasn't working overtime. Adam had enjoyed the forays into nature and become an advocate for environmental concerns as an adult, but now he wondered if his mom would have preferred a little pampering. Their camp gear had been primitive. She'd cooked over a grill on the fire and while he and his dad had done chores to help out, it couldn't have been easy for her.

"How about your web designing?" he asked Cassie.

"Hard to say. Maybe by then I'll be in so much demand that I won't have to live in a metropolitan area. I already have customers from different states. Online business is the face of the future. With Skype and other tools, meeting in person isn't necessary."

Cassie's comments made her more of a mystery than before. But then, Adam enjoyed cities and had trouble understanding why some people didn't. Cities were invigorating, with something continually going on.

"So that's your dream," he murmured. "A home in the wild."

"I suppose you could call it that." Cassie seemed to tear her gaze from the distant mountain. "But it won't happen for a while."

"I understand your brother is a park ranger at Mount Rainier National Park. You must be close if you share his love for nature."

Cassie opened her mouth as if to respond, then closed it as Adam's parents pulled into the parking lot. She went to her car and roused the twins, who tumbled out yawning.

"Uh, hey, Adam," Glen said while his sister waved.

The senior Wildings got out of their truck, Dermott looking distinctly uncomfortable. It didn't surprise Adam; his father wasn't an overly social man.

"Hi, Elizabeth," Glen called, seeming to shake himself wider awake. "And, uh, Dermott. This is my sister, Tiffany."

Tiff grinned at them. "Glen has been really smug that he won't be outnumbered today. You know, guys and gals."

Adam's jaw dropped when his father gave her a cordial smile. "I felt that way after my son left for college. Then it was just me with my wife and daughter."

"I didn't know Adam had a sister."

"Her name is Sophie."

"Cool. My name is boring. There are a *gazillion* Tiffanys. We have four in my grade."

Dermott's smile broadened. "Don't put it down. I like Tiffany. Sophia was my grandmother's name. Sophia Carlotta. *Her* great-grandmother came from Spain."

"Awesome."

CASSIE WATCHED HER niece effortlessly charm Adam's father and shook her head. Glen had told them both about a "snarky" comment made by the elder Mr. Wilding and it was typical of Tiff that she wanted to fix things... which meant making friends.

Elizabeth and Glen had immediately put their heads together and begun talking, making Cassie wish that he had a stronger relationship with his grandmother. Her parents lived across the Puget Sound, in a wooded area outside of Port Townsend, but her dad worried constantly about his immune system since he'd had a liver transplant. It made them reluctant to spend time with the kids...or anyone, for that matter. Visitors seemed to be regarded as walking germ factories.

They drove to the convention center in Adam's SUV and were directed to a reserved parking area, courtesy of the VIP pass she'd received. The large hall for the exhibitors was still moderately quiet since they hadn't opened yet to the public.

Tiffany immediately left with Dermott Wilding, while Glen and Elizabeth headed in the opposite direction.

"I wonder where Tiff is taking my father," Adam mused.

"She's hoping to find someone who worked on *The Martian*. She wants to discuss aspects of the movie—scientific accuracy and why they changed certain elements from the novel. She has a whole load of questions."

Adam frowned. "Tiffany is interested in the sciences?"

"She won first place for her science fair project this year. I think she has visions of being like the woman in that song, 'Carlene,' but wants to skip the nerdy high school phase."

"I have no idea what you're talking about." Adam looked so perplexed that Cassie almost laughed.

"You must not listen to country music. One

of Phil Vassar's hit songs was about encountering a hot redhead in a sports car who turns out to be the whiz kid that he'd known in high school. She has a PhD but is now modeling for money. I'm sure you could find it online. The song has a great beat."

"So you like country music and want a house surrounded by nature. Interesting, I've probably just doubled what I know about you personally."

The comment raised a red flag for Cassie, but she wasn't trying to put up a front any longer, the way she had for Michael's sake. He hadn't approved of her small town roots, saying the people he worked with expected him to be with someone sophisticated and classy. He acted as if anyone who hadn't always lived in the city was somehow lacking.

What wasn't classy was Michael's attitude.

Cassie shook the memories away.

She didn't love Michael any longer, but it still hurt that he'd wanted her to put on airs and pretend she was someone she wasn't. Most of his coworkers hadn't been the nicest people.

"There's truth in country music," Cassie said lightly. "Not every song, but often."

"I'll take your word for it."

"Okay, what are your musical preferences?"

Adam shrugged. "Can't say that I have any. Jazz is good, but I rarely play anything."

"Are your folks the same?"

Curiously, his mouth tightened. "My sister and I listened to classical music when we were studying and before tests. My parents were told that it helped students do better, particularly with mathematics."

It wasn't the question Cassie had asked, but she didn't challenge him. "I've heard that, too. I play Beethoven or Mozart when I'm working on a complex programming problem. Also Handel's *Water Music*. Ooh, and Gregorian chants. They're great."

Adam's tense expression eased. "You don't require the kids to listen with you?"

"No, I wouldn't want to cause a riot." She let out an exasperated breath. "As to the 'require the kids to listen' part of your question…what is that supposed to mean?"

"It's none of my business."

"That hasn't stopped you so far," Cassie muttered, thinking about the probing he'd done the day they'd met. "If something is bothering you, please spit it out. I don't like mind games."

"No games. I'm just starting to think I misinterpreted something. When did Glen decide he wanted to be a doctor?"

"Jeez, I don't know. Years ago. I remember when I was visiting in San Diego, he announced that he was going to cure malaria. He'd watched a TV documentary about the medical teams around the world who fight the disease and was inspired by them."

"I'm impressed."

"I know. It's wonderful that it meant so much to him. Since then, he's just gotten more and more determined, though now he's torn between medical research and practicing medicine. He gets really frustrated because so many people say it's a whim and to enjoy being a kid before making such a big decision for the future. I tell him to ignore them and decide for himself."

ADAM WINCED, REALIZING he'd been wrong about Cassie and he looked at her with renewed respect. While she might be unsure with parenting issues, she was trying to do right by her niece and nephew.

"Okay, confession time," he said. "I mentioned my parents expected me to become a lawyer. They talked about it as long as I can remember. And they dreamed of me ending up someday on the US Supreme Court. It meant everything to them and they still wish I'd followed through with their plans. I have to admit that I wondered whether you were putting the same pressure on Glen. I apologize for that."

Cassie blinked. "I want the kids to succeed, but how and what they do is up to them." Her face was reflective, rather than insulted. "I'm uncomfortable with the modeling, but that's because I'm not interested in fashion and I worry Tiff will become obsessed about her weight and appearance. It helped to meet Nicole George and see how grounded she seems. Do your parents feel better about your career now that you've become a talent agent?"

Adam made a noncommittal gesture. "Hard to say. They don't understand the work and it isn't what they wanted for me."

"But becoming a lawyer was their plan, not yours," Cassie pointed out reasonably. "And you started modeling to help with your mom's medical expenses."

"That doesn't matter to my father. He's happier now that I'm a businessman, but he still seems to harbor that vision of seeing me on the Supreme Court. When I was buying the agency with my partners, he even suggested I apply to law school instead."

Cassie wrinkled her nose. "That's his ego and pride talking."

Adam stiffened, though he knew she was right.

"I know something about parental pride and ego," Cassie added hastily. "Three years ago, they decided my father needed a liver transplant, but he wouldn't let me or my brother be tested as potential donors. He said a man doesn't take something like that from his children. It was crazy. The portion of the liver donated regenerates in a couple of months and donors have an excellent recovery rate."

Adam suspected the admission about her father's health issues was difficult for someone as private as Cassie. "How about your sister?"

Cassie rolled her eyes. "I hate to say it, but she didn't volunteer to be tested. On the other hand, with her drinking, I doubt Marie's liver is in any condition for a donation, which she may have realized."

More and more people were coming and going through the main doors of the large hall, flowing around them, so they began wandering down the aisles, checking out the various vendor stalls.

"How is your father now?" Adam asked after

a few minutes of looking at science fiction–related merchandise.

"Better. Dad was on the transplant list for a long time, but he was able to have the surgery before his condition became critical. Now with the immunosuppressive medications, he worries about catching colds and getting other infections. Anyway, he retired and they've become quite reclusive."

"I see." Adam cast a glance at Cassie and wondered if she'd inherited a reclusive tendency from her parents. A house in the mountains surround by nature? As strongly as he felt about protecting animals and the environment, it didn't appeal to him.

"Cassie, that's you, isn't it?" called a voice, breaking into Adam's thoughts. "I'm T'Pring Belson."

"Hi, T'Pring." Cassie shook hands with the forty-something woman who'd approached them. "T'Pring, this is Adam Wilding. He and his parents came with us to see the convention."

"Excellent. We had massive advance ticket sales through the website, which naturally attracted even more exhibitors. You did a wonderful job and will be getting a nice bonus."

"I'm glad you're pleased."

The woman rushed away and Adam cocked his head. "T'Pring? That's from *Star Trek*. It must be a stage name."

"No, T'Pring is her real name. Her Facebook page explains that her parents were *Star Trek* fans and wanted to call their daughter something unique. Apparently they weren't the only ones. I was curious so I searched online and found quite a few T'Prings, both with the original spelling and with the apostrophe removed."

"I had no idea. So, you get a bonus if the advance sales are sufficient?"

"It was part of the agreement, though I mostly wanted to ensure I had passes for the twins and their friends. Glen claims these events can be difficult to get into. He always wanted to attend Comic-Con down south, but couldn't score a ticket."

Adam stopped to look at a display of *Star Trek* uniforms and command insignias. In the corner of the hall, he saw his father and Tiffany, deep in conversation with an exhibitor. A few stalls away, his mom and Glen were mock dueling with *Star Wars* lightsabers.

It was as if Adam had fallen down a rabbit hole and nothing made sense. He'd known his mother enjoyed science fiction—she was the one who'd introduced him to writers such as Asimov and Heinlein—but not to the point she'd enjoy a sci-fi convention. As for Dermott?

Adam glanced at his father again. If anything, he'd expected Dermott to drag his feet and turn the outing into an exercise in patience. Yet it was nothing like that so far, perhaps due to Tiffany's fresh eagerness.

"Tiffany sure seems to get along with my dad," he murmured.

"You sound amazed. Is your father difficult?"

"It depends on the circumstances. He's great if you're a construction worker. I don't suppose Tiff lives a secret life as a carpenter?"

"Hardly." Cassie's tone was dry. "She used super glue on the hinges to put her display boards together for the first level of the science fair, reinforced by duct tape. It wasn't impressive, but she pulled it off by artistically covering everything with a fabric drape."

Adam chuckled. "That's one solution. I'll have to look into putting the information about the award in our promotional material. There are several local advertisers who'd love knowing about it. Is her interest in the medical arena like her brother?"

"Nope, earth sciences. You know, I'm not sure how many people realize how important science fairs have become. Kids are willing to look outside the proverbial box and researchers are paying serious attention to their work. Colleges also recruit at the more senior level."

Just then the doors of the exhibit hall opened and visitors began rushing inside, many dressed as characters from sci-fi and superhero movies. Amateur costuming had become amazingly sophisticated and many of the participants looked as if they'd walked off a film set.

"Watch out for the Klingons," Cassie joked.

Adam was intrigued. He wasn't a gifted photographer like his partner, Logan Kensington, but he began snapping pictures, trying to get a good selection of his parents and the twins, as well as the costumed attendees.

It was a surprise to find himself in Cassie's company, but since the twins had unexpectedly paired off with his parents, it would be rude to leave her alone.

ELIZABETH WAS HAVING more fun than she'd had in ages. Glen didn't treat her as if she was fragile or an invalid; he was a great kid with boundless energy and curiosity.

It was how things should have been with

Adam at the same age. Instead they'd focused too much on building for the future rather than getting to know him and finding out what he wanted to do with his life. The same with Sophie.

"Hey, don't be so gloomy," Glen ordered.

"Did I look gloomy?"

"Sort of. Aunt Cassie says it's okay to be glum sometimes, but smiling makes you feel better."

"I like your aunt."

"She's pretty great." Yet his face scrunched briefly with emotion before smoothing out.

"What was that funny expression about?" Elizabeth asked.

"Nothing. I just…sometimes I wish my mom was more like Aunt Cassie. Well, except she eats a ton of salad and fruit and vegetables," Glen added hastily. "It's *boring*. She won't even get granola bars because they have so much sugar. And she buys a fruit preserve instead of regular jam for peanut butter sandwiches."

It seemed as if he'd needed to say something critical about his aunt, probably as a sideways defense of his mother, who must have serious issues if the kids weren't living with her.

Elizabeth just nodded, though she sympathized with both Glen and his aunt. "My husband and I didn't enjoy any of the same food when we got married. I didn't know how to fix the Spanish and New Mexico–style dishes he'd grown up eating and couldn't tolerate spicy food myself. It took a while to sort everything out. I'm sure you and Cassie will do the same."

"I guess. I'm getting used to Aunt Cassie's cooking and she tries to make some of the stuff we like. Oh, *awesome*." Glen pointed to someone down the aisle. "She's dressed like Jaylah from *Star Trek Beyond*."

The woman was garbed in the character's warrior costume, her face boldly painted white with jagged black stripes.

"I didn't enjoy *Star Trek Beyond* as much as *Star Trek Into Darkness*," Elizabeth confessed. "What do you think about the new reboot?"

"It's pretty good. I like all the new actors. I hope they keep making the movies."

"Same here."

Elizabeth looked over to where her son and Glen's aunt were talking. She'd hoped the outing would start the process of bringing the family closer, but she couldn't force it to happen. Adam and his father were both impossibly stubborn, though she was certain they'd deny it.

"Is Cassie totally opposed to junk food, or is it mostly at home?" Elizabeth asked.

"Mostly at home. She doesn't say we can't have it, like with our friends or something, but she's got a thing about healthy food. Organic, too. I think it's because our grandpa has been sick a bunch."

"That makes sense. I brought sandwiches and fried chicken and other things for lunch. Hopefully she won't disapprove too much."

Glen's eyes gleamed. "Nah, she'll be okay. It sounds great."

Elizabeth tried to keep a straight face. He was normal teenage boy with a huge appetite. It was a refreshing reminder of Adam's teen years. No matter how hard she'd tried to keep him filled up, he'd stayed lean and perpetually hungry.

She glanced around the hall, feeling the old tug, the wish to be part of the sci-fi world as a writer. She'd noted a couple of prominent authors were doing book signings during the convention and had indulged in a brief, silly vision of being one of them.

"Hey, what's up?" Glen asked.

She hesitated, then decided there wasn't any reason to keep her writing a secret. "Being here reminds me of fantasies I had as a girl when I discovered books by Jules Verne and Robert Heinlein. I started weaving my own stories in my head and then had to write them down."

"Cool. Can I get one of your books at the library?"

Kids could be so accepting, without all the questions that adults tended to ask. "I'm afraid not. I never sent anything to a publisher. Some of it is just in notebooks. I have stacks of them, going back to when I was nine years old."

"Can I read some?"

Elizabeth instantly felt vulnerable. Few people had ever read her stories. "I don't think you'd like them—too old-style."

"Maybe I would."

She didn't say anything else because Adam came over with Cassie. "Enjoying yourself, Mom?"

"Oh, yes. I planned to attend a science fiction convention last year before I retired, but it didn't...um, didn't happen. I was disappointed." She stumbled over her words, not wanting to explain how she'd won tickets in a contest at work but had ended up having gall bladder surgery instead. Unlike her heart operation years ago, it had been relatively minor, but the last thing she wanted was to remind Adam she'd had another health issue.

"I didn't know that." Adam sounded puzzled. "You should have told me. There have been a number of conventions in California and I could have arranged for you to go."

"It wasn't a big deal," she returned. "I always thought it would be exciting to be an astronaut, too."

"So did I," Cassie said.

Her nephew stared. "You did?"

Cassie bobbed her head. "That's why I studied both astrophysics and computer science in college. But I…well, I didn't end up applying to the program."

She looked uncomfortable and Elizabeth guessed it was a difficult memory. "I understand your father has been ill," she said to change the subject. "How is he doing?"

"Much better. I've never been to Albuquerque. What's the first thing that struck you about Washington?"

"The color. New Mexico is beautiful, but red and yellow earth tones dominate everything. Here everything seems to be green. Even the ground is covered by green, especially in the woods."

Cassie grinned. "We *are* the Evergreen State.

The forest understory is heavy. Salal bushes, huckleberries, ferns… It goes on and on."

"Glen mentioned your brother is a park ranger. You must share some of his interests."

"A few."

"Wait a minute," Adam interjected. "I'm confused. You studied astrophysics, but you're a web programmer who wants to live in the mountains someday? Isn't that a little—"

"Odd?" Cassie finished for him. "Maybe. What can I say? I'm complicated."

There appeared to be an undercurrent of tension between Cassie and Adam, which piqued Elizabeth's interest. Cassie wasn't the least bit like his fiancée, whose lively energy had seemed to fill every room of the house when they'd visited Albuquerque together. Losing Isabelle had been a terrible blow and Adam hadn't been the same since.

Elizabeth frowned in thought as she watched her son and Cassie together. The young woman seemed nice, but it was unlikely he'd get involved with someone so different. Not that he'd dated seriously since Isabelle's death. Adam didn't confide in his mother very often any longer, but he'd told her that much. It was awful to think he might never find anyone again.

Elizabeth looked over at her husband, who

was laughing. He wasn't a perfect man, but he was perfect for her. Well, *most* of the time. Love didn't mean your partner didn't drive you crazy on a regular basis.

She smiled fondly.

Okay, Dermott was stubborn, proud and opinionated—he was also loving, faithful and determined to take care of his family. There were worse qualities to have in a spouse.

CHAPTER SIX

EIGHT DAYS AFTER the sci-fi convention, Cassie put her laptop and the spare battery into a carrying case and called to her niece and nephew.

"Time to go, we don't want to be late."

Tiffany raced down the stairs and waited for her brother, so excited she was hopping from one foot to the other. Glen followed more slowly, his backpack slung across one shoulder, looking decidedly less thrilled than his sister. He'd seemed pleased about getting his first job; now he looked sick to his stomach.

"Are you all right?" Cassie asked.

"Yeah."

She almost asked if he'd changed his mind about modeling, but was that the right thing to do? Would it make him more uncertain about the decision he'd made, or would it show how much she cared? Backing out at this point might be problematic, but if it was what he wanted…? At the same time, it was also important to honor commitments. The questions were enough to keep her occupied 24/7.

"Do you think they'll have food at this thing, or do we have to wait until they're done to eat?" Glen asked.

Somehow, she doubted his uneasiness stemmed from concern about filling his stomach.

"I don't know, but I've packed snacks just in case," she assured.

Glen nodded, though the strain in his face didn't get better. Obviously it was one thing to decide to be a model, another to actually walk in front of a camera.

"Let's *go*," Tiffany urged.

Cassie hiked an eyebrow at her nephew. "How about it?"

"Okay."

He squared his shoulders like a soldier facing battle and she tried not to grin. She'd had a stable, quiet childhood but still remembered the ups and downs of adolescence. Everything had felt as if it was the end of the world or the beginning of something fabulous.

Cassie felt a flash of wistful regret. When was the last time she'd felt as if something fabulous and amazing could be on the horizon?

The photo shoot was on the edge of downtown Seattle and when they arrived, the crew was setting up their equipment in a parking area. It appeared to be quite a production, though not particularly glamorous. She also suspected a fair amount of boredom would be involved.

"I'm Mr. Piligian's assistant, Penny Chandler. He's the photographer," said a young woman. "You must be our models."

"Yes, ma'am," Tiff agreed eagerly. "I'm Tiffany Bryant and this is my brother, Glen. And my aunt."

The photographer's assistant winced slightly, possibly from being called ma'am. The woman couldn't be more than twenty-five and probably wouldn't appreciate being tagged as a ma'am for a long time to come. Cassie sympathized. She'd discovered that a few people still saw someone's "aunt" as a comfortable, gray-haired woman—the way they were often portrayed in Hollywood's classic television programs or movies.

"I'm Cassie Bryant," she introduced herself.

"Hi." Penny held something out. "Wear this badge to show you're supposed to be here."

"Thanks." Cassie shifted the shoulder strap for her computer bag and clipped the badge to the belt loop on her jeans. "Where do you need Tiff and Glen?"

"The wardrobe supervisor and his assistant will be here shortly. The kids will need to change into their first costumes and then go to makeup."

"Makeup?" Glen repeated in an unusually high tone.

"Yes, of course."

He looked alarmed. "That's for girls."

"Glen, stage makeup is normal," said Adam from behind Cassie. "Everyone in front of a camera wears it."

"Everyone?"

"Even famous movie stars," Cassie explained quickly.

Glen didn't seem reassured, but he went with the wardrobe supervisor when she arrived, along with Tiffany. Tents had been erected similar to the temporary cabanas Cassie had used when on a college break in the Caribbean. A faint nostalgia went through her. Her college roommate had talked her into going to the Caribbean on spring break and it had been one of the best weeks of her life. Sometimes she wished she could have stayed there, floating in the warm crystalline water, free of the heartache and self-doubt that came later.

Cassie pushed the memory away and looked at Adam. "Hi. You mentioned you'd try to visit the twins' first booking. Something about passing on professional standards?"

"Yes, but it's more than that. The previous owner of Moonlight Ventures is a wonderful guy, but he did a huge amount of hand-holding with his clients and tenants. We want to approach the business in a different way, so we're trying to break that mold. Nonetheless, I wanted to be available in case you or the kids had any questions or concerns."

"Such as wearing stage makeup?"

Adam laughed. "I suppose that's something we should add to the reading material about the realities of being a model."

"For teenage boys, at least," Cassie said wryly. "I don't think Glen anticipated that when he decided to give modeling a shot. He simply saw a chance to make money for medical school. On the other hand, maybe it's best he didn't know until the last moment."

"I suppose." Adam's face didn't have the strained expression he'd worn in the past when Glen's ambition to become a doctor was being discussed. It was understandable now that she knew Adam's parents had tried to pressure him into becoming a lawyer.

His initial companionability at the sci-fi conference had been a surprise. She'd expected to spend most of the day wandering around on her own or with the twins. Instead, after the first few minutes when she'd found herself paired with Adam, they'd stayed together as a group.

Elizabeth was a pleasant woman and while her husband had initially come off as gruff, he'd smoothed out as they got better acquainted. As for Adam? He'd been pleasant, but had mostly stayed out of the conversation. Cassie hadn't been able to decide if there was a reason for his silence.

It was just as well. He'd seemed more human when they were talking, not simply a gorgeous man who operated in a world that was too unfamiliar for comfort. Truth be told, she'd rather feel uncomfortable with Adam Wilding. That way she wouldn't get any nonsensical ideas.

Her reflections fled when Glen appeared in a swashbuckler costume.

"Very dashing," she called.

He pulled a rapier from his belt and waved it around. "Pretty cool. On guard."

Still, the costume concerned Cassie because she wondered how they planned to dress Tiff. A low-cut gown from the same period? If so, they'd have to think again. But when Tiffany came out of the second tent, she wore a trendy prom dress that was suitable for her age.

"Are you breathing a sigh of relief?" Adam whispered in Cassie's ear.

His breath feathered across her skin and a tingle of awareness went through her, stronger than she could have imagined possible from such an innocent contact.

"Yes. Among your other talents, have you become a mind reader?" she asked, telling her pulse to stop jumping. She didn't want to like Adam that way. Even supposing he became interested in her, she couldn't risk upsetting the twins' lives again so soon. Maybe she was being judgmental, but she didn't want to remind them of the way Marie had run around, bringing home men she'd just met and knew nothing about.

"It was mostly a guess based on the protective mother-bear look in your eyes," Adam explained.

Mother bear? The description pleased Cassie. "I didn't know I was being that obvious."

"This is the twins' first modeling job. You being concerned is natural." Adam waved his hand around the area taken over by the film crew. "The advertising concept is to emphasize the game company's advances in the next generation of their programming. And to suggest their competitors are behind the times, of course."

The fees being paid to the kids had seemed eye-popping—more than Glen could earn mowing lawns over several summers—but now Cassie could see they were commensurate with the overall cost of the production. "This is an expensive way to promote sales for a new computer game."

"They can afford it. Ten years ago, Mindspinder Games became one of the hottest startups in the software industry and quickly became competitive on the national level. They're huge."

"Glen enjoys their programs, so he liked it when they wanted him and Tiff to do a job. But I'm curious, you said there would be a go-see before they'd be hired, but there wasn't."

Adam shrugged. "The owner saw the promotional photos of Tiff and Glen on the website and called about them a week ago last Friday. I mentioned they were going to the sci-fi convention and he decided to attend, too, and take a look. Shane Wolcott told me that he doesn't find go-sees productive. He prefers seeing models interact naturally."

"So you turned Saturday into a business

trip." Cassie tried to suppress a faint, illogical disappointment.

"To an extent, since I knew someone interested in hiring the kids would be there."

She swallowed, knowing she didn't have any reason to be upset...yet was. "Why didn't you tell me that someone would be observing Tiff and Glen? I wouldn't have told them."

WHILE ADAM HAD seen a flash of protectiveness in Cassie's eyes earlier, he'd recognized little else. What made her so guarded?

He cleared his throat. "Shane didn't want anyone except me to know in case you coached the kids."

It was true, though Shane had acknowledged Cassie might need to be told to prevent misunderstandings...the kind that could ensue if she noticed a strange man watching or speaking to her niece and nephew.

"I have no intention of coaching Glen and Tiffany," Cassie returned in a sharp tone, "now or in the future. We've already had shades of this discussion. Have I been a stage mom in any way?"

"No, of course not."

"Then kindly keep me in the loop from now on. You can have your office manager call or email. It shouldn't be too difficult or time-consuming. I don't want to always wonder if someone could be observing them anonymously."

Once again she was suggesting their contacts be limited to electronic communication or through another individual. With some women, he might start wondering if she was trying to prompt his interest by playing it cool, but that hardly seemed to be Cassie's style. The most logical explanation was that she either didn't like or trust him. Or both.

It shouldn't bother him, but it did. He was generally considered a nice, respectable guy.

"All right," he agreed. "In the spirit of keeping you in the loop, I'm hoping the results of the photo shoot will convince Shane to cast the kids in a national television commercial. He's mentioned the possibility. Just don't get your hopes up or tell Glen and Tiffany. This business is volatile."

"I understand."

"Good. Would you like to get something to eat or drink?"

"Coffee would be great."

They walked across to the food truck. Adam recognized the name of the caterer; according to Nicole, it was one of the best in the Seattle area.

It would be a long day of shooting. Judging from the size of the costume rack, Pat Piligian planned to do a wide variety of contrasting photographs. He was a perfectionist, and if more than one photo ended up being used in Mindspinder Games' print advertising campaign, the kids would be paid accordingly.

"What can I get for you?" asked the caterer.

"Coffee," Cassie said.

"We have both Seattle's Best Coffee and Starbucks. Would you like a latte, espresso or something else?"

"The brand doesn't matter, just whatever is ready to go."

After they'd both gotten their order, Adam sent her a glance. "I thought everyone in Washington was devoted to specialty java. I've never seen a place with so many coffee stands, shops and carts."

She wrinkled her nose. "I work at home and make terrible coffee. The odds are excellent that *anyone* else makes it better than I do."

Adam chuckled. "Why don't you fill a thermos every morning at your local gourmet stop?"

Cassie rolled her eyes. "Because it's expensive and you can get hooked on those fancy coffee drinks. A friend of mine was having financial troubles and couldn't understand why. I figured out she was spending over four hundred bucks a month on lattes. That may not sound like much to you, but to her, it was the difference between making her bills or getting further behind each month."

"Surely it wasn't that high."

"Actually, it was more, but nobody believes me. She didn't, either, until I made her do the math. Think about it…she got a tall, extra hot, double shot mocha latte three or four times a day. All these drive-through coffee stands make it easy to stop for a cup when you're running around from one task to the next. They cost at least four dollars and she always gave them a dollar tip."

"Four hundred a month sounds like a lot for a beverage, even for me, whatever that comment was supposed to mean."

"I shouldn't have said that. I suppose most people think supermodels lead fabulous lives, where money isn't an issue."

"I made a good living in front of the camera, but I didn't live extravagantly. I saved and invested the majority of my income. I grew up in a working family and know the value of money," Adam returned.

For some reason, it felt important that Cassie understood. While he enjoyed his share of luxuries, he'd never lived as if he was rolling in wealth; he'd always known that sooner or later the bucks would stop coming in. The luxury his success in modeling had given him was being able to choose *when* to change the direction of his life. Modeling was fine, but he'd been ready to take on something new, which was exactly what Moonlight Ventures represented.

"My parents worked, too," Cassie murmured. "Mom was a dental technician and Dad was a jock…that is, he taught high school PE and coached football."

Adam lifted an eyebrow. "A jock. Is that how you see him?"

"It's mostly how he sees himself. Or did." Cassie looked down the bustling city street that Pat Piligian planned to use as a backdrop for his photographs of the twins. "He even played professional football for a while. Being ill has been hard on him, and when we talk, it's always about the active outdoor life he led before getting sick."

"I didn't realize a liver transplant required someone to be sedentary."

"The first twelve months there are restrictions on certain types of activity, but Dad is beyond that." Her smile seemed forced. "It takes time to adjust and feel comfortable around people again. And to trust your body. This isn't something they ever contemplated happening, but I'm hoping he'll figure it out. Mom, too. It takes time," she repeated.

Feel comfortable around people again?

Interesting comment and it was similar to something else Cassie had said about her parents; obviously she was worried for their emotional state. Were they equally concerned about her? Or maybe she was reserved because she'd been dealing with so much with little family support, Adam mused. Her father's illness would be difficult enough to handle, but she'd also become guardian to two children because her sister was unfit to mother them.

Was anyone offering Cassie the emotional support *she* needed? Not that it was his business, but staying detached was proving more difficult than he'd expected it to be—at least in this particular case. Maybe it was because his sister's kids were twins, too, or because he had minimal experience being on the other side of the agent-client relationship.

"I'm sorry things have been tough with your

folks," Adam said, realizing he'd been lost in thought. "How far away do they live?"

"Not too far as the crow flies, but they're near Port Townsend, which is across the Puget Sound. When I go, it's usually south to the Tacoma Narrows bridge, and then up the west side of the Sound. It's a fair drive, so now that I have the twins, we mostly visit by phone."

"Was your dad a good coach?"

"The team frequently had a winning average. He was okay working with students. It was the parents he found challenging. But ultimately, he probably would have been happier as a fisherman or a tug boat operator or something similar to that. He used to talk about it when I was growing up."

Adam raised his eyebrows. "Those are pretty solitary occupations."

"I know." She stirred restlessly. "Are you sure that Tiff's makeup will look age appropriate? I'm not trying to be difficult, but when I first brought her and her brother to Washington, she had two plastic shoeboxes filled with the poorest quality makeup I've ever seen. Truly awful stuff."

Cassie smiled ruefully.

"Marie let them do or watch anything they wanted," she continued, "whenever they wanted. While I've curtailed some of their less than great habits, I can't turn everything into a battle."

Her comments underscored the challenges she faced with her niece and nephew. Admiration went through Adam. Tiffany and Glen had gone from a horrible living situation, which nonetheless had left them to do as they pleased. Now they were in a decent home, but it had restrictions they must be chafing against.

"Tiff's makeup will be professionally done. I get your concerns. Criticizing never occurred to me," he said firmly. "Anyhow, I'm not a father, so I doubt my opinion is valid in the first place."

"That hasn't stopped other people from critiquing my decisions, even strangers." Her tone was resigned. "I guess it goes with the territory. They mostly want to be helpful, without realizing how frustrating it can be. Well, sometimes they're just busybodies."

"No doubt." Adam noticed someone coming toward them. "Hey, Shane," he called. "Shane, this is Cassie Bryant, the twins' aunt. Cassie, Shane Wolcott is the owner of Mindspinder Games."

Shane shook hands with Cassie. "Hello. I'm

delighted your niece and nephew are doing an ad for us."

"I understand you used the sci-fi convention as an…um, alternative go-see."

"Yeah, I'm a computer geek. With all the hours I spend programming, my social skills have suffered, so I'm more effective just observing potential models. And their attractive aunt, of course."

Adam restrained a snort. A few months ago he'd flown up to attend a charity ball in Seattle. Shane Wolcott had shown up looking as if he was a suave diplomat. He was brilliant, sophisticated and possessed a lethal charm that most women seemed to enjoy. His "aw, shucks" routine must have been adopted for Cassie's benefit. To Cassie's credit, it didn't appear to have cut any ice with her.

"I'm glad you like Tiffany and Glen," she said, pointing to where the kids were having makeup applied. "They've been looking forward to this photo shoot."

If anything, Shane seemed even more intrigued. He probably wasn't used to a member of the opposite sex being impervious to his charm.

Join the club, Adam thought. Not that he'd tried to charm Cassie, but she rarely let down her guard. Admittedly, she'd been friendly at the sci-fi convention and had gotten along with his parents. Revealing their expectations about his career and his concerns about Glen could have been a mistake; instead it had led to an enlightening chat about her father and male pride.

"What do you do?" Shane asked. "Adam didn't tell me."

"I'm a freelance website designer and manager."

Shane gave her a megawatt smile. "A woman after my own heart. Tell me one of the sites you've created. I'll have to visit it."

"The website for the sci-fi convention."

The interest in his face intensified. "That's a great design. It was a brilliant idea to create a role-playing game for users who wanted to win a discount on their tickets. I hear the website had four times the normal number of visitors. Is there any chance you'd be interested in working for Mindspinder? I could use someone with your creative vision."

"I'M PRETTY BUSY with my business," Cassie explained, trying to ignore how much Shane's polished, flirtatious style reminded her of Michael.

"At least let me call to discuss the possibilities," Shane urged. "I'm open to a variety of working arrangements, including part time and freelance."

"All right." Cassie gave him one of her cards, though she figured he was mostly making polite conversation.

Computer games had never particularly interested her, but since becoming guardian to Tiff and Glen, she'd learned more about them. Mindspinder was a company she especially liked since they relied more on complexity than violent imagery.

Rather than casually dropping her business card in a pocket, Shane Wolcott tucked it into his wallet. "I'll be in touch," he promised.

Adam cleared his throat, almost seeming annoyed. "Cassie, you previously mentioned wanting to work on your laptop while the kids were at shoots. What do you need in terms of seating?"

"I can use one of those, if there are enough." She gestured to a stack of wood-and-canvas director's chairs.

"Surely we can do better than that," Shane interjected. "I'll check with the coordinator and have something delivered if necessary."

"Please don't bother. I'll be fine," Cassie protested.

"It isn't a bother."

He left and Cassie released an exasperated breath. "I don't need any special consideration and I really don't need anybody thinking I'm being demanding."

Adam gave her a quirky grin. "Since you have to be here all day without compensation, making you comfortable is only right."

"Glen and Tiff are being compensated. Quite generously. I had no idea that modeling fees could be so high."

"It depends on how well-known they are, who's hiring them and how broad the exposure will be. National ad versus local ad, that sort of thing. Their next job could be for a great deal less," Adam cautioned.

"I understand. By the way," she said, "you should be aware that Glen and your mom have chatted a couple of times on the phone. Apparently they exchanged cell numbers at the convention."

"What do they talk about?"

"I'm not a spy, I don't listen to what he says," Cassie said wryly. "But I suspect he may sub-

consciously see her as a surrogate grandmother
and that she misses her grandkids."

"I suppose. It was a shock when my folks arrived and said they were renting an apartment
for a few months. As a rule, I go see them in
Albuquerque, not the other way around."

Shane returned while Cassie was debating
what to say. She had a feeling Adam wasn't
thrilled about his parents being in Washington,
but to her, it seemed a good step forward. She
was certain her own parents would be happier
if they'd leave the isolated little bubble they
were living inside.

"I'll be going now. Please ask Penny Chandler for anything you need," Shane urged. "I
wish I could stay, but I have a meeting at nine."

"It was nice meeting you," Cassie said
quickly.

"The same here," he returned. "I'll be in
touch."

"I'd better get going as well," Adam told her
after Shane was gone. "You have my cell number, Cassie. Call if you have concerns or issues."

She breathed a sigh of relief when both of
them were out of sight and she could get to
work. Being around two such high-powered

men made her feel as if all the oxygen was being sucked out of the air.

ADAM WOULD HAVE preferred staying at the photo shoot. He told himself that it was because he missed the behind-the-scenes world of modeling, but it was more than that—because of Cassie, he was having trouble keeping his personal feelings from interfering with his job.

He was particularly unhappy that he'd felt a flash of jealousy when the owner of Mindspinder Games tried to charm Cassie. He was equally unhappy about his relief when she'd seen through Shane Wolcott's easy charm. Shane was a decent guy, but he saw an attractive woman and couldn't help pouring it on. Yet it was clear that he'd seen something special in her...the same intriguing quality Adam kept glimpsing.

His hands tightened on the steering wheel. *Enough.*

Admiring Cassie's devotion to her niece and nephew was fine, but he was the twins' agent, that was all. It was something Kevin McClaskey had forgotten as he tried to be everything to his various clients. But even more important, Cassie was a prickly woman who'd metaphorically posted No Trespassing signs around herself. Adam couldn't imagine anything more frustrating than to get involved with someone like that.

His heart had already been shredded enough when he lost Isabelle. He didn't need to invite more pain by starting to care for the wrong person.

CHAPTER SEVEN

ELIZABETH HUMMED AS she finished a batch of tamales. She wanted to stock Adam's freezer with them, along with containers of his favorite chile verde. She still hoped to return every few months and replenish his supply, even though things weren't going well between him and Dermott.

She sighed.

It had been over a week since the science fiction convention and she could hardly keep her husband and son together in the same room for longer than it took to eat a meal.

Oooooh, they were both so stubborn it made her mad. Did Dermott honestly think he'd have more in common with a son who was an attorney or judge than he had with a son who was a talent agent and former model?

Not likely.

Yet in many ways they were so much alike. Surely the two of them could find common ground if she pushed hard enough.

Outside the window, she saw the owner of the small apartment cottage they'd rented. Dermott was nearby, happily doing repairs to the buildings that had gone untended. The owner was nice, he just wasn't handy and didn't want to charge higher rent to his tenants. In exchange for Dermott's work, they were now staying for free. It pleased her husband to make old things useful again and it meant they'd probably remain in Washington longer.

Her phone chirped and she saw a text message from Glen, probably about the photo shoot that he and his sister had done for a computer company.

Glen was the one who'd asked if they could talk sometimes. She wouldn't have tried to push a friendship on him, even though she wondered if connecting with him might help her understand Adam better. She'd admitted that to Glen and he'd looked puzzled before laughing about it. Maybe, with everything he'd already gone through in life, he'd learned that laughter was healing.

Elizabeth read the message from Glen.

Weird day. Bunch of costumes, like Halloween.

Did Tiff have fun? she texted back.

Won't stop talking abt it uh gotta go dnnr ready.

Bye, she replied, knowing he was probably already racing to the dinner table. Food was a top priority for Glen. Adam had been the same at that age. Keeping him fed had seemed like a full-time job.

As if in response to the thought, she saw Adam drive in and park. She'd invited him for the evening and was hoping it wouldn't be yet another tense meal.

She stepped outside and kissed his cheek. "Hello, there."

"Hi, Mom. Hope you don't mind, I didn't stop to change. I came straight from the office."

Dermott harrumphed from where he was scraping paint from a window sill. "Yeah. I'll bet you call that a suit."

Adam's mouth tightened. "This is called business casual, which is appropriate for what I do."

"Surely you can't think a suit jacket over jeans is suitable for business."

"It's what the managers wore at the teleservice center where I used to work," Elizabeth interjected quickly. "But a lot of them didn't wear ties the way Adam does. You look nice, son."

"Thanks, Mom."

She was proud of him and wished Dermott could feel the same. It wasn't just that Adam was handsome, he had a good heart and cared about people and the environment. When he'd become so successful as a model, she'd worried they would start seeing him in the scandal sheets, attending wild parties and accused of using drugs. But while there had been periodic pictures of him with the women he dated and speculation about his marriage plans, they'd seen little else.

Until Isabelle.

Before her death, the attention had largely been positive about a beautiful, glamorous couple with a bright future. After she died, the paparazzi had speculated all sorts of scandalous possibilities. They'd even hounded them in Albuquerque, digging into their past, printing stories about Sophie's teenage pregnancy, marriage and swift divorce, though it had nothing to do with Isabelle.

Sophie had hated it, yet the articles had also mentioned her business—orders for New Mexico–style Christmas ornaments had flooded in, perhaps a form of support for getting victimized by a relentless press.

"Mom, is something wrong?"

Elizabeth blinked. "No, I'm fine. I made pot roast for dinner and tamales for your freezer."

Adam grinned. "Can't I just eat them?"

"Of course. I can always make more."

"Maybe I should get a full-size freezer."

"Go right ahead. I'll make sure it's full before we go home."

"Sounds great."

Despite his words, Elizabeth suspected he wouldn't get the freezer—he was too concerned about her overdoing. But since the two men she loved most in the world were already at odds for the evening, she pushed her frustration away and concentrated on getting through the meal.

ADAM DEBATED WITH himself the next morning, then picked up the phone and dialed Cassie's number. She worked at home, so it wasn't a surprise to get her rather than voice mail.

"Hey, Cassie, it's Adam."

"Oh, hello. Is something up?"

"I'm doing a television commercial for the Virgil Wildlife Conservation Center this week and wondered if Tiff and Glen might want to be in the background shots. It's pro bono, but it would be good exposure for them and might lead to other jobs."

There was a long silence at the other end of the line and he pictured Cassie in his mind. She'd just spent hours at a photo shoot and was probably wondering if shepherding her niece and nephew to modeling jobs was going to become a full-time activity. It was a valid concern—after all, she needed to make a living, and working on her laptop at a photo shoot couldn't be as productive as working in her own office.

"No pressure," he said quickly. "I just wanted to offer the opportunity."

"It seems worthwhile on more than one level. Does the wildlife place know you want to bring the kids?"

"I haven't asked in case you weren't interested, but including them shouldn't be a problem. I'll clear it and let you know if there are any issues. They didn't expect to shoot the ad for a couple of months, but a film crew that does work for public TV had a slot open up this week unexpectedly. They're doing the shoot for free, so obviously the wildlife center wants to jump on the offer."

"I see." There was another silence. "What

risks would there be for the kids? Will they come in contact with the wild animals?"

"Risks should be minimal. It's unlikely they'd interact with the wolves. There's an approved script, which means they won't have speaking parts unless the director makes changes, which might put them closer to the animals. I can't even guarantee any footage of them will make it into the ad because of how they put these things together, so it's all right if you say no," he assured, "I won't be offended."

"No, that is, I'm not refusing, just evaluating my schedule. Are we talking about one day, or more?"

"Just one. On Saturday. That's all the time the crew has available. They're flying in from Alaska and doing a thirty-six hour layover in Washington. They have to leave on Sunday for Greenland to shoot a special on global warming, so believe me, they'll be done. Probably by one or a little later."

"Um, okay. I'm in the middle of a new design, but I should have the basics done by then. I need to check with the kids, though. Do you want to hold, or should I email their answer?"

"I can hold."

Several minutes passed before Cassie came back on the line. "Tiff is thrilled and Glen thinks it would be cool to see the animals. Where and what time?"

"I'll pick you up," Adam astonished himself by saying.

"That isn't necessary. We can meet you there."

He thought fast to come up with a valid reason for them traveling together...aside from his big mouth. "Both the film crew and the wildlife center are passionate about environmental responsibility. Arriving in separate vehicles doesn't seem appropriate. I even plan to take my sedan, since it's more gas-friendly than the SUV."

"We could meet at the agency."

"The agency and my loft are in the city. Your place is on the way to the center, and since the twins hate getting up early, this means they can be in bed a little longer."

Another long silence followed. "All right. You have our address."

"Yes. The film crew wants to get set up before the center opens for visitors, so I'll be at your place at 7:00 a.m. I can have you sign the paperwork for Tiff and Glen before filming begins. It won't be a regular contract, just a release."

"Fine. What should the kids wear? I'm assuming this is a low budget affair, so there won't be a wardrobe department or anything."

Adam chuckled. "You assume correctly. Casual dress is appropriate—jeans and T-shirts, that sort of thing. They won't want anybody in the ad who's too dressy. It wouldn't fit. Tiff and Glen should just look the way kids normally dress. However, avoid stripes or polka dots. Sometimes they don't film well."

"All right. I can also bring extra clothes, just in case. We'll see you Saturday morning."

"Right."

He heard a soft "goodbye," followed by the sound of the call being disconnected. A wry smile creased his mouth. Cassie was a woman of few words.

CASSIE PUT THE phone down and drew a tight breath. She hadn't expected to see much, if anything, of Adam. He must represent dozens of clients; he couldn't spend a large amount of time with any particular one, or in this case, *two*.

Yet so far he'd gone to the convention, spent over an hour at the shoot for Mindspinder Games and now had invited Tiff and Glen to be in a television commercial for an environmental cause. Was he taking such a strong interest in her niece and nephew to prove that modeling could be a viable source of college money?

The question made Cassie roll her eyes.

Adam Wilding didn't need to prove anything to anybody. It was unfortunate his father still clung to the wish he'd become a lawyer, but Adam was plainly successful. Someday his father would surely recognize that. Moreover, it wasn't fair to assume Adam did everything in reaction to his parents.

Cassie's fingers hesitated over her computer keyboard, then she accessed the Moonlight Ventures website again. She genuinely felt it had an overdone, gimmicky quality, but the design of the site wasn't what she was looking for, it was the page about Adam. On it, his photograph was darkly sophisticated—sort of a James Bond look.

Not approachable.

Men of Adam's caliber belonged on movie screens with leading ladies as beautiful as Nicole George, not dealing with everyday people. On the other hand, their website *was* selling something—the ability of the agency to make their clients as glamorous and successful as the people who ran it. So maybe the photo was intended to convey a "you can be like this, too" message. It all depended on what Moonlight Ventures was trying to say about itself.

The page about Adam didn't provide much personal information; it was mostly about his professional credits and experience. But from the additional research she'd done on Adam Wilding, she had learned more than she had any right to know—his fiancée's death should have been respected as a private grief. Instead, stories about him and his family had been rampant.

It was hard to imagine the pain of losing someone so suddenly. Ironically, from all accounts, Adam's career had prospered even more afterward. Perhaps it had been the darkness in his eyes, the depth of emotion both revealed and veiled in his face.

Her business line rang and she absently picked it up without checking the caller ID. "Bryant Web Designs," she answered.

"It's Adam again."

Cassie nearly dropped the receiver at hearing his deep voice. It was like reading a book, only to have one of the characters actually speak to her.

Adam Wilding is real, she reminded herself.

"I called your business line to be sure we could talk privately," he continued. "Yesterday, when you mentioned Glen and my mom connecting, I should have asked if *you're* okay with it."

Cassie straightened, trying to decide if Adam was the one who might be uncomfortable.

"I don't see a problem, unless you do," she answered quietly. "I've asked Glen not to put any undue expectations on your mother."

"Expectations?"

Cassie got up and closed the door of her office. The twins didn't eavesdrop as far as she knew, but the same as Adam, she didn't want to take a chance of them overhearing accidentally.

"For one, my parents aren't involved with his life because of Dad's health," she explained. "As I mentioned yesterday, I think Glen might be seeing Elizabeth as a surrogate grandmother."

"Mom wouldn't mind that."

"Perhaps, and Glen is sensitive and mature for his age. I'm sure he'd appreciate having someone else who's stable and reliable as a confidant. But it wouldn't be fair to Elizabeth to expect as much from her as if she really was his grandmother. Besides, she doesn't live here permanently. She's on vacation."

"Surely he has teachers he can confide in, at least during the school year."

Cassie touched the snow globe her niece and nephew had given her for Christmas. Inside was an idyllic miniature world, like a Christmas card, the kind her niece and nephew had never known. Her heart ached as she looked at it, wondering if they'd sent her a subconscious appeal when they'd chosen the gift. *Please give us this world.*

She questioned how well Adam could understand as an outsider. While he'd been pressured regarding his career, his childhood hadn't been dominated by a neglectful, alcoholic mother and an overloaded school system that couldn't keep up with so many children in troubled homes. Glen and Tiff might appear to be normal teens, but they had a wealth of ghosts haunting them. It added an extra challenge to her efforts at being a parent.

"I'm not sure Glen trusts teachers," she admitted finally. "While he tried to protect Marie, a part of him may also feel his teachers should have realized what was going on and taken action sooner. Emotions are complicated. Regardless, Elizabeth is new in Glen's experience. She's an older woman who doesn't have a stake in his life, who's also warm and sympathetic."

"That doesn't explain why Tiffany and my dad connected so well at the sci-fi convention. He's a good guy, but I wouldn't call him warm and sympathetic."

Cassie pursed her mouth, wondering if Adam knew his father had made a snide remark to Glen the day they'd met. Perhaps it was best not to mention it.

"Tiff is a peacemaker. She may have thought he wasn't comfortable and wanted to smooth things over."

"I see. Anyway, I think it's okay for Glen and my mother to be in contact. He's a teenager. It's been a while, but I remember being that age," Adam said with a hint of humor. "He isn't going to spend a huge amount of his time talking to my mom."

"If their friendship isn't a concern for you, it isn't one for me. At least right now," Cassie added. She closed the tab displaying the Moonlight Ventures website—it was disconcerting to talk to Adam with his image on her computer screen...especially *that* image. "Is there anything else?"

"Nope, that was all. It's just a bit strange to have—"

"Our personal lives intersecting?" she finished.

He cleared his throat. "Yeah. I always had a good relationship with my agent, but I never met Betsy's family or went to a science fiction convention with her. I've always preferred keeping my business and personal lives separate."

"I imagine everything will settle down and be normal soon. In the meantime, I'd better get back to work."

"Er, yes, of course. See you on Saturday."

Cassie put the phone on her desk and got up to open the door again; not wanting Tiff and Glen to feel shut out. In the beginning, it had been hard to focus with two active kids in the house, but she managed better now... partly by working in the early morning before they got up.

Footsteps thundered down the staircase a few minutes later and Glen appeared at the office door.

"Hashtag's dad is taking him to the Tacoma Sandpipers' game. He called to invite me to go 'cause they got an extra ticket. Is that okay? They're coming over right now, just in case."

Hashtag was Glen's closest friend, Richard Griffith, but after years of being called

"Richie," he preferred the nickname he'd gotten at computer camp. Cassie knew the Griffiths through the boys' friendship and the parent-teacher association, but she wasn't sure of the protocol for an outing like this. Parents had usually spoken to her before issuing an invitation. Still, the twins were teenagers and probably needed to start being more independent.

"*Pleeease* let me go," Glen pleaded when she didn't respond right away. "I'll be polite and won't make any problems."

"It isn't that, I was just trying to decide if I should talk to Mr. Griffith first. Remember what I said about being new to taking care of kids when you first came? I know it's been almost a year, but I'm still learning, so please be patient."

"I'm sure it's okay."

Cassie hesitated a moment longer, then took money from her wallet and gave it to him. "Okay, but buy your own food and offer to pay for parking. And let them know you appreciate being included."

"Thanks!"

The doorbell rang and she went outside to thank Jerry Griffith herself for inviting Glen. He was a nice guy struggling to accept that his son preferred computers over outdoor sports. Luckily both boys loved baseball and they enjoyed watching the local farm team most of all.

Back in her office, she considered what to do about Tiffany. Balancing the special treats her niece and nephew received wasn't always easy. That was probably a challenge faced by any multiple child household, but it seemed particularly acute with the twins…partly because she was too aware of everything they'd gone through with their mother.

As if on cue, Tiffany appeared at the office door. "Aunt Cassie, can't we go to the game, too, or do something else?"

Cassie glanced at her computer screens. She was busier than ever with two new contracts, but could work late tonight to try to catch up.

"Tell you what," she said slowly, "I ordered a family membership to the MoPOP and the package arrived a few days ago. Would you prefer spending the afternoon there?" The MoPOP was the Museum of Pop Culture at the Seattle Center—very trendy and popular with the students at Tiffany's school. They'd gone once and her niece had wanted to return ever since.

Tiffany gave her a brilliant smile. "That would be totally awesome."

GLEN CRAMMED HIS stomach with french fries, hot dogs and ice cream at the ball game, cheering the Sandpipers between visits to the concession stand. He felt a little bad that he hadn't asked Mr. Griffith if Tiff could come with them, but it was a guys day out. At least that's what Hashtag called it.

Was that what Aunt Cassie would call being sexist?

He didn't know. But it *had* to be okay for guys to sometimes do things together just as guys. Tiff and her friends liked fooling around by themselves and nobody said *they* were sexist. Anyhow, Mr. Griffith had already gotten the tickets when Hashtag called to invite him, so she couldn't have come.

Glen waited through one of the concession lines with his friend and they got another hot dog. He wasn't hungry any longer, but the chance to eat hot dogs didn't come every day.

"Are you going to play with a wolf at that photo thing on Saturday?" Hashtag asked as they hurried back to their seats. Glen had explained about the wildlife commercial he and Tiff were doing with Adam, but he'd made his friend promise not to tell anyone else since he still wasn't comfortable with being a model.

"There's no way Aunt Cassie will let us play with a wolf," he replied doubtfully.

"Bummer."

Glen shrugged. It was weird that he felt both good and frustrated that his aunt was so protective. Yet it also made him squirm, especially when Aunt Cassie talked about not knowing much about raising kids and asked them to be patient while she learned. Tiffany said it was great that Cassie didn't pretend to know everything, but it was different for him. His sister didn't have a reason to feel guilty about upsetting everyone's lives.

He groaned as the Sandpipers' batter popped the ball into a high fly, then shouted a cheer when the third baseman fumbled and dropped it. The batter got all the way to second base, making it just under the throw, and the fans in the stadium went wild.

"We're lucky. That doesn't happen very often," Mr. Griffith declared. He was crazy about baseball and even watched classic baseball games during the off-season, much to Hashtag's disgust. Glen agreed. Why watch a game that couldn't make any difference to the stats?

Hashtag got a faraway expression and took out his phone, probably to look up the statistical probability of a fly ball being dropped.

"You agreed, no electronics," Mr. Griffith said.

Hashtag sighed, but he slipped the phone into his pocket without arguing.

Sometimes Glen envied his friend for having a dad. Mr. Griffith was nice and did stuff with his son, while Glen didn't even know his own dad's name. But it was just as well, he figured, the guy would just cause more problems—after all, if his mom had liked him, he couldn't be worth much.

The thought wasn't new, just one that always made Glen feel lousy. He wanted to love his mom, he really did, but a lot of the time he didn't even like her.

The Sandpipers won an hour later and Glen got up to leave with the others.

"Dad, would you let me play with a wolf?" Hashtag asked as they headed for the car.

Mr. Griffith lifted his eyebrows. "You want to play with a wolf? I can't even get you to toss a stick for Bodger."

Bodger was the Griffiths' English sheepdog. He looked like a giant white and gray mop.

"Bodger can't see a stick through all his fur. I just wondered," Hashtag told him quickly.

"But would you? I mean if the wolf was safe and sort of tame."

"I suppose. Wolves are terrific. You'd have to fight me for the chance to do it, though," Mr. Griffith kidded as they got into his SUV. "I'd want my turn first."

"Tell your aunt what Dad said," Hashtag whispered to Glen as Mr. Griffith focused on the cars waiting to exit. "Maybe she'll lighten up."

Glen wasn't sure, but he had an idea that might work. Aunt Cassie really liked Elizabeth and might listen if someone else's mother thought it was okay. So maybe he could ask Elizabeth if she agreed with Hashtag's dad, then invite her to the photo shoot and see what happened.

CHAPTER EIGHT

THE DRIVE TO the Virgil Wildlife Conservation Center was quiet at first. The kids immediately fell asleep in the back seat of the sedan and Cassie didn't say anything in case Adam preferred silence while his mind woke up to the day.

"Have you ever been out here?" he asked finally.

"No. I've heard about the rescue work they do, but wasn't aware they allowed visitors."

"It's new. Their focus is still on wildlife rescue and conservation, but they know it's also critical to educate people about the importance of keystone species."

"You mean predators, like mountain lions and wolves. My brother has talked about that. Devlin says keystone species have a disproportionate impact on the environment relative to its population."

Adam nodded. "Except keystone species aren't all four-footed predators. Various fish, such as salmon, are keystone species, along with other animals."

"For someone who loves city living, your concern for wildlife is…incongruous," she murmured, echoing something he'd said in one of their discussions.

He chuckled. "Touché. But city people can be concerned about the environment, even if they'll never see a wolf in the wild or a bear digging for grubs in a rotten log."

"Have you?" Cassie asked.

"Seen a wolf or bear in the wild? Bears, many times. Wolves are tougher. They're actually rather shy of people, but I'd love to see one in its natural habitat. In the meantime, I have places like the wildlife center to visit."

Adam's enthusiasm was engaging; no wonder he was often asked to do ads about issues such as wolf conservation. She'd once seen a nature special where he'd done the introduction and narration. At the time, she'd figured it was a public relations move, but now she realized it stemmed from a true interest.

They pulled into the wildlife center's parking area fifteen minutes early and she saw they were the first to arrive.

"The center doesn't have anyone here at night?" she asked.

"They do, but staff and volunteer parking is around the side of the building."

Cassie glanced back at her niece and nephew. They hadn't stirred. "How did you get interested in wildlife conservation?" she asked.

"I've always been fascinated by nature, also by archeology, for that matter. My family didn't take fancy vacations as a kid, but when we weren't visiting my dad's grandparents, we went camping. As I got older, my friends and I would go hiking on the weekends. When I was fifteen, I was able to join a summer archeological dig for three weeks. I felt like Indiana Jones in *Raiders of the Lost Ark*."

"That sounds fun. It didn't tempt you to become an archeologist?"

Adam's expression tightened. "My father—"

"Oh, right," Cassie said quickly. From what he'd told her, declaring he didn't want a legal career would have caused a huge uproar in the Wilding family. Apparently the uproar had been bad enough once he was an adult. "It's never too late."

He shook his head. "I'm happy being a talent agent. But now that I'm not traveling so much, it might be interesting to take a few classes. I'm impressed with the University of Washington campus in Seattle."

"I loved going there."

Her time at the university had been wonderful, except for her last year in graduate school when she'd met Michael and given up her dreams to make him happy. That was the hardest part when she remembered him, knowing she'd lost sight of herself and what she wanted. It had been like looking into a mirror and no longer recognizing the person looking back.

Suddenly uneasy, Cassie got out and drew several deep breaths. She was vaguely aware of Adam getting out as well.

"Something wrong?" he asked.

"Not really. I—" From nearby, an eerie howl rang through the air, interrupting her. The haunting cry made her skin tingle. "Wow. Are there wolves this close to the parking area?"

"One of the enclosures comes right up to the building, where visitors can observe the pack from behind picture windows. That's Bravo Pack. They aren't as shy of people as the others."

"So they have more than one wolf pack here."

"Yeah. One of them is part of a breeding and release program. They're kept separate and can only be observed by webcam. The other two packs are rescues that can't be released for various reasons, usually because of past injuries or too much socialization with humans."

"I love the sound. Gives me goose bumps."

"A WOLF SONG echoes through the soul," Adam murmured.

Cassie cocked her head at him. In the car, he'd noted a faintly distressed expression and was pleased to see it had faded.

"Echoes through the soul?" she repeated. "I would have never guessed you were a poet."

"I'm not. Maybe I read that somewhere."

"Ah, you mean you can't admit to having romantic, poetic leanings."

"I'm just honest. In high school, my creative writing teacher usually wrote on my papers, 'technically correct, lacks imagination.'"

"Ouch."

"At least I wasn't unfairly accused of plagiarism. My girlfriend was questioned whether she'd actually authored a particular sonnet because he thought it was too good to have been written by someone her age. Juanita was devastated. I totally lost it when she began crying."

Cassie frowned. "He questioned it without proof, just because it was good? That's appalling. Kids can do amazing things. We don't give them enough credit."

"I know. I told him he owed her an apology, but he didn't appreciate being challenged, especially in front of a whole class, so the school suspended me for three days. My parents were furious with me."

A light breeze was blowing and Cassie brushed a strand of hair from her cheek. "Surely they were proud that you'd defended your girlfriend."

"They were, but I gave you the sanitized version of what happened," Adam admitted. "I didn't get physical, but I was really foul-mouthed. I knew better, but I was full of self-righteous outrage. Mom and Dad approved of me defending Juanita, but they were appalled at how I did it."

Cassie shot another glance into the car at Glen and Tiffany and stepped farther away. "Um, I know what it's like to be called in for a parent-teacher meeting about inappropriate language," she said softly.

Adam was surprised. "Which...er, one of the twins? I'd hate for an advertiser or film crew to be put off with that sort of thing. Whether it's fair or not, they prefer teens with a clean-cut image."

Cassie put her chin up. "You may be their talent agent, but that's private. Regardless, the three of us have discussed that while they live with me, certain words aren't acceptable. Learning to respect boundaries has been tough, but they're learning."

"Surely their old school didn't allow that kind of language, either."

Cassie gave him a cool look. "Apparently it was a chronic issue. It's difficult for a child not to repeat what they keep hearing at home and is never told not to speak like that. Marie didn't care what the school said, so it was hard for them to care, either."

He shouldn't have been surprised. Before coming to live with their aunt, the twins hadn't grown up with the best role model. Whether it affected his strategy as their agent was another question.

"The truth is," Cassie continued, "I can't make Glen and Tiff forget the bad things they've gone through. I'm not sure I should, even if it was possible."

"Oh?"

"We're all the sum total of our experiences. I've always disliked fantasy novels or science fiction shows where they erase a character's memory of events with the argument it would 'complicate' their life. Even if it was possible, what gives someone the right to decide that for someone else? It's like erasing part of a person's identity."

Adam had never given the idea much consideration, but he understood what Cassie meant. "I get what you're saying."

"I hate that my niece and nephew went through so much. I wish I could have done something about it, but those are their memories, for good or bad. Their experiences belong to them, not me. To take them away now would change who they've become."

"I see."

Cassie was a curious woman with strong opinions. While he felt attraction, he wasn't sure how well he liked her—she was awfully closed and prickly—but Glen and Tiffany seemed fond enough of their aunt. That was what mattered. Hopefully, their mother wouldn't decide to seek custody again.

Another single wolf cry floated through the air, then was joined by another, then another and another. The sound was a beautiful, wild, musical quartet.

The back door of the sedan open and Glen emerged, followed by Tiffany on the other side, her eyes wide. "Ohmygosh," she exclaimed, "those are wolves."

"Yup." Adam's lips twitched. Apparently it only took a chorus of wolf howls to rouse two sleep-loving teenagers; he should give a recording to Cassie to use when she had trouble getting them out of bed.

Glen yawned. "Man, it sucks getting up early on a Saturday."

"But we don't mind," Tiffany announced with a glare at her brother. "That's what models and actors have to do."

"Uh, yeah." Glen rubbed his stomach. "Is there anything to eat?"

Cassie reached into the car and took out one of the insulated bags she'd brought. "Breakfast burritos. They should still be hot."

Glen's face brightened. "PBJ muffins, too?"

"PBJ muffins, too."

Adam accepted a burrito filled with a mixture of eggs, peppers and cheese. He liked spicy food and was glad to find Cassie had provided salsa to dress up the meal. Her large thermos of steaming coffee was also welcome. At the Mindspinder photo shoot, she'd claimed to be lousy at making it, but the brew was drinkable and went well with the PBJ muffins, which turned out to be whole-grain muffins filled with peanut butter and jam.

"They're one of the few things I bake," Cassie said when he complimented her. "You make a huge batch of the batter and it can keep in the fridge for several weeks."

Adam had just finished eating when someone emerged from the main building. "Hi," he called. "We're here to do the commercial being shot today."

"Vince Owens, head of security," the man explained as he approached them. "The film crew phoned. They've been delayed with a flat tire and our administrator is treating an injured cat."

"Mountain lion or bobcat?" Cassie asked.

"Domestic, though this one seems to think it's a panther. People bring us strays that are injured or sick when they don't know where else to go. Dr. Shaunessy doesn't turn any animal away. At one time or another, we've all been pressed into service as vet technicians."

"That's cool," Glen said.

The security man grinned. "I think so, and it makes a work shift move faster to know you've done something constructive."

Leila Shaunessy came out a few minutes later. When Adam was moving to Seattle, his friends in various environmental organizations had urged him to offer his help in promoting her rescue and conservation work. Since agreeing to do the video, he'd visited the center a number of times so the animals could become accustomed to his scent and presence. Particularly Mojave, one of the alpha wolves. He was an amazing animal—intense, smart and able to control his pack with little more than a warning glance.

"Morning, Leila," he said. "Let me introduce Tiffany and Glen, and their aunt, Cassie. Everyone, this is Leila, administrator and founder of the Virgil Wildlife Conservation Center. She's also a great veterinarian, originally hailing from Ireland."

"I appreciate all of you doing this commercial." Leila stopped and smiled. "Actually, since we aren't soliciting money, naming it a commercial or advertisement doesn't sound quite right. I'm just not sure what else to call it since this is the first time we're doing something for television. The thing will air in thirty to sixty second segments on various channels... any stations I've convinced to give us the time for free, that is."

"How about calling it a short educational video?" Cassie suggested.

"That's better. I'm not saying we don't welcome donations, though we have a generous endowment for our rescue and conservation work, but our purpose right now is to inform people."

"Mr. Wilding and I were discussing the importance of keystone species on the drive out here," Cassie said.

Adam's eyebrows shot up. He'd intentionally used first names when introducing everyone, and yet Cassie had called him "Mr. Wilding." She was incredibly frustrating. He still didn't believe it was advisable to get too friendly with his clients' guardian, but surely he and Cassie had gone beyond that sort of formality.

On the other hand, maybe he was just over-reading the situation. She was such a challenge to understand, his brain might be looking for explanations where none were needed.

The film crew arrived and Adam went over to greet them. He'd already consulted with everyone about having Tiffany and Glen in the television spot. They liked the idea, but a great deal depended on the twins; if they couldn't behave naturally, there was no value to including them.

It would also help him know if they had any natural ability as actors.

He glanced back at Cassie, wondering if she would be interested in appearing in the wildlife shoot as well, only to decide he'd asked her enough questions today.

GLEN HAD ALREADY figured out that being a model meant a bunch of just hanging around and being bored. He didn't mind if there was something to do, so he'd brought one of his games. Besides, the ad was mostly about the center and Adam was doing narration, so he and Tiffany wouldn't have much to do.

You'd think a short video wouldn't take long to shoot, but he hadn't thought a few pictures for Mindspinder Games would take long, either. Instead it had taken *all* day, with them changing in and out of costumes and getting into silly poses.

"Do you have a regular clinic to treat the animals?" he asked Leila as the film crew began unloading equipment.

"Yes. Would you and your family like a tour?"

He turned to his sister and aunt, a funny, nice feeling in his stomach. They *were* a family. Maybe different than most of the kids at school, but that didn't matter. "Do you want a tour, Aunt Cassie?"

"Sure."

"Me, too," Tiff said.

Adam was helping unload equipment and said that filming wouldn't begin for a while, so they went into the building. It was bigger than it seemed from outside, and the front part was like a museum, with windows for visitors to watch one of the wolf packs. Right now the wolves were over the hill and out of sight, though they could be seen on three webcams.

The vet clinic was in a long wing that angled out in the rear. Glen looked around and thought it wasn't very different from a human clinic. They had an X-ray room and a lab and treatment areas. Also jars with long cotton swabs and the other junk you saw at a doctor's office.

"What do you do when you have to take care of a sick bear?" Tiffany wanted to know. "They're gi*nor*mous and wouldn't fit on one of these tables. Or through the door. And what if they wake up?"

Leila chuckled. "I treat bears outside in one of the enclosures. As for a patient waking up in the middle of treatment, I'm very careful about things like that."

"Oh. What's the weirdest animal you've treated?"

"Hard to say, but probably a hedgehog. A motorist brought one in, thinking it was a strange baby porcupine, when it was actually someone's lost pet. Hedgehogs aren't native to the North American continent."

"My brother wants to be doctor, but being a vet would be *waaaay* cooler. Glen, don't you want to be like Dr. Doolittle and talk to the animals?"

"That's just a silly kids movie," Glen muttered.

Sometimes what Tiff said really bothered him. She was the same as everyone else, teasing about him wanting to be a doctor. Aunt Cassie and Elizabeth were the only ones who didn't act that way.

He hoped Elizabeth would be here today, but in her last text, she'd said she was still trying to convince Dermott to go. Anyway, he felt funny about inviting her. It might seem as if he was trying to trick Aunt Cassie into letting him get close to the wolves. Okay, so he wouldn't ask about petting them, then nobody would ever know.

"It would be nice if we could talk to our patients," Leila said. "Perhaps the hardest part of my work is being unable to explain what I'm doing and offer reassurance. I might also get more cooperation that way. Glen, it's something to think about if you move forward with medical studies and consider pediatrics as a specialty. Babies don't understand why you're giving them a vaccine or doing something else, the same with my patients."

"Uh, yeah."

He tried not to get frustrated about her saying *if* he moved forward with medical studies. At least she wasn't as negative as his teachers and the principal at Salish Junior High had been in the beginning. After seeing his old class records, they'd told Aunt Cassie that he and Tiff were high school dropouts in the making and nothing they'd seen suggested the outcome was likely to change.

Man, had she gotten ticked. He'd have used a different word, but Aunt Cassie didn't like him saying that one.

He and Tiff had sat outside the principal's office that time when Aunt Cassie had gotten called in for a talk about a letter received from their old junior high. They'd heard her say how wrong it was to pigeonhole kids and that nobody was going to keep her niece and nephew from succeeding because of the past. Also that their old school was from the Dark Ages and had no business sending a separate letter from the official records and she was seriously considering legal action against them. After that, the principal had apologized and promised to throw away the other school's stupid letter.

It was rad having her stand up for them that way.

"This is the surgical recovery area," Leila said, bringing them into a room lined on both sides by stainless steel kennels, some larger, some smaller. She pointed to one of them. "And there is our latest patient. She's quite a handful."

Glen looked inside and saw a skinny kitten with a bandage covering its foreleg. It was black except for white whiskers and a white bib. Her fur was rumpled and she seemed to have runny eyes. She looked at Leila and hissed.

It didn't seem to bother her. "As I said, she's a handful. Most of my patients don't appreciate what we do for them, but at the same time, it's good when they have spirit."

"She's great."

Glen stuck his fingers between the bars and wiggled them at the kitten. It limped over and leaned against his forefinger, a loud purr coming from its throat…while still glaring at the veterinarian. Glen wanted to take the kitten home more than anything, but how could he ask

Aunt Cassie? Their mom hadn't allowed them to have pets in San Diego; she'd said it was too expensive and too much work and trouble.

He put his other hand up, pressed flat against the bars, and the kitten rubbed as close as it could, purring so hard it rumbled up to his wrists.

"She's chosen you," Leila said in her distinctive brogue. "That's quite a compliment. Cats can be very selective about the humans they accept."

"Glen, do you want him?" It was Aunt Cassie and he nodded jerkily, feeling guilty and happy at the same time. He didn't know how she felt about pets, just that she didn't have one right now.

"I'll take care of him," he promised.

"I know. What is the center's policy about adoption for cats you've rescued?" Aunt Cassie asked Leila.

"Normally at the end of each month we transfer any that have come in to a no-kill shelter, but there isn't a rule that says I can't let one be adopted here. However, I'll need to keep her for treatment awhile longer before she goes anywhere. In the meantime, she'll have all her shots and be fixed. Black cats are often overlooked in shelters, so it would be nice to see this one find a home, preferably where she can live indoors."

Tiffany looked unhappy. "Why are black cats overlooked?"

"There are a number of reasons. One is that some people still believe they're bad luck, though where I grew up in Ireland, it's quite the opposite. But it isn't just black cats who have a hard time finding homes—black dogs also spend more time in animal shelters than other dogs."

"That's awful." Tiff immediately looked as if she was going to start crying.

"I agree, but we often get them here at the wildlife center. People just dump them or abandon them."

Tiff sniffed. "Do you have any now?"

"We have a batch of puppies, but they aren't black. They're around the corner, through the door marked Kennels. Go ahead if you want to visit them. They need socialization."

Tiffany hurried away and a minute later Glen heard her let out a small shriek of excitement. "*Ohmygosh, ohmygosh.* They're *darling.*"

CASSIE CLOSED HER eyes for a moment. She had a feeling that the household was about to expand by both a cat *and* a dog. After all, she couldn't let Glen have a cat and not let Tiff have a dog, and how could she drag him away from the kitten when he'd plainly fallen in love with it?

It seemed as if she had to say no an awful lot. No to the bad words they were accustomed to saying. No to the junk food they wanted. No to them staying up all night and sleeping all day. No to having every channel available on cable TV and watching whatever they wanted, no matter what the rating. There was some really weird stuff on a few of those channels, especially after midnight, so it was easier not to have them in the cable package than to load on parental controls the way she had with their computers.

The twins were good kids, but that didn't mean they were happy about the boundaries they'd never experienced before living with her.

"You look as if you're solving a puzzle," Adam's low voice murmuring in Cassie's ear made her jump. She'd expected him to stay with the film crew.

"Not exactly. Do they need the kids now?"

"We still have a few minutes. Where's Tiffany?"

"Playing with a litter of puppies. We should get her."

They found Tiff sitting in one of the kennels with happy, sandy-colored puppies jumping on her in gleeful excitement.

"I'm sorry, I should have asked, how are you set up for animals?" Leila asked softly.

The best time to ask would have been before the kids fell in love with the idea of adopting, but Cassie didn't say so. "The cat will live inside and we have a house with a fully fenced yard. Most of the neighbors have dogs, so it shouldn't upset anybody if we add another to the mix," she returned in an equally low tone.

"Excellent."

Cassie squared her shoulders. "Tiff, do you want a puppy?"

Her niece looked up. "Oh, *yes*. But I want a black one because of what Leila said."

Cassie's eyes burned and she blinked to keep from crying. Tiffany had a big heart and it wasn't surprising she'd choose a pet that might have a harder time finding a home otherwise.

"All right. You need to remember that a dog requires more care than cats, including the need to be walked and bathed. You'd also need to clean up after it, both in the yard and when you take him or her out for a walk. Are you prepared to do all that?"

"Yes, I promise."

"Okay, we'll go to an animal shelter where you can pick one out. Today, if we have time after the photo shoot is done."

Tiffany smiled happily. "Thanks, Aunt Cassie."

Adam had gone into the kennel to kneel beside the puppies, chuckling at their eager bids for attention. It was easy to imagine him doing something like this with his own children one day. Of course, Cassie didn't know whether he wanted to get married after losing his fiancée in such a sad way. But it would be a shame if he didn't. He related well to the twins and was the kind of man that kids enjoyed.

Cassie told herself that the speculations about Adam were normal. Surely it was natural to wonder about him, especially since he could have so much impact upon the twins.

There was nothing personal about it.

CHAPTER NINE

ELIZABETH SHIVERED WITH excitement as they drove out to the wildlife center. Glen's invitation had seemed an ideal opportunity to see Adam working, and she knew that no matter how her husband still felt about the modeling, he was proud of their son's public service efforts.

Really, if they would just talk more, they might see they weren't that far apart on the important things.

At the wildlife center, she and Dermott got out of the truck. It was a few minutes after nine and a number of vehicles were in the parking area.

"I don't see why we have to keep surprising Adam," Dermott grumbled as they walked toward the main building. "Maybe he doesn't like surprises."

"You're the one who doesn't like them, dear."

Elizabeth had checked and knew the wildlife visitor center opened at 9:00 a.m. Inside, the broad windows with a hillside beyond drew immediate attention. She was still getting used to how green it was in Washington. Pictures didn't do it justice.

There wasn't any sign of Adam in the visitor area and she looked through the large picture windows, hoping to see cameras and whatever else was involved with making a commercial. But everything seemed quiet except for a single wolf walking over the crest of the hill.

Elizabeth watched, thrilled at the sight. Proud, ears pricked forward, alert, the animal was utterly regal. He stared down the slope with an unnerving intensity.

Other visitors saw him as well and they crowded up to the windows, exclaiming and pointing.

A young man stepped forward wearing a shirt with the VWCC logo on the front. "Hi, I'm Tim Rowdon, a weekend volunteer here at the conservation center. The wolf you're seeing is Mojave. He's four years old and the alpha wolf of Bravo Pack. They're part of our public relations team. While they can't be released into the wild for various reasons, they help us educate people about the importance of wolves to the ecosystem."

"I heard Mojave was raised like he was a pet dog," someone called from the back.

Tim bobbed his head. "That's right. He was found following a woodland fire at just a week old. His burns were treated and he was bottle fed by a rancher in Wyoming, then was transferred here two years ago. Since he's imprinted on humans and there's nerve damage to one of his hind legs, it was decided not to attempt returning him to the wild."

"He looks pretty wild to me," said one of the women, shivering. "It feels as if he's looking right at me."

"Yeah, *through* me," added the man next to her.

Tim grinned. "I know that feeling. Though raised by humans, Mojave's wild instincts are impressive. He's always aware of his surroundings."

The corners of Elizabeth's mouth twitched. Many people were afraid of wolves. She'd felt that way as well, but Adam had told her that a healthy, full-blooded wolf rarely, if ever, attacked a human being.

A ripple of disappointment went through the onlookers when Mojave raised his head, seemed to listen for something, then spun and raced back over the hill. Sighs went through the crowd around the window as they dispersed, giving Elizabeth a chance to speak to the volunteer in private.

"Hello, I'm Elizabeth Wilding. My son is supposed to be here, doing a commercial for the center. Adam Wilding…? Also Glen and Tiffany Bryant." She gestured to Dermott. "My husband and I were hoping to see some of the filming if it isn't too much trouble."

"Wait here while I make a call."

Elizabeth suddenly felt unsure as the young man stepped away and took out a cell phone.

Maybe surprising Adam hadn't been such a good idea. For some reason, she'd thought everyone would be out in front with a big group of onlookers. Glen hadn't known what to expect, but he'd said that lots of people going by on the street had stopped to rubberneck the Mindspinder photo shoot.

She'd even brought a large quantity of food, hoping it would be enough to feed lunch to everyone involved in making the commercial. Food was a good icebreaker—after all, everyone had to eat.

While Adam hadn't invited them to the wildlife center the way Glen did, he had mentioned the reason he'd be busy today. Now she wondered if having his parents appear unexpectedly would make him uncomfortable. He was a grown man, not a child wanting his mom and dad to show up and watch him compete at a track meet.

She didn't have much time to think about it before Tim returned. "Our administrator asked me to escort you. They've started filming, so we'll need to be quiet when we get close."

Elizabeth called to Dermott and they followed the young man through a door marked Authorized Personnel.

"What do you do when you aren't giving time to the conservation center?" she asked Tim.

"I'm a mechanic. Someday I hope to own my repair shop, but right now I work for my uncle."

"That's a fine skill. The world needs mechanics," Dermott said. "You'll always have a job somewhere."

"Yes, sir. That's what Uncle Chet tells me."

Elizabeth smiled. "How did you start volunteering?"

"Well, my uncle repairs the VWCC vehicles and I got interested. And, uh…" He stopped and his ears turned red. "There was a girl I liked. She doesn't work here any longer, but I still stayed. Okay, we're getting near where they're filming, so we'd better stop talking."

They walked over the top of a small rise and Elizabeth saw something that nearly put her heart in her throat—Adam was inside the fence, cameras focused on him, crouched next to a wolf.

ADAM GAZED INTO Mojave's eyes, thrilled that the magnificent animal had come so close.

A faint noise broke Mojave's concentration and his head turned. One of the females had stepped out of cover and he released a low, guttural sound. She edged back behind a tree.

Adam waited until the wolf's attention was back on him before rising to his feet. Though Mojave had lived as long with humans as he had with other wolves, it didn't seem wise to startle him—his instincts as an alpha appeared to be in first-rate condition.

He went quietly to the gate, aware the crew still had their cameras focused on Mojave. He'd done part of the narration for the educational video—as Cassie had tagged it—but there was more left to do. And they might want it done again in different settings, looking for the best impact possible.

It was only when he was outside the wolf enclosure that he looked around…and saw his parents. Mom was pale and his dad was watching Mojave in apparent fascination.

Adam pinned a pleasant expression on his face and headed toward them. It was his own fault; if he hadn't wanted to risk them showing up unexpectedly, he shouldn't have told them about doing the educational video.

"Hey, Mom, Dad. I didn't know you were coming out here today."

"I invited them," Glen volunteered. His face turned uncertain. "Uh, I hope that was okay, Adam. I mean, this wasn't like a regular job."

Leila stepped forward before he could say anything. "Mr. Wilding, Mrs. Wilding, you're quite welcome. In fact, it would be great if you could help us out by appearing in some general scenes for our video. We were just discussing how nice it would be to have more people for it."

"That would be fun," Elizabeth said. The color in her face had rushed back. "Right, Dermott?"

"Yeah," Dermott agreed, though Adam could imagine the silent dialogue running through his father's head about dignity and respect. But nobody had asked him to wear a bathing suit and strike poses, and the video was for a good cause—Dad might not study the issues surrounding wildlife preservation, but he agreed with the objectives.

"That's wonderful."

While the director obtained releases from the elder Wildings, Cassie stepped closer, away from the twins. "I'm sorry if Glen did something inappropriate," she said softly. "He didn't tell me about inviting them, so I couldn't run it past you. I'll talk to him."

"It's okay," Adam assured her. "I was just surprised to see my parents here. Glen obviously understands he shouldn't do it for a regular modeling assignment, and that's the important thing."

Her smile was wry. "Boundaries, again. Ironic, right? We want kids to think the sky is the limit for what they can achieve, and we still have all these rules we want them to follow."

Adam laughed. "We're surrounded by paradoxes. Speaking of which, did you really want to become part of the space program?"

"I gave it serious consideration. If you look at the roster of astronauts on NASA's website, you can see from their biographies that they have a variety of educational backgrounds and experience. Some have been in the military, others not. I don't know if it's something I'd want now, but at the time it was a dream."

And dreams are important, Adam thought.

It was curious that Cassie's new hope of living in the mountains and her old hope of going into space seemed so far apart. But then, both involved a certain amount of solitude, so maybe they weren't so different.

He cleared his throat. "I'm impressed that Tiffany decided to wait to get a dog, rather than taking one of the puppies in there."

"Apparently black dogs spend more time in shelters than other dogs. Tiff is very soft-hearted. Glen, too, he just doesn't show it as much, though you should have seen him react to that kitten Leila was treating. Soooo, our household is about to expand by both a puppy and a kitten. I've never dealt with puppies before. Don't they leave a lot of puddles on the floor before they learn that's what bushes and fire hydrants are for?"

The corner of Adam's mouth twitched at the resigned note in Cassie's voice. "If memory serves, that's the way it works. I haven't had a puppy since I was a kid, but I recall my mother being frustrated with Puddles's maturing process."

"Seriously, your dog was named Puddles, or is that a joke?"

He chuckled. "Joke. Her name was Angel.

Actually, while she had a few accidents, it wasn't too bad. You could ask my mom. I was four at the time, so no one handed me a mop."

"Angel? That's nice. What breed?"

"Mutt. As in unknown heritage. Dad brought her home from a construction site where she was living on scraps from everyone's lunch. She was probably part Lab, part terrier and part who knows what."

"Is Angel the reason you care about wolves so much?"

Adam shrugged. "Not exactly. After I started to make a name for myself in modeling, a consortium of ranchers wanted me to make a commercial for them. The script talked about the financial losses they'd suffered from wolves, so I did my research. While a couple of calves had been lost between them, they'd been fully compensated by an environmental group. I refused the job, the information got out somehow, and several conservation organizations contacted me, expressing their appreciation."

"You became their hero."

"I wouldn't put it that way, but I started doing free work on their behalf and things developed from there. People like Leila are the ones who work every single day to change attitudes and save the animals. I just help out every now and then."

"That's nice." Cassie stirred restlessly and he recalled she hadn't brought her laptop.

"I noticed you didn't bring your computer today. Didn't you want to get some work done?" he asked.

"I wasn't sure how feasible it would be out here."

"I'm sorry."

She smiled faintly. "Surely taking care of your clients' guardian isn't part of your duties as an agent."

"It's just that I appreciate the time you're taking to help the wildlife center," he said.

It was true, but it was also true that things continued being complicated with Cassie and the twins. Yes, he felt a certain responsibility toward her as his clients' guardian. After all, she was devoting a fair amount of time to Glen and Tiffany's new career, while still running her business. He also admired her decision to put their entire modeling fees into a trust fund.

And he was undeniably attracted to her.

It didn't make sense. She was a prickly, unfathomable woman who practically had Don't Trespass written on her forehead. From the little she'd told him, it seemed clear she was wary of getting hurt again. He understood—losing Isabelle had left wounds deeper than he'd ever imagined possible. But starting to care for someone with so many emotional barriers would be the same as inviting more heartache. Yet even knowing that, she intrigued him.

Cassie looked at her niece and nephew, then turned back to him. "Tiff and Glen were thrilled you asked them to be involved in the video. And I...er, have been thinking about our discussion earlier, about the school and their language. I shouldn't have said anything. I hope it won't affect how you work with them."

"Don't worry about it," Adam urged, bothered by the hint of uncertainty he saw in her eyes. "I want them to be a success, and that isn't going to change because I found out one of them did the same thing that got me in trouble as a teenager."

"I GUESS THAT would be a little hypocritical," Cassie murmured, the edge of tension easing in her stomach. Her feelings remained mixed about Glen and Tiffany becoming models, but she was just as worried about messing it up for them.

"Yeah. You know, it's okay to trust me, Cassie."

Trust?

It didn't come easily to her, but she nodded. "Sure. This is new to me, that's all."

She didn't have time to say more because the director came over to consult with Adam, then took him away to do another clip for the film.

"Isn't it exciting?" Elizabeth asked, looking decidedly more excited than her taciturn husband. "You're going to be in the video, too, aren't you?"

"Afraid not, I'm pretty camera shy."

"Oh, but you're so lovely."

Cassie didn't feel lovely, but she smiled and thanked the other woman.

Elizabeth was unquestionably sincere, but Cassie had seen too many photos of Michael at company parties and events while he was schmoozing management, and the pictures usually showed her next to him, looking decidedly uncomfortable and out of place. Then he'd critiqued how she looked and offered "advice."

Michael had probably loved her in his own way, but that didn't help much when someone pointed a camera at her and she remembered all her insecurities.

But she was happy to go watch as Adam worked in front of the camera, while the director put the twins and the Wildings in the background, almost as if they were kids having fun with their grandparents. The only difference was the fact they were sometimes inside the wolf enclosure, although in a slightly recessed space. She didn't mind standing inside next to the cameraman, but she was nervous for the kids.

Leila said they had tranquilizer guns ready in the very unlikely possibility that the wolves were a problem. The general visitor didn't get this opportunity and both of the kids were thrilled, so she'd bit her tongue and agreed. One thing she was certain of was that Adam would never put Glen and Tiffany or his parents at risk. So it had to be okay.

Since the wolves didn't follow direction, shot after shot was taken as the director tried to get exactly the right feel.

Cassie couldn't help agreeing whenever the cameraman focused on Dermott, saying how well he photographed. She'd brought her own camera and extra SD cards, so she had been taking plenty of pictures herself. And it was true. Dermott photographed very well. Around sixty, he was a handsome man. Adam looked a lot like him.

"That's incredible," the director whispered two hours later as Mojave approached Dermott and the two locked gazes. Adam must have recognized something special was happening, because he backed away to stand next to Cassie as they watched.

Long minutes passed while something unspoken seemed to pass between man and wolf.

When Mojave returned to his pack, Dermott shook his head and the sensitive microphone picked up his words. "I never knew it could be like that." Then he jerked and looked toward everyone else who was watching. "Sorry I opened my big mouth and messed that up for you."

"Not on your life," the director exclaimed. "That's exactly the kind of thing I was looking for."

"Oh, I… Well, I'm glad I didn't ruin anything."

Dermott started walking toward his son, his eyes still wide and full of amazement.

Cassie poked Adam in the side. "Go tell him what you're thinking, instead of just standing there." She scrunched her nose. "Oops, that's none of my business."

"I'm always afraid he'll misinterpret."

"But not saying anything can be misinterpreted, too."

"Right."

Adam stepped forward to meet his father. "That was an incredible moment, Dad."

Embarrassment crossed Dermott's face. "You aren't going to make me into one of your models, are you?" he answered gruffly, but with the faintest hint of humor in his eyes.

"Of course not." Adam's voice was tight and his smile stiff.

The twins and the elder Wildings went back to where the director wanted them.

Adam looked at Cassie. "See what I mean?"

She made a face at him. "No, I don't. You're the one who misinterpreted things. Your dad was making a sly joke and you missed it entirely."

Adam's eyes opened wide. "He was? I never thought he had a sense of humor."

"He was definitely kidding around. Maybe you're the one without the sense of humor," Cassie suggested.

"Come on, you don't believe that. Wasn't the thing about Puddles a *little* funny?"

"Sure. A sense of humor is a survival skill in today's world, but maybe you haven't had an opportunity to show it, or don't think you should on the job. Or maybe it's subtle, like your dad."

"I—"

"Adam," the director called. "Can we do that last shot with you again?"

"Okay." He grinned at Cassie. "Maybe I need to laugh more."

"Couldn't hurt."

Retreating farther into the background, Cassie inwardly scolded herself. What was she thinking to offer opinions or advice to Adam Wilding? But it had seemed as if Dermott had wanted something from his son, so maybe it wasn't just Tiffany who wanted to fix things for people.

She needed to keep her distance from Adam. He lived a high-powered life with savvy, successful people in careers she barely understood. But he was also intelligent, caring and good-looking enough to still startle her with it.

Honestly, this kind of guy should come with warning signs.

ADAM HAD TO force himself to focus and do what the director wanted. The crew needed to finish so they could get ready for tomorrow's flight to Greenland, and it wasn't fair if he didn't give them his full attention. Nor did he want to be anything except his best in front of his parents. For the first time in his life, he was acting, in a sense, in front of them, with his father taking part.

And the weirdest thing of all was his father's shifting attitude. Dad *had* been joking, and instead of joking back, Adam realized he'd taken it as the same old negativity and responded accordingly.

"That's a wrap," the director finally called. "You guys have been terrific. We should have enough for several different television spots. We'll know once our film editor does her thing."

While the twins returned to the clinic with Leila and his parents, Adam went over to Cassie.

"How did you recognize what was going on with Dad when I didn't?" he asked in a low voice.

"I... Some of the time it's easier to see things from the outside than when you're up to your neck in it."

"There's always been such a tug of war between us. Maybe I've forgotten to look for anything but the next bombardment."

"Things won't ever change unless you stop doing that," she said, looking extremely uncomfortable.

Adam cocked his head. "What's the matter?"

"It's just that your parents aren't any of my business and I shouldn't have said anything in the first place." There was a hint of distress in her voice.

"Why does that bother you so much?"

"You're the one who prefers not having your personal and professional lives mixed up with each other."

"True, but there are unique circumstances involved here that I didn't anticipate. Isn't there a saying about life is what happens while you're making other plans?"

A ghost of a smile curved her soft lips. "Are you trying to prove that you *do* have a sense of humor?"

"I'm dismayed that you implied I didn't have one. Perhaps I need to amp up my vitamin B, or pull out a few of my favorite movies to remind myself. I'm a classic film buff and screwball comedies are some of my favorites."

The strain in Cassie's expression appeared to ease and her smile came more naturally.

"Yeah. I do that, too. It's good therapy, watching comedies."

"Do you have any favorites?"

"I like a mixed bag of stuff on TV. Movies are nice as well, though I usually don't have time to watch longer stuff. How about you?"

"The same. I have great old films on DVD, like *Bringing Up Baby* and…" He hesitated. "I used to get a huge kick out of the classic *Addams Family* show, too."

A pang hit him. He and Isabelle had often kidded around about the old television series. She'd say something in French and he'd start kissing her arm the way Gomez did when his wife spoke French on the show.

"You look melancholy all of a sudden," Cassie murmured.

"My fiancée and I had a running joke that came from *The Addams Family*." He paused, but then said, "She died before we could marry." He wasn't sure why he'd explained.

"I'm sorry I reminded you of something painful."

He shook his head. "It's a good memory. Isabelle had a zany sense of fun. I try to remember things like that, rather than how it felt to lose her."

"I ran across several online articles about

the two of you when I was researching Moonlight Ventures. She was beautiful, but the picture I saw in your office was nicer than the others."

Adam thought about the photo. He'd tried telling himself that he shouldn't put it out and had finally set it on the credenza behind his desk. Maybe it hadn't been the best idea—he wanted to move on, and constantly seeing a reminder couldn't help.

"I took that myself," he explained, "the day we got engaged."

"Do you think about her often?"

"Not as much as when it first happened, but I'll never forget how much I loved her."

Cassie frowned faintly. "Why should you? Even if you fall in love again, real love ought to be remembered."

"Do you have something that good to recall?" he asked.

"Nothing significant," she said in what seemed to be a deliberately light tone.

It was almost as if he could see Cassie's defenses going up again and Adam was frustrated. For a brief moment, she'd forgotten to hide from him. Not that he needed to know the

Cassie behind the mask—he already knew she was the wrong woman to get involved with.
So why was he so disappointed?

CHAPTER TEN

CASSIE TRIED TO ignore the energy she sensed from Adam as they walked into the clinic. They found Glen communing with his kitten, and through the open door to the kennel area, Tiffany could be seen once again covered by a pile of wriggling, excited puppies.

Pulling her camera out again, she snapped more shots of the kids, wanting to capture the abandoned pleasure on their faces.

"That reminds me," Adam said, "I've been meaning to ask if you have photos of Glen and Tiffany when they were younger. It can be useful sometimes."

"There aren't many. I checked my sister's apartment and didn't find much. Naturally I took some pics whenever I visited, but they aren't studio quality or anything. Very casual."

It frustrated her to think that Glen and Tiffany's childhood had gone largely unrecorded by their mother. With smartphones, it was so easy.

"How about annual school shots?"

"They…uh, lack personality." While Cassie appreciated having the school photos, they revealed lonely, hurting kids and she didn't want strangers to see the twins that way. "The lack of early childhood pictures won't work against them, will it?"

"Don't worry, it's just another resource. Occasionally a casting director will ask if any are available, but it wouldn't be a deciding factor. Anyhow, I can always take a look at the ones you snapped informally if see if they'd work. For future reference."

From the sudden discomfort on Adam's face, casting directors might be something he regretted mentioning. "Casting director" sounded as if it was connected to acting rather than modeling, so he might be concerned about building up Tiffany's hopes about becoming an actress. Cassie just hoped he wasn't keeping another secret from her, the way he had about Shane Wolcott of Mindspinder Games attending the sci-fi convention to anonymously evaluate the kids. It gave her an uneasy sensation to think someone had been watching them—would she have caught on if she had better parenting instincts?

"In case I didn't say it earlier," Adam continued, "I want to thank you for giving me more insight into my dad. I suppose I've never considered that the way I react might be part of the problem between us. Maybe if *I* change, it will help. At least I'll give it a try."

"I'm glad what I said wasn't too much of a problem."

To avoid any more conversation, Cassie moved closer to Glen so she could get pictures from a different angle. She was glad when Adam headed for the exterior door they'd come through earlier. Keeping him at a distance was the wisest course.

A FUNNY TINGLE traveled up Glen's arm from where the kitten was licking his fingers. It was weird. He hadn't even known that he liked cats. Not that he'd hated them, either, just that he didn't know one way or the other.

Leila had said the kitten had chosen him. That was cool. Hopefully, Oreo wouldn't forget him in between visits, until he could take her home. That's what he'd decided to call her, Oreo.

Aunt Cassie snapped several pictures of him and Oreo. She took lots of pictures, at home and whenever they went somewhere.

"She seems to love you already," Aunt Cassie told him. "Not that I'm surprised by that."

"Yeah, well, thanks." He felt embarrassed about turning into a pile of goo over a tiny fur ball. "I'm calling her Oreo. Leila already wrote it on her chart."

"Great name."

"Hey, everyone," a voice called. "Adam's mother brought lunch for all of us. We're eating in the visitor picnic area."

Glen reluctantly pulled his hand back and followed Aunt Cassie as she headed for where Tiff was playing with the puppies. As much as he'd like to stay with Oreo, he wouldn't want to hurt Elizabeth's feelings by not eating the food she'd made.

And he was also hungry.

He ran back to the kitten. "I'll be back soon," he promised. She let out a meow and settled down, being careful of her injured leg. Maybe he was imagining it, but her big eyes seemed to understand.

Outside there was a covered patio with picnic tables. At one of them, Elizabeth was pulling containers of food from bags and a large cooler. She looked really happy as members of the camera crew thanked her and said they'd like to take her with them wherever they went.

"Three cheers for Mrs. W," one guy yelled and a chorus of hurrahs went up.

"Thanks, I'm starving," Glen said when he got to where Elizabeth was serving out mountains of macaroni salad and sandwiches. There was a big container of vegetables and one with fruit, too, but he ignored them.

"I enjoy feeding people," she replied softly. "I just hope that Adam doesn't mind me butting in like this."

"He seems okay with it." Glen's mouth was already full, but he talked around a bite of sandwich as he pointed at Adam, who was holding a plate and talking with the film director. Tiff sat with Dermott at a picnic table.

"Elizabeth, this is wonderful," Aunt Cassie said, coming to the table. "You have a real gift for food and kindness."

Glen hadn't known that older ladies could blush, but Elizabeth turned pink and looked pleased. It was strange. He had a grandmother and barely knew her. Elizabeth was sort of how he'd thought a grandmother would be. Well, she cooked and she listened, but he never would have imagined a grandma loving science fiction and that kind of stuff. And she wasn't pretending about it, either.

He'd asked again about reading some of her stories, but she was sort of shy about anybody seeing her stuff. It was probably like when he didn't tell people that he was going to be a doctor, since they usually looked at him as if he was silly and pretending.

He waved at Elizabeth and Aunt Cassie, then went to sit with Tiffany. It had turned out to be a terrific day.

CASSIE TOOK HER plate and went to join the kids who were sitting with Dermott. "You all did a wonderful job," she told them. "I could never be that natural with a camera pointed at me."

"I just focused on the kids and the animals," Dermott told her. "Hope it does some good for the center and education and all that."

He seemed relaxed, though he stiffened when his son joined the group.

"Jonathan thinks he's got some really good material," Adam told them.

"Four and a half hours of filming to get a minute or two." Dermott shook his head. "I never gave any thought to what happens behind the scenes in a commercial or film, but it takes much more than I expected to make it work."

Holding her breath, Cassie hoped Adam wouldn't turn down the opening his father seemed to be offering.

Adam made a face. "Yeah, before I got

started in the business I figured it would be short and sweet."

"It sure isn't," Glen added. "I couldn't believe how long it took the other day for just a magazine ad. Mindspinder video games are the bomb, but making the ad was…" His voice trailed and Cassie wondered if he was trying not to say something negative about modeling in front of Adam.

"I'm guessing it must be boring, at least part of the time." Dermott's tone was dry. "But not when you have a live wolf around to keep things spiced up."

"Some of it was Dullsville at the Mindspinder job," Tiffany acknowledged. Vegetables were piled on her plate, with only a small amount of macaroni salad and half a sandwich. "But I loved it anyway."

Adam had sat next to Cassie and she could see the tension in his fist that he'd laid on the bench next to his leg. That was probably understandable since he was trying to talk to his father in a new way.

It also made her wonder if there was a new approach she could use with her own parents. At times, she almost felt like an orphan. She had to do something about that. She missed seeing her parents in person; surely they felt the same.

"I guess all work has aspects that aren't as much fun," Adam speculated. "Is that how it is when building houses or doing repairs, Dad?"

"Naturally, though I might have enjoyed it more if I'd been in charge."

"You knew more than most of your bosses, so you should have been in charge. I'll always remember the time you got fired for pointing out the foundation on a house was messed up. I was awfully proud that you'd stood up for what was right. That house would still be standing today if you'd been the contractor building it."

There was a startled, yet pleased expression on the older man's face, but he shook his head. "I probably couldn't have made a go of it with my own business."

"I'll bet you could have done it," Cassie interjected. "In fact, you still could. There's a crying need for people to have a reliable company to handle small repairs and construction jobs—kind of an all-around handyman service. It's so hard getting something done on my house. Everyone wants the big jobs and doesn't want to deal with anything small. Then when you *do* get someone out, it costs a small fortune. Recently I wanted a ceiling fan installed in my home office, but the estimate from the electrician was absurd."

"I've considered something of the sort," Dermott acknowledged.

Adam leaned forward. "You might also work as a consultant. When my partners and I start expanding, we'll be the same as a lot of businesses and won't have the expertise to discuss it with construction personnel. When the time comes, I'd figured on giving you a call to see if you'd mind helping us, but not every business has that kind of resource."

"I'd be happy to give you a hand, if you'd think it would be useful, but I'm too old to start my own company."

"Nonsense," Cassie said stoutly. "It's never too late to pursue a dream." Then she felt like kicking herself. Once again, she was sticking her nose into something that wasn't her affair. Even worse, she was sticking her nose into Adam's family and she'd already realized it was wiser to put insulation between them. What had happened to her today? It was as if all the filters in her brain had been removed.

"Cassie's right," Adam agreed.

"I used to have other dreams, too," Dermott started to say, and Cassie was afraid he was going to mention his hopes of Adam becoming a lawyer. But after a moment's hesitation, he continued. "But they didn't work out. And, uh, maybe it's just as well."

Knowing what she did about Dermott's "other dreams," Cassie thought it a major triumph that he didn't use the moment as an opportunity for a dig at his son. She was afraid Adam would overreact, but he only smiled.

"Think about it, Dad," Adam urged. "A handyman company specializing in small jobs for homeowners sounds worthwhile. Even if there are already places in Albuquerque doing that, there must be room for another. You could even run it out of the house, taking job orders and coordinating schedules with workers whose skills you already know. They could provide their own tools and act as subcontractors."

"Maybe."

"And social media is an inexpensive way to start advertising," Cassie said, breathing easier. She didn't need this drama and she wasn't good at it. At the same time, she couldn't help hoping that things would get better for Adam and his father. They both seemed like decent men…a little too obstinate for their own good, but decent.

Naturally, she'd want family harmony for

anyone. It wasn't for any other reason, such as starting to care about him.

She wasn't that stupid.

ELIZABETH LOOKED AT the picnic table where two of the people she loved best in the world were sitting and talking. Surely the day had been healthy for her husband, who'd truly seemed to enjoy helping with the video. And he'd been good at it. Wasn't it possible that Adam got some of his photogenic ability from his father? That might seem fanciful, but she didn't think it was impossible. They certainly shared the same dark, handsome looks.

As she watched, Glen swung out from the table and headed toward her, plate in hand.

Elizabeth chuckled. *Hungry teenager alert.*

"Is there enough for seconds?" he asked hopefully.

"More than enough."

He loaded up on sandwiches and another mountain of salad.

"Don't you think a few vegetables would be a good idea?" she asked.

Groaning, he put a few carrots sticks on his plate. "How about that?"

"Add some broccoli or celery and you won't have to be completely embarrassed when people say, 'But Dr. Bryant, do you really think proper nutrition makes a difference?'"

With a grin, he tossed two broccoli flowerets on his plate and dribbled ranch dressing over them.

"I like when you say Dr. Bryant. Some people act like I'm blowing smoke when I talk about medical school."

"It's your dream," she said softly, "and it's up to you whether you make it a reality."

He frowned. "That's strange. They were talking about dreams and stuff over at the table just now."

"Really?" Anxiety clutched her stomach. Dreams were a messy subject in the Wilding family, filled with pitfalls.

"Yeah, Aunt Cassie and Adam are telling Dermott that he isn't too old to start his own business."

The tension eased. Elizabeth absolutely agreed. Her husband had retired too early. "I've always thought he'd be good at it."

"Are you gonna come sit down and have something to eat?"

"I suppose so."

He waited while she put food on a paper plate and walked with her to join the others, where her son and husband seemed to be chatting amiably. Perhaps one of her own dreams might be an inch closer to coming true if Adam and Dermott cooperated.

A faint depression swept over Elizabeth. This wouldn't be the first time she'd built up her hopes only to have them knocked down again. But she had to keep trying.

ADAM WASN'T SURE whether surreal or bizarre best described the day. His parents confounded him, but he thought it might be Cassie who was the biggest puzzle.

He'd spent his entire working career around beautiful women, and they'd varied widely, as all women did. The ones who were open and confident without being vain had attracted his highest admiration and liking. His partners, Nicole and Rachel, fit that category, different as they were from one another in other ways.

But with Cassie, he was confronting a woman who made little of her appearance and didn't seem confident about much except her web designs. She was also reserved, wanting little more than to retreat into isolation, the same as her parents and brother.

Yet she'd been sensitive enough to pick up on his dad's awkward overture. And taking care of Glen and Tiffany wasn't just a duty she was resigned to doing, she really loved them. But why he found her so intriguing was the mystery.

Shaking his thoughts aside, he finished his lunch and returned to the food table for one of his mother's fudge brownies.

His mother followed him, her brow creased. "Adam, dear, I want to apologize. Your father said we shouldn't surprise you and then I also brought all this food. It must seem as if I'm trying to horn in on your life."

"It's fine, Mom." He bent to give her a quick hug. "In fact, it was great. We couldn't do it if this had been a regular modeling assignment for Glen or Tiffany—sometimes there's a closed set and it also wouldn't look professional for the kids to have visitors. But Jonathan, the director, says what happened with Dad is going to make the video a real standout."

Her brow smoothed. "I think you got your amazing looks and photogenic quality from him."

"Uh, yeah." It was a new thought, but not unwelcome. Adam hoped he was like his dad in other ways, too. Maybe not the stubborn part, but Dermott was honest, determined, practical and caring.

His mother leaned toward him. "Adam, Dermott wants to invite Tiffany and Glen to drive up to Mount Rainier with us this afternoon. After all, we're already halfway there. But I said we should ask you before we say anything."

"It's up to Cassie, but there's no problem on my end. I know she promised Tiff she could get a puppy today if there was time, but there's always another day for that."

Elizabeth went back to the table and he watched as she drew Cassie away for a brief conversation. Cassie nodded and they next talked to the twins, who lit up with delight.

It meant he and Cassie would be returning alone. Not that it made any difference; after all, the twins had been fast asleep on the way to the wildlife center. Still, being genuinely alone together would change the dynamics.

A short while later, the film crew helped clean up and then left, effusively thanking Elizabeth for lunch. After saying goodbye to the animals, Glen and Tiffany jumped eagerly into the back seat of Dermott's truck. Adam was left with Cassie, who showed every sign of having withdrawn into herself again.

"I hope it's all right that my folks invited the kids along," he said as they headed for his sedan.

"It's fine. They're crazy about Mount Rainier."

"Earlier in the week you mentioned potential issues about Glen being in contact with my mom. It just occurred to me that you might be concerned about them getting close to people who are temporarily in the area. My parents love New Mexico too much to move to the Northwest."

Cassie shrugged. "I'm afraid Tiffany and Glen are accustomed to people going in and out of their lives. My sister's boyfriends were like a continually revolving door. I doubt any of them lasted for long."

"Ouch. Do they get anxious when you date?"

She tensed visibly. The question hadn't been haphazard; he felt an inexplicable compulsion to see behind her barriers.

"I don't date," she answered in a flat tone.

"Why not?"

"Is it necessary to explain? Do *you* date?"

"Occasionally. It took a while after Isabelle died to want to, then I finally realized she wouldn't have wanted me to bury myself along with her."

Was it his imagination, or had there been a slight quiver of emotion in Cassie's jaw? Yet all she said was, "That's real love."

"I agree. So, what's your excuse for avoiding the dating game?"

Cassie glared. "If you must know, it's partly for the kids, but I also got burned on a guy I loved and who I thought loved me, but then all he wanted was to turn me into a corporate clone of the Stepford variety. I tried for three excruciatingly long years, but I couldn't change that much."

"He wanted you," Adam said, "but *not* you."

"Exactly."

"How did he want you to be different?" Adam couldn't resist asking. He knew he should just drop the subject, but curiosity was overriding good sense.

Cassie sighed. "He wanted someone outgoing, but not pushy, pretty and well dressed, but who didn't outshine anyone else, someone who collected all the pertinent gossip and reported it back to him so he could use it to get ahead. I don't know, there always seemed to be plenty of me that needed changing."

"Only in his outdated opinion. I didn't realize the old stereotype about corporate spouses was still around."

Cassie looked more uncomfortable than ever. "It probably depends on the company.

And most of it may have been in Michael's imagination—his idea of how to get ahead. He was quite ambitious."

Adam was silent as they got into the car and buckled their seat belts. "So when you broke up with him, you retreated to your computers just like your parents retreated to their isolated lives," he observed at length.

"I... Maybe."

"You shouldn't give him so much power. He sounds like a jerk."

Cassie restlessly shifted in her seat. She was wearing worn jeans and a blue T-shirt, her long hair was natural and simply clipped away from her face. Except for a gold locket, she wore no makeup or accessories and Adam suddenly realized how much it suited her. Makeup would just detract from her fine complexion, and her eyes were striking enough without enhancement.

"Michael isn't a totally horrible person," she said defensively. "I don't like thinking I would have kept trying for so long if he wasn't worthwhile on *some* level. Besides, he may have honestly believed we had the same goals and were working together to reach them."

Adam almost suggested she hadn't wanted

to accept the truth, but that might come off as criticism. Besides, who was he to say? People weren't all good or bad; they were usually a combination.

"So you anticipated marrying him," he commented instead, "and out of affection and loyalty, did your best to become what he wanted."

"Yes. We were never officially engaged, but Michael often talked about when we'd get married. He never said he was holding off because I wasn't getting it right, but I kept wondering if that was the reason."

Three years of pressure to become someone else could definitely make a woman defensive. And it bothered Adam to recall that when they met, he'd noted that Cassie didn't try to "jazz" herself up, as he had phrased it. He'd almost considered it a negative quality. Had she gone that direction because of her boyfriend? No, Adam had a feeling it was her natural style. But then he wondered something else. Maybe her longtime boyfriend had simply wanted her to come out of her shell and embrace her own beauty. Cassie could have interpreted that badly and believed he found her wanting.

"What ended it for you?" Adam probed,

needing to understand, rather than make assumptions.

She stared through the side window, as if to keep him from being able to see what was in her eyes. "We went to a party at his boss's big country house. There was heavy drinking and people backstabbing each other when they got a chance. It made me nauseous to think Michael wanted me to fit in with them. But the worst part was when his boss suggested there were ways I could help Michael get ahead. He winked and told me about a sweet little hotel where we could be alone. When I told Michael about it, he joked about how it would put him on the fast track to a vice presidency...only he wasn't really joking."

Anger slammed through Adam. No matter what her boyfriend's original motives might have been, he was slime, through and through.

"That's disgusting. A real man would have told his boss off and quit on the spot."

"I don't think Michael was a bad man at first, but he got co-opted by a place where people did anything to get ahead, no matter what the cost. I told him he was a better person than that and how there were plenty of businesses that didn't operate that way. But he couldn't see it, so I broke it off. I hoped he'd see the truth, but we never spoke again."

Admiration vied with the anger in Adam's veins. Cassie's voice was regretful, as if she felt sorry for the jerk and wished she'd been able to save him from himself. It said a great deal about her caring, honest nature.

"Personally," he said, "I think you're being kinder than he deserves."

This time Cassie faced him, her changeable eyes now dark and troubled. "That's nice of you, but I still feel as if I messed up somehow."

"After three years of being told you weren't right the way you already were, maybe you just got in the habit of thinking it was your fault."

A wisp of a smile curved her soft lips. "You could be right. Thanks for the insight."

"It's only fair. You opened my eyes earlier about my dad."

Suddenly she started gently laughing and it transformed her face. She was very pretty.

"What's so funny?" he asked.

"I'm not really sure. Today is just so incongruous. Or maybe *weird* is a good description."

"Earlier I was thinking it was surreal, or possibly bizarre."

She grinned. "What other words might fit?"

"Let's see—*strange, peculiar, wacky*?"

"Those are pretty good," she agreed. "How about *offbeat, nutty* or *absurd*?"

He started the car.

"What we need is a good thesaurus. I could look it up online, but maybe it's better as a mental exercise."

"True, though my mom loves the thesaurus on her computer."

"Glen mentioned that she writes."

"Yeah, it's a hobby, though she's often written in a notebook, rather than the computer."

As he drove from the parking lot, they heard a wolf howl.

"Do you think that's Mojave?" Cassie asked.

"I'm no expert, but it sounds like him."

"At least he seems comfortable in his world," she said. "Since he was raised by humans, do you think he misses having close human companionship?"

"Maybe at times, but probably less now that he's found a mate. Did you know that many wolves mate for life?"

Cassie bobbed her head. "I heard that once. I guess they're better at love than humans."

"Sometimes. But I'm not giving up hope."

Cassie didn't respond, but sat in silence, her face solemn and reflective.

CHAPTER ELEVEN

AS THEY DROVE BACK, Cassie thought about the list of words they'd exchanged to describe the day. They all fit. The last thing she'd expected was to open up to Adam, though she didn't know and wouldn't ask why the day had seemed strange for him as well.

For her own peace of mind, she needed to restore their professional relationship. Adam was the talent agent for her niece and nephew, which was the proper topic for discussion between them.

"You mentioned casting directors. Do you think acting is a possibility for Tiffany or Glen? I know that's what Tiff wants. Should they have acting lessons?"

"Possibly, although, a lot of young actors don't have formal training. It shouldn't be a problem if they have natural ability." A wry expression crossed his face. "I've had a nibble of interest from a producer who's putting together a television movie that could become a family series. But you can never predict if any inquiry will come to anything. Regardless, the kids will be able to audition if they want."

"I'm glad it's family oriented. Is the movie a drama?" she asked, appreciating that he hadn't rushed in with warnings not to tell the twins.

"Yes, with comedic elements."

"Did you ever consider acting?" The question was a little personal, but it also explored his experience, which surely was applicable.

"Getting tied into such a rigorous schedule wasn't attractive, though that isn't why I turned down the biggest part I was offered. I told my agent no because I would have played a student in his first year of law school."

"Oh."

"Yeah. I figured it would be hard on my dad if he saw it."

"Kind of like poking a wound. That was nice of you."

Adam let out a short, humorless laugh. "What's nice and what's self-protective? I didn't want to hurt him, but I didn't want to reopen the debate, either."

They kept getting into personal territory, no matter what, although it was nice to hear a man who was able to reflect on right and wrong and his own motives for making choices.

Cassie drew a shaky breath. She already found Adam physically attractive—who wouldn't? But she didn't want to find his character equally appealing. Even if she could get past her personal demons, it wasn't credible to think he'd ever have any interest in her. He was a man who could date and marry a woman of extraordinary beauty and accomplishment.

It wasn't that Cassie considered herself plain or stupid, but she knew she was ordinary and wasn't going to stand out in a crowd.

Adam rubbed the back of his neck. "Do you mind if we stop and get something to drink? I'm pretty thirsty."

"No problem."

He pulled off the road at one of the funky little grocery-tourist shops that could be found all over the Northwest. She opened the door and slipped out as he came around to her side; he seemed somewhat chagrined.

"Is this awkward?" she finally asked.

He made a face. "My dad brought me up to open doors for ladies and to follow traditional customs. You probably see that as old-fashioned and sexist."

"Actually, I think it's a nice courtesy unless someone thinks I'm too helpless to properly open a door or take care of myself. Then it would be old-fashioned and sexist."

His expression turned thoughtful. "So it's all in the motivation. Do you accept men at face value until you have evidence one way or the other?"

"That's probably best for most things in life."

"Not if doing it gives a guy three years to shred your self-confidence," he returned harshly.

Cassie stared at Adam, who seemed equally shocked by his own words.

"Maybe you're right," she returned, her voice tight and controlled, "but that's a pretty brutal way of putting it. I already know I was wrong to stick it out that long, so you don't have to emphasize my mistake."

Now he seemed appalled. "I didn't intend it as a criticism. The truth is, you were nicer than he deserved."

His hand came up and gently brushed against her cheek before he bent and put his lips gently against hers. She started to kiss him back, then pulled away.

"No need to feel sorry for me, and I don't need my ego stroked," she said without looking him in the eye. "Let's find something cold to drink. Then I should get home. With the kids gone, I might be able to catch up on my work this afternoon."

Adam stepped backward. "Yes, of course." Now he seemed as carefully businesslike as she was trying to be. "I don't want to forget how much time you've already put in today, or act as if I'm not grateful."

"I did it for the kids and partly for the wolves and wildlife center, so you don't have cause for gratitude one way or the other."

Despite his brisk manner, he still held the door of the store open for her and insisted on paying for a bottle of mineral water. But this time she wondered if it was about being a gentleman, or if he just pitied her.

Why on earth had she told him so much about herself?

GLEN POSED IN front of the Mount Rainier Sunrise visitor center along with Tiffany and the Wildings while another tourist snapped a picture of them with Elizabeth's smartphone.

"Thanks," Elizabeth told the woman when she handed back the phone.

"Not at all. It's wonderful to see grandparents and their grandkids doing things together."

He almost expected Elizabeth to explain they weren't related, but she didn't seem to care.

Tiffany headed off with Dermott to look at wildflowers while he and Elizabeth went to read a plaque.

"Uh, you didn't mind that lady thinking we were a family?" he finally asked.

"Why should I? Did you?"

"Nah. My own grandma, she's nice and all, but I can't talk to her. I was thinking this morning how you were sort of what I used to imagine a grandmother would be like, except for the science fiction stuff. That's *waaaay* cooler than I ever thought a grandma would be."

"Thank you. That's quite a compliment."

"I still want to read some of your stories."

"I'm not sure it would be interesting to you, though it would be nice to get a teenager's opinion."

"Maybe you could email one to me."

"I'm having trouble getting on the internet."

"Call Aunt Cassie. She's a whiz on computers."

"You're a good kid, Glen."

He made a face. "Not everyone thinks so." But he didn't want to talk about how teachers and some other people figured he was heading for something bad because of his mom.

"Can we go to the gift shop? I wanted to look for Aunt Cassie's birthday present."

"Is it soon?"

"In a few weeks. I don't think she's paying any attention. My grandparents stay away from people because of Grandpa's health so they won't do anything. Uncle Orville is cool—he's Aunt Cassie's godfather—but she doesn't have the kind of friends that might make a big deal. The thing is, she did this totally awesome pizza party for our birthday and I don't know how to tell her thanks for everything."

Elizabeth smiled. "Why don't we plan a celebration? If you want, we can also let Dermott and Tiffany in on the fun."

He wanted to hug her, but felt weird about the idea.

ADAM GRIPPED THE phone receiver and counted to ten, then to twenty. He hadn't slept well in the days since the informational video was filmed at the wildlife center. His brain felt foggy and he didn't know what to say to his mother about the invitation to a surprise birthday party for Cassie.

"Adam, dear, are you there?" Mom asked.

"Uh, yeah."

"Can you come to Cassie's party?"

"To be honest, I'm not sure she'd want me there."

"What did you do?" It was her Mom voice, the one he remembered from years ago, when she'd known he was the one who'd hit a ball through the window or was responsible for the eight-ball pattern shaved on the dog's side.

"I said the wrong thing," he admitted, "or maybe she just took it the wrong way."

"Fortunately, Cassie isn't small-minded and will likely forgive you either way. Besides, isn't there a big audition for the kids later this morning?"

Glen must have told her. His folks seemed up on most of their activities.

"That's right," Adam acknowledged, "a casting director wants to see both of them."

"You're going, right? It's their first acting audition—or do agents avoid them?"

"I don't go to everything for my clients, but this is a fairly big deal, so I expect to be there for part of it."

"Good. Then you'll see Cassie and can smooth things over."

Resignation settled over him. "I'll do my best."

"And you'll come to her party? Her godfather will be there, too, but I don't know about her parents and brother."

"Yes, I'll come."

"Remember, Cassie doesn't know about it, so don't say anything. I'd better go. Love you." Her voice was bright and cheery.

"Love you, too."

He put his phone away, knowing he might as well accept that his client relationship with the twins and Cassie probably wouldn't ever be strictly professional, especially while his parents were in the Seattle area. But it wasn't as if he'd started a precedent. Everything with his other clients, both new and established, was going according to plan.

The situation wouldn't bother him that much if it wasn't for Cassie—she'd gotten under his skin.

Why had he kissed her?

She'd interpreted it as a pat on the head, a kind of consolation prize out of pity. But that wasn't the case... He'd wanted to kiss her. In fact, he would have pulled her into an even longer embrace if she hadn't ended it so quickly. Yet she'd responded, brief as it had been.

Strange. On the way to the wildlife center, he'd questioned whether he even liked her; five hours later he had wanted nothing more than a slow, sweet kiss. The day must have been an anomaly.

An hour later, he headed to the studio where Glen and Tiffany would be meeting the casting director, who'd been intrigued, both by their pictures and by them being twins.

"Hi, Adam," Tiffany bubbled a greeting. Adrenaline was obviously running high.

"Hey," Glen said. He seemed calmer than his sister but still energized.

Cassie smiled evenly and Adam could see her barriers were perfectly resurrected. He should be relieved, but he also wondered whether understanding Cassie better would help him find a manageable place for her in his head. Not that it was right to categorize people, but he was having trouble sorting out his feelings about her.

The producer and director were professionals and moved things along. Other kids and teens were there as well, looking excited and hopeful. They were given scripts and asked to do cold readings, then to try acting out a scene. At first Tiffany was paired with a younger girl, while Glen was put with a pretty brunette his own age. After a while, the groupings were remixed and the readings continued.

"Is this the regular way these things go?" Cassie asked quietly.

"I haven't been to a huge number of them,

but enough to know that each director has his or her own style. Sometimes screen tests are done in private, but they're obviously looking for chemistry between actors and actresses. And flexibility."

He was glad to see that both Tiffany and Glen had settled down and were focused. To his eyes, they were doing a good job.

"The kids can definitely perform," he commented.

"They learned early how to put on an act."

It was a sobering reminder of the struggles the twins experienced before moving in with their aunt. Adam had never lived with a troubled, alcoholic mother, but he could well imagine the situations where Tiffany and Glen might have pretended their way through the unpleasantness. It had been bad enough knowing about it when he first became their agent; now that he knew them better, what they'd endured offended him on an even deeper level.

"It's a strange twist," he murmured, "that what was a burden for them might work in their favor now."

Today Cassie's eyes seemed dark and mysterious, cool and remote. "Life is ironic and the cosmos has a weird sense of humor."

Another hour slowly passed as the auditions

continued. Adam told himself that staying was the right thing to do as an agent. But the kids were fine and he was sure there weren't any issues with the TV crew. He just didn't want Cassie to be there alone. She hadn't brought her computer or even a book to pass the time; she simply stood and watched.

As the minutes passed, however, tension seemed to grow in her posture. Maybe it was his imagination, but she looked as if she hadn't slept any more than he had, and he found himself wondering if she'd been kept awake, thinking about their kiss. It was ridiculous to wonder about something like that—they'd briefly kissed, nothing more, yet he was reacting as if he was Glen's age instead of a grown man.

"I've been thinking," Cassie said finally and his pulse jumped. "It will be hard on Tiffany if they want Glen and not her."

Ironic amusement rumbled in Adam's gut as reality settled around him.

"Do you want it to be a package deal or nothing?" he asked, forcing himself into a professional mode.

"Not at all. As you know, Glen had a go-see last week by himself, and Tiffany had one yesterday. They won't always be paired up and it's probably best if they aren't—emotionally, I mean. I don't want them to become dependent on each other. But Tiff is the one who wants to act the most. Glen is intrigued by the idea, but he won't be upset if it doesn't happen."

Adam cleared his throat. "They need to keep in mind that when a director doesn't choose a particular actor, it doesn't mean there's anything wrong with them. They're looking for certain types and whether actors have chemistry together."

"I know, and they've been testing dozens of kids. This is the third day of auditions, so logically, most of them won't get chosen. But teenagers don't care about logic." Hints of conflicting emotions flickered across Cassie's face. "I want to encourage them to have dreams, to think anything is possible, but another part of me wants to protect them from disappointment. On top of that, when you read about what happens to some child stars when they grow up, I have to ask if any television show is worth it."

Adam drew Cassie to one side when a technician came hurrying toward them carrying a boom. One of his business partners had been badly injured on a modeling set. He didn't know the particulars, Rachel didn't like talking about it, but he'd heard the incident started with a poorly fixed lighting boom.

"I understand," he said. "Growing up is hard enough, so adding anything just complicates it further. But most child actors turn out fine. Not only that, but Tiffany and Glen aren't starting as young children."

"True. But part of staying grounded depends on the grown-ups in their lives, which means I'm in shaky territory."

Adam no longer had doubts about whether he liked Cassie. He liked her for many reasons, including her intelligent concern for the twins and the other people she encountered. Her lack of confidence bothered him, but that was mostly because he knew where some of it had originated.

"You aren't in shaky territory," he said firmly. "From what I've seen, Tiffany and Glen couldn't be in better hands."

"You didn't think so when we first met." The lift of her eyebrow was wry and knowing.

"As I've explained, there were personal biases I had to navigate, but it didn't take long to realize the truth."

Adam didn't know if he was relieved or disappointed when Cassie's attention returned to the set. Glen and Tiffany had finally been paired together, acting out a scene over what was intended to be a breakfast table. They both displayed excellent timing for both drama and hints of humor, yet it seemed completely natural. What's more, they appeared to have already learned their lines, with little need to refer to the script.

He inhaled deeply and caught the faint hint of peaches and vanilla from Cassie. Shampoo? A perfume? He didn't know and shouldn't care…but it was the same elusive fragrance he remembered from their kiss.

CASSIE HADN'T COUNTED on Adam staying for so long at the audition and she was conflicted. Having their agent present as support was probably a confidence builder for Glen and Tiffany, but for herself, she found it unsettling. Especially when she'd convinced herself that she'd dealt with his kiss and didn't have to think about it again.

Tension made her throat ache, but she tried to look reassuring whenever the kids glanced in their direction.

The casting director walked over half an hour later. "Hi, I'm Richard Reynolds," he said to Cassie. "Since you're standing with Adam

Wilding, I'm guessing you must be Tiffany and Glen's aunt."

"Yes."

"Ordinarily I'd send a message through Adam, but since you're both here, I'm going to take a shortcut and say I'd like both the kids back tomorrow to see how they interact with the adult actors. Can you be here at ten?"

Cassie's heart was in her throat. "Yes."

"Great. I look forward to seeing you then." Richard hurried back to the set.

"That's a good sign," Adam said in a low voice.

"I know, but I'm not sure how to feel about it."

Tiffany and Glen soon came dashing toward them, looking pleased and happy.

"Mr. Reynolds just said something about tomorrow," Tiffany said. "Are we coming back for more?"

"That's right."

"Cool," Glen breathed. "This is loads better than modeling." He glanced contritely at Adam. "Uh, sorry."

Adam shook his head. "No need to apologize."

Glen looked at Cassie. "I'm hungry. There were donuts, but can we get some real food?"

"Of course."

"How about letting me take all of you to lunch?" Adam suggested.

"Can we?" the kids asked Cassie with hopeful expressions.

She nodded her consent, though the last thing she wanted was to spend more time with Adam. And to think she'd thought their contact would be limited.

As the kids raced ahead to the parking area, she tried to clear her mind. "I realize that working with us has been awkward. With the kids getting acquainted with your parents, you've ended up putting in far more time than you do with other clients."

"I'm making peace with it. Maybe this is something both our families have needed."

"You mentioned the previous owner did a lot of hand-holding with clients, but I don't expect that." Cassie had almost taken his comment as an assurance he wouldn't be constantly around, and yet so far, he'd been very present in the kids' careers.

Adam's face seemed deliberately neutral. "It never occurred to me that you were in need of hand-holding." He pulled her to a stop until she faced him. "Cassie, I need you to understand that I didn't feel sorry for you the other day, no matter how it sounded. You had a rough time with your creep of a boyfriend and you've taken on responsibilities now that some people would run away from. But feeling sorry with someone is different than feeling sorry for them." He grinned. "You're good with words, so you must see the difference."

She nodded. Pity would almost be easier, because it was understandable. Computers were her specialty, not good-looking guys. She never knew where she stood with them.

"Okay," she managed to say.

"You'll give me the benefit of the doubt?"

"I'll do my best."

"Thanks."

CASSIE WAS GLAD Adam didn't come to the auditions on Thursday. He texted her afterward to say that the director had promised to let them know about casting, one way or the other, in the next twenty-four hours. She was doubtful about the twenty-four hour promise, so she deliberately didn't tell Tiff and Glen.

On Friday afternoon, she was deep in a design, trying to fit the client's style to the program. The kids were busy with friends, offering a longer period for uninterrupted work.

As if mocking her, the doorbell rang. She sighed, wondering if it was Dermott Wilding.

He'd done a number of odd job repairs around the house. It was sweet and endearing, but she felt bad because he wouldn't accept payment.

Instead it turned out to be Adam Wilding standing on the front porch.

"Hi," he said. "I wanted you to be the first to know they want both Tiffany and Glen in the TV movie. They're moving fast on this one, so work may start as early as next Wednesday. I'll be busy negotiating the contracts in the interim. I'll email you the details when I get them."

A mixture of alarm and excitement shot through Cassie. "That's wonderful. Can you also email them to my godfather, for him to take a quick look? I attached his contact information to the representation agreements and I can let him know they might be coming."

"No problem. It's a terrific opportunity for Tiff and Glen, though there's no guarantee the movie will be picked up as a series pilot, or even that they'd keep the same actors for the series." He cocked his head as if he was studying her.

"Is something wrong?"

"No, this is just happening quickly. Um, please come in," she said awkwardly, unsure of the protocol involved. Of course, protocols were getting knocked six ways to Sunday by the twins becoming friends with Adam's parents. The elder Wildings had even taken Glen and Tiff on two additional outings, one to the Seattle Center and the other to the wildlife center, where Glen had finally been able to bring home his kitten to join the dog Tiffany had already adopted. "I just need to keep Glen's kitten from going outside."

"I'd heard that Oreo had been liberated. But I can't stay. I just wanted to tell you the news. If the network picks up the movie as a series, it may be used as a mid-season replacement. That would mean, at the very least, steady work for several months."

Cassie frowned. "What about school?"

"They'll provide a tutor on the set, similar to homeschooling. Depending on the size of their roles, it could be full or part time, with them still attending high school some of the week."

"Now I remember—the pamphlet you gave us explained it was a possibility for extended jobs."

This probably meant she wouldn't see Adam that much from now on. The kids would be working for however long the movie required, and possibly on the series if it came through, so there wouldn't be much need for him to come around. Cassie promised herself that once she got accustomed to not seeing him, she'd be convinced it was a good thing.

She forced a smile. "It's too bad the kids aren't home. Glen is at a pool party and Tiffany went to a movie with friends."

"That's all right. I could have called, but I wanted to tell you in person. When are you going to give them the news?"

"You should get the honor if you want it," Cassie said. "It's because of you that they're getting this chance."

Adam looked pleased. "I'd love to."

"How about tonight?" she suggested. "They should be home by seven."

"Sure. But now I'd better get back to work."

He headed for his car, which was parked in the driveway. They'd had a completely pleasant and professional conversation. Still, she had the oddest feeling he was disappointed, as though there were words that he'd wanted to say, or to hear, and they hadn't been spoken.

Better sense asserted itself and Cassie rolled her eyes. Adam was the twins' agent. The relationship had gotten tangled because of his parents and personal revelations that should never have been made, but anything else was a product of her imagination.

BACK AT THE OFFICE, Adam checked his email and found one with video files from the Virgil Wildlife Conservation Center filming. Jonathan was a workaholic, passionate about environmental issues and had probably been working with the film editor at night, even while filming all day in Greenland.

Adam decided to bring the videos to Cassie's house that evening.

It had been thoughtful of her to let him tell Glen and Tiffany the news about the movie. Under normal circumstances, he wouldn't anticipate it that much. While it was always nice to tell a client they had a job, he would have likely phoned or emailed the news to anyone else. But he'd wanted to see Cassie's face when she heard, alone if possible. That way, she could more comfortably discuss any reservations.

Okay, maybe he'd also wondered if she'd grab him for a celebratory hug or perhaps a victory dance. But that sort of spontaneity wasn't her style.

At exactly seven, he rang the Bryant doorbell again, which was followed by pounding footsteps and Tiffany opening the door.

"I saw you out the window," she explained. She grabbed him by the hand and pulled him into a comfortable living room where Glen was playing with his new kitten and Cassie was sitting with a book. Earlier in the day, her hair had been snugly confined in a French braid. Now it fell over her shoulders in a rich chestnut cascade.

"Look who's here," Tiff announced.

"Hi, Adam," Glen greeted him. He put Oreo on his shoulder and sat forward. "What's up?"

"I have a DVD you might enjoy seeing," Adam told them.

Cassie's brow creased in confusion, but she simply gestured to the DVD player in the corner and used the remote to turn on the television.

With a leap, Tiffany landed on the couch next to her brother, so Adam took the armchair nearest Cassie.

In a moment, the wildlife video came onto the screen. There were squeaks of excitement from Tiffany. Glen was quieter but obviously pleased as they watched a sample of their work at the wildlife center.

"That's amazing," Tiff declared when the different clips had played. "I never saw myself on TV before."

"In that case—" Adam paused for dramatic effect, glancing at Cassie and winking "—you'll have to get used to it, because they want you both for the movie."

This time, Tiffany shrieked with joy.

"Wow," Glen exclaimed, then he looked at Cassie. "Aren't *you* excited?"

"Yes. I heard about it earlier, but thought Adam should be the one to tell you."

"This is amazing." Tiffany sighed.

"I have everything for root beer floats to help us celebrate," Cassie announced.

Glen put Oreo down and jumped up from the couch. "Can we have them now with Adam?"

"Sure. Why don't you get the mugs out?"

The kids raced toward the kitchen and Adam turned to Cassie. "I can't tell if being in a movie or having a root beer float is the most thrilling news for them."

"Ice cream is just the cherry on top." She looked rueful. "With this news and a sugar high from root beer floats, I have a feeling they won't be in bed until after midnight."

He extended a hand to help her from the couch. She seemed to hesitate before letting him pull her upright. Her soft chestnut hair brushed his bare arm and Adam couldn't resist lifting a finger to touch it.

"Your hair changes color," he murmured,

"the same as your eyes. It's chestnut tonight but turns fiery in the sunlight."

Her throat flexed visibly as she swallowed. "Sunlight changes most people's hair, bringing out gold or red highlights."

"Perhaps."

Cassie swept the wavy masses over her opposite shoulder. "I don't usually wear it this loose and wild, but I worked off excess energy in the garden earlier, so decided to wash it when I came in. I've been letting it dry and got involved in my book."

"It's beautiful."

"Nice of you to say, but I've always wished I had hair like one of your business partners—Rachel or Nicole, I mean. Theirs is much more striking than plain old brown. For a while I dyed it, but that's a pain when it's long."

He couldn't imagine Cassie as a blonde or dark brunette. "Your natural color suits you."

"It's easier, so that's a good thing."

Adam had meant it as a compliment, but he wasn't sure she'd heard it that way.

CHAPTER TWELVE

CASSIE TOOK CLIPS from her pocket and fastened her hair out of the way. "There, now I can play the proper aunt."

Adam's eyes lit with humor.

"Hey, guys," Glen called from the kitchen, "aren't we going to have any?"

"Coming," she replied, then glanced at Adam. "I didn't intend to hold you up. It just seemed nice to plan something the kids love as a celebration. I'll explain if you need to get going."

"Would you rather have me leave?"

"Not at all, I'm just trying to respect the personal versus professional issue."

He shrugged. "Agents celebrate with clients. Besides, I haven't had an ice cream float in years. What kind of root beer did you get?"

"A local all-natural brand."

"It's nice to know you're consistent."

"Not that consistent—the ice cream isn't organic or even all natural. For years, I looked for the exact right kind that doesn't have too much air beaten into it or a bunch of emulsifiers or whatever it is that makes it wrong for floats. Well, the way *I* like them. It has to be solid enough that the root beer forms ice crystals when you pour it on top. You let everything sit together for about fifteen seconds and then dig in."

"You have a recipe? This I have to see."

He followed her to the kitchen where Glen and Tiffany were impatiently standing next to the counter. Four large glass mugs were waiting.

"I couldn't find the root beer," Glen said.

Cassie winked. "That's because I hid it in the vegetable drawer. I figured it was safe from discovery in there, especially since tonight was pizza night."

Tiffany giggled.

Adam had stopped right behind her and his arm was lightly pressed against her lower back. When he chuckled, the movement sent a shiver up her spine.

Truthfully, she wished Adam hadn't stayed to share the treat…or was she fooling herself? It hadn't been necessary to mention the floats; she could have waited until he was gone. Only an idiot wouldn't guess the kids would invite him to stay.

Glen dug in the vegetable drawer for the bottles of root beer while Cassie went to the freezer in her pantry for the vanilla ice cream. She returned and pulled off the top.

Tiffany looked at Adam. "Aunt Cassie knows the absolute *best* way to make floats, but they're only for super special occasions."

"The ice cream has to be really frozen hard," Cassie said, "so it's a challenge to scoop it out."

"I'll do that part," Adam offered.

The muscles in his arms and shoulders flexed as he scooped ice cream into the mugs. Cassie told herself to breathe—there was nothing unusual about a strong man. But she still spilled some of the soda while pouring it into the mugs.

There was no denying she found Adam physically attractive; if only his other qualities weren't so likeable and tempting as well. She'd already wasted three years trying to fit in where she wasn't comfortable and was always being judged for her inadequacies.

Even in the wildly unlikely scenario that Adam became interested in her, his world was far too sophisticated and upscale for her. She'd never fit into it or with his friends, and there was no reason to get depressed about the truth.

ON SATURDAY, ELIZABETH and Dermott took the kids over to Bainbridge Island to celebrate them being cast in the TV movie. Elizabeth had never ridden on a ferry before and was pleased she didn't get seasick. They'd invited Adam and Cassie to join them, but both had declared the need to catch up on work.

"Aunt Cassie works awful hard," Glen said after they ate lunch at a place overlooking the Puget Sound.

Elizabeth nodded. "I admire her. I called a few days ago, the way you suggested, and she walked me right through the internet problem I was having on my computer. She's so good at describing everything."

"Yeah, she could be like those geeks who drive around and troubleshoot problems, but she prefers designing websites. She did a bunch of free stuff for the computer lab at school, though. The computer science teacher, Mr. Allen, didn't have a clue. But she was nice to him about it."

Elizabeth smiled. "I'm sure she was. Since my internet problems are fixed, I could send my novel if you're still interested."

"Awesome. I never knew a writer before."

His enthusiasm was nice. Having Glen, Tiffany and Cassie around was helping her be a little less homesick for Sophie and the grand-children; talking on the phone just wasn't the same as seeing them. But since Adam didn't live in New Mexico, and she and Dermott couldn't live in two places at once, she'd be missing part of her family no matter what.

After lunch, they began exploring the town, but Glen immediately started edging Elizabeth away from the others.

"It's cool that we got the parts in that TV movie," he said finally. "And that it might turn into a series."

"It's a great opportunity."

"Yeah, if I make a lot of money, it could pay for college. The thing is, I really want to be a doctor, but I know how Adam was going to be a lawyer, then he started modeling and never went to law school. Dermott sounds funny when he talks about that."

Elizabeth felt a wave of sympathy. Glen wasn't an average teenager. She already knew he'd survived twelve difficult years with an al-coholic mother. What was more, he obviously had mixed emotions about being relieved his mom was no longer in his life.

"Your situation isn't the same," Elizabeth said carefully. "I don't believe Adam ever truly wanted to be a lawyer. It was his father's dream and I thought it was a wonderful idea, too. That isn't to say that things might be different if I hadn't needed surgery. For one, the family might not have fallen apart and... Well, that's not the issue here. Adam chose the life he wanted and I'm glad for him."

"But don't people get screwed up by making the wrong stuff important? I don't want to start acting and put medical school off and then find out it's too late."

Elizabeth reached over and squeezed his elbow. "Glen, some people get to be a lot older than you before realizing they can make that kind of mistake. I'm sure you're going to make the right choices, whatever those choices might be."

"I know about mistakes. Well, I don't know if it was a mistake exactly, but..." His voice trailed.

She waited for him to start again. Obviously something was chewing on him and he might be hesitant to share it with someone he'd only known a short while. Still, she was willing to listen, even if it raised ghosts from her own past.

Was it possible to bring good out of the mistakes she and Dermott had made?

"It's all right if you don't want to explain," she told him after the silence had gone on awhile. "Perhaps you need to discuss it with your aunt."

"I *can't* tell Aunt Cassie."

"Whatever it is, I'm sure she'd understand."

"But if I hadn't called the social services people, she wouldn't be stuck with us now." He looked miserable as the words rushed out. "Mom was drinking like crazy and some of her sleazoid boyfriends scared me the way they looked at Tiff. So I called because I thought Mom would try harder if they talked to her. Instead, they wanted to send us to a foster home."

Elizabeth's heart ached at the pain in Glen's face. "That didn't happen because your aunt wanted you to live with her."

"Yeah, but she had to give up her rad sports car and share her house, and now she has to spend all this time taking us to jobs and it's my fault."

Elizabeth hurt even more for him. "What you did was right and brave and I know your aunt would agree with me."

"I thought I was helping."

"Children of alcoholics often feel they have to fix things and take care of people. But you were a kid and shouldn't have needed to rescue you and your sister. I hope it doesn't offend your dignity by saying you were a kid at twelve, and that you still aren't completely adult at thirteen."

A ghost of a smile crossed his face. "It's cool. Aunt Cassie understands about me wanting to be a doctor, but she also says I shouldn't rush to grow up."

"She's right. That's why you should let Adam and Cassie help you sort things out. You know, about the acting and how it might affect what you want to do in the future. And you should do it before a contract is signed."

"I don't know," he said doubtfully.

She saw Tiffany coming down the sidewalk with Dermott and knew the private moment was nearly over.

"Think about it," Elizabeth urged. "Adam and Cassie want to help. As for that call you made… I'm sure your aunt will understand. Keeping it a secret isn't necessary."

He jerked his head, but it was neither a yes or no, then started walking toward his sister.

Elizabeth was grateful Glen had confided in her. Hopefully, something good would come from it.

ON MONDAY MORNING, Adam arrived at the office well past opening time. He'd spent a significant part of the weekend working out the twins' contracts with the studio, negotiating a healthy amount for them both. It was far better than he'd thought possible considering their inexperience.

"Sorry I'm late, Chelsea. Anything come up?" he asked the office manager.

"The movie company sent the finalized Bryant contracts to us. I've forwarded them to the Bryants' attorney. He called and says he should be done with them today. He also wants you to know how much he appreciates your communicating with him over the weekend and sending the initial drafts. Entertainment contracts aren't his specialty, but he was able to consult a friend from law school who told him everything is within line."

"Excellent."

"Anyway, they're on your desk. Cassie also called, asking for an appointment for her and her nephew. Glen wants to talk, but she doesn't know what it's about. Your morning was free, so I told her to come at ten thirty, unless she heard back from me."

"Sounds good," he said, keeping his face neutral. In the privacy of his office, he immediately checked his cell to see if he'd somehow missed a call or email from Cassie. He hadn't, and his frustration rose.

He should have kept his mouth shut about wanting to keep his business and personal lives separate, then maybe she'd trust him enough to make contact directly. He'd finally accepted that there was nothing business-as-usual about his relationship with the Bryants. For that matter, he'd be at Cassie's home that evening to attend her surprise birthday party.

While Adam waited for Cassie and Glen, he went through submissions from potential clients. They got hundreds for every individual the agency decided to sign. If he started a literary arm to the agency, it would grow even worse.

"Hey," Rachel stuck in her head to say. She was here for the week to work and look for a place to live.

"Hi, how's the hunt going?"

"I found a place I really want in an area that isn't in the city. It's roomy, in converted industrial space and just blocks from Lake Washington. I'd have a huge balcony with a view, but no yard to maintain."

"Sounds perfect."

"Or as near to it as I'll be able to get. Keep your fingers crossed that my offer is accepted. It's empty, so I should be able to move in quickly."

He held up both hands with fingers crossed. "There's a pal."

She started down the hallway and he heard her give a friendly greeting, followed by Cassie's answer in return.

Adam went to meet them at the door. "Good morning. So you just met the fourth member of our team."

"Rachel seems nice," Cassie said. "Is she here full time yet?"

"She will be soon. I'm looking forward to having all the partners here together. It'll be good for Moonlight Ventures, but we're also close friends."

"I suppose trust is a key factor in making the business successful. It might be fun to have partners…if it was like that."

Adam didn't know if she was simply saying something polite, or if she'd really enjoy working with people. She'd chosen such a solitary profession. Cassie was talented. He had looked at a range of websites she'd designed and was impressed with how unique they were. Each seemed to be a distinctive reflection of her clients' tastes.

"Rachel used to be a model, didn't she?" Cassie asked.

"That's right."

"Man, is she pretty," Glen said enthusiastically. "Like, *super* pretty. I wanted to say something, but I felt like a dope. She's different from Nicole," Glen added. "I guess all models don't have to look the same."

"Beauty comes in various forms."

"Yeah, or you wouldn't have been interested in Tiff." The normality of his brotherly scorn was reassuring.

Cassie shook a finger at her nephew with a mock-stern expression until he grinned. But after dropping into a chair, he just sat and stared at the carpet. Adam didn't prompt him, figuring he'd talk when he was ready.

After a couple minutes, Glen did, meandering from subject to subject the way a teen can, explaining how fun he thought acting was going to be. It was going to be money for school and he'd never earn that much at any other kind of job...but he was afraid it might mess up becoming a doctor.

"You were supposed to go to law school and didn't," Glen eventually muttered. "Elizabeth says she doesn't think you ever really wanted to be a lawyer, but I'm still worried about what will happen."

"My mom is right," Adam agreed, relieved his mother at least had realized a career in law wouldn't have worked for him. "I never wanted to be a lawyer the way you want to be a doctor, so it wasn't the same for me."

"But I've read about actors who got sidetracked when they first planned to do something else."

Thinking carefully about what to say, Adam nodded. "That happens, and it isn't terrible if someone finds a different career they love too much to leave. Basically, we need to talk as we go along, reviewing your priorities. One thing we can do is structure contracts so you won't get caught in a long-term agreement that limits your choices."

"Can we really do that?"

"Of course. And let me repeat, this isn't like my own situation. I'd already decided against studying law when I started modeling. It turned out to be a good career, but I went into it by accident since I wanted to make extra money when my mom got sick."

"That's why? It's weird—she acts as if she messed up everyone's life by needing surgery."

Adam jerked. *"What?"*

Glen instantly looked worried again. "Uh, maybe I shouldn't have told you that."

"It's okay. I just didn't realize she still felt that way. How do you know?"

"From stuff she's said. I don't think she meant to talk about it."

"I appreciate knowing." Adam smiled, though he had a tight sensation in his stomach. "Who knows, the way you listen to people, perhaps you'll end up in psychiatry."

"Nah." Glen shook his head. "I want to cure diseases."

"That's an exciting goal."

Glen turned to Cassie, his face no longer looking as if the end of the world was imminent. "I'm hungry. Can we get a burger on the way home?"

"I'd like to talk with your aunt about something," Adam told him. "There's food in the lounge. If you look in the very back of the bottom cupboard to the right of the refrigerator, you'll find my personal stash of dried fruit and nuts. There are a few chocolate chunks thrown in for flavor. Help yourself."

"Thanks."

Adam closed the door behind Glen and sat next to Cassie. "He's quite a kid."

"You handled that well," she replied, her eyes filled with admiration. "I appreciate it."

In a strange way, he felt as if he'd been knighted.

Cassie nearly sagged in relief.

She'd been anxious ever since Glen had asked if they could meet with Adam, though he hadn't wanted to tell her why. She'd understood—some things were so hard to talk about, you didn't want to keep repeating yourself. She was pretty sure there were other things he still had on his mind, but this was a beginning.

"Your godfather will let us know today if he has any concerns about the final contracts," Adam said. "I don't think he anticipates any problems, so I'll come over first thing tomorrow and get your signature. The start of filming has been moved to next Monday, but I want the paperwork finalized as quickly as possible."

Adam was all business and Cassie tried not to be disappointed. Honestly, she was reverting to girlish adolescence around him...wishing for something that was impossible. Hearts were slow to heal and, apparently, even slower to learn.

"Fine," she said evenly. "Anything else?"

"Actually, my partners and I want you to redesign and manage our website. Provided you have time and are interested."

For a brief moment, Cassie wondered if Adam was pursing the idea because of the twins' angst about her taking them to jobs.

On the other hand, the agency's website definitely needed a major overhaul and she was earning a name in the field.

"I'm sure I can work Moonlight Ventures into my schedule."

"Wonderful." He grabbed a file from his desk. "We've put together a list of what needs to be part of the site structure. Also our ideas and preferences and what we don't like about our current website. I'm afraid it's quite a bit of information... We've been unhappy with the current design for a while, so we've had time to put our thoughts together."

His fingers brushed hers as he handed over the file. The sensation lingered, like tiny sparks of electricity.

"I'll take a look to get an idea of how much work the design may entail and how it will fit with my current commitments."

"Excellent. I imagine we'll need to have meetings while you're doing the design. Maybe I could come to the movie set while the kids are working."

Cassie winced internally, wondering if she should have accepted the job so quickly. For some reason it hadn't occurred to her that redesigning the Moonlight Ventures website would mean spending additional time with

Adam. If anything, she would have pictured consultations with Nicole or Rachel, or even Chelsea, the office manager.

"Fine, if it's all right with the movie people. I don't want to presume anything with them. In the meantime, I'd better collect Glen and go home," she said, proud of how professional and objective she sounded.

Glen was in the lounge and seemed much happier than he had at breakfast that morning.

"Adam was great," he said when he was fastening his seat belt in the car. "Guess I made too big a deal out of it."

"No. I want you to feel you can discuss anything you're worried about. Is there anything else on your mind?"

Cassie waited because it was one of those moments when her instincts said something else was going on. After a minute or two, Glen's face twisted up.

"Well, there's this one thing. Elizabeth told me that children whose parents are, uh, alcoholics sometimes feel as if they have to fix everything. What if wanting to be a doctor is only about that? I mean, I don't think it is and maybe it doesn't even make a difference, but I still wonder."

Cassie hurt for him and was proud at the

same time that he was trying to evaluate his objectives and be rational.

"Elizabeth is right," she said quietly. "A lot of psychological stuff can go on when a kid has a parent with problems. But it's also true that everyone is affected by things from childhood. You probably don't know that your grandmother is afraid of water because she nearly drowned as a little girl. She won't even get on a ferry and hates crossing bridges."

Glen's mouth scrunched up while he thought about it. "That sucks. If I had to choose, wanting to heal people is better than being afraid of water."

"I agree. Do you remember when you first wanted to be a doctor?" Cassie asked.

"It was that TV show."

"That's right. You cared about kids who were sick and wanted to help. If that's a problem, I wish more people had one like it."

"Thanks." He reached over for an awkward hug.

As she started the car, Cassie still wondered if he'd talked about everything that was bothering him. But opening up had to be his decision. Besides, he and Tiffany would go back to their therapist in the fall. They'd seen him weekly during the school year, and he'd suggested taking the summer off to see how they adjusted.

"Shall we go to the store and pick something out for dinner?" she asked.

"Tiff is cooking, remember? We're supposed to stay out of the kitchen. It's dumb. She wants to be an actress, but doesn't want an audience when she's trying to cook."

"Cooking isn't the same as performing. But we're going to eat whatever Tiff makes, no matter what."

"I guess. Anyhow, there's peanut butter."

It was on a cheerful note that they headed home. Cassie was grateful. Things were getting easier with the kids. Not that there wouldn't be more problems, but she wasn't as nervous about dealing with them as she used to be.

Inside the house, Glen scooped up Oreo, who purred and settled down on his shoulder; the kitten's fierce attachment had survived two weeks in the VWCC kennels. Surprisingly, Tiffany had picked an adult black spaniel mix at the animal shelter rather than a puppy. Lady was an easygoing dog and had already formed a comfortable friendship with Oreo. The two were a huge amount of fun and Cassie wondered why she hadn't gotten a cat or dog a long time ago.

Glen headed upstairs and Cassie went into her office. She put the Moonlight Ventures file on her desk and stared at it. Part of her wanted to immediately jump into a design for the agency, but she had other commitments that came first. Besides, she needed to study the material to be sure she knew what Adam and his partners wanted, and then talk to them to be sure she'd gotten it right.

With music playing to blend out other noises, she quickly prioritized what needed to be done and got started.

Her business phone rang a few hours later and she saw Mindspinder Games on the caller ID.

"Bryant Web Designs," she answered.

"Hi, Cassie, it's Shane Wolcott. Sorry it took this long to get back to you. I was out of the country for meetings with foreign distributors and things got crazy."

"No apology needed." She actually hadn't expected to hear from him again, unless it was in connection to the twins.

"But I am sorry. I was sincere about the offer to work for my company. We have great pay and benefits and I don't care if you run your own business at the same time."

Cassie already had more work than she could handle, which was why she'd arranged to subcontract website maintenance to Giselle. Now she was talking to another college friend about the same arrangement.

"That's flattering, Shane, but I'm fully booked."

"Look, Cassie, you've got talent. The game you devised for the sci-fi convention website shows the creativity we look for at Mindspinder. I understand the organizers want to use your design for other conventions around the world."

Cassie didn't know how he'd learned that particular piece of information, but he was right. Soon after the convention, she'd accepted a huge contract to adapt the website to other venues. It represented easy money since the changes would be relatively simple. The agreement had also helped her breathe easier about finances, which were obviously going to be affected by the twins' modeling and acting careers.

"The thing is, I like you, Cassie," Shane continued, an unexpected warmth in his tone. "I don't care if you can only give me a few hours a month. Surely you have time for a little freelance consulting."

Even over the phone, his charm was evident.

He was also hard to turn down. She'd never been headhunted by a major company before and it was tempting.

"Well, Tiff and Glen have just gotten parts in a TV movie, so let me see how things sort themselves out in the next few weeks. I have to be at the site whenever they have a job."

"I understand. An arrangement can be as flexible as you need it to be. Look, I've got your email address. I'll send you an offer and consulting fee schedule. You won't be disappointed. In the meantime, I hope you don't mind if I stay in touch."

"That's fine."

"Good. We'll talk soon."

Wow. Cassie put the phone down. If there was one thing she was completely confident about, it was her web designs. But Mindspinder was a computer game company...hardly her arena. Still, she'd had fun designing the role-playing game for the sci-fi convention and had already come up with several variations to keep it fresh, along with a whole new game. Maybe it would be good to accept some consulting work. Staying fresh was important.

"Aunt Cassie?"

The unexpected voice made her jump and

she spun around in her office chair. Tiffany stood at the open door.

"Hey, Tiff, is dinner ready?"

There was an air of suppressed excitement in her niece, a happy one so the kitchen probably wasn't flooded...the way it had been the first time she'd tried to cook.

"Yeah, I thought we'd eat on the patio."

Yawning, Cassie stood and stretched. "Good idea. I haven't come up for air all afternoon."

With Tiffany following her, she went to the rear door and opened it.

"Surprise," a chorus of voices exclaimed. "Happy birthday!"

Cassie's heart thudded and she gulped, realizing there weren't as many people in her backyard as it sounded. It was just the twins, her godfather and the Wildings. Including Adam.

She pulled in a breath. "Wow."

Elizabeth came forward and kissed her cheek. "Happy birthday, dear. I hope you don't mind, but it was too much fun planning to resist."

The yard seemed filled with balloons and streamers. The scent of barbecued food wafted through the air and she saw a decorated cake with a freezer of homemade ice cream next to it.

Cassie blinked back tears and accepted a hug from the older woman. It had been a long time since she'd paid attention to her birthday.

Dermott waved a spatula from the barbecue grill she hadn't been able to assemble. "We have all sorts of good things and we're ready to serve," he called.

Tiffany and Glen kept hugging her and Uncle Orville patted her shoulder. Only Adam stood to one side, his gaze hard to read.

"The guest of honor needs to sit down," Elizabeth urged. "The kids and I will bring out the rest of the food."

"Happy birthday," Adam came over to say when she was alone again. "You looked mildly panicked for a minute."

"Just because it was unexpected. I don't have a phobia about groups, whatever you may think."

"Not that exactly, but doesn't your family have a retreat-from-the-world attitude?"

"Don't knock what you haven't tried."

She had no chance to think about it further because the food started landing on the table.

"Personally, I like barbecued steak," Dermott said, setting vegetable shish kebabs on her plate, "but Glen says you might prefer these."

"They look fabulous. I'm impressed you figured out how to put the grill together—I tried for hours before giving up. Clearly I'm not mechanically gifted."

"Nonsense. It turns out the company included the wrong hardware in the assembly package, but I found parts at the store that work."

"You're terrific."

Dermott's shoulders straightened and he looked pleased.

The food was delicious and the gathering cheerful. It was another surreal occasion, but Cassie was getting used to them.

ADAM THOUGHT CASSIE was taking the unexpected social event fairly well. Of course, she cared too much about her niece and nephew to do anything except receive their efforts graciously.

"Your brother was going to come," Elizabeth explained over homemade ice cream and cake, "but he called a few hours ago and said he was needed on a search and rescue team to look for a pair of lost hikers. I hope they'll be all right."

"Few people know that part of the back-country as well as Devlin," Cassie said. "He's found a number of lost hikers."

"That's good to know. We also invited your parents, but I don't think the invitation got there in time."

Adam shot a glance at Cassie's godfather and spotted a disgusted look in the other man's eyes. They'd talked over the weekend while working on the contract. Though Orville Calloway had been circumspect, Adam had caught hints that he was annoyed with his old childhood friend.

What had Cassie said about her dad? *It takes time to adjust and feel comfortable around people again.* Still, surely celebrating their daughter's birthday with her would be a good step toward adjusting. But then, Adam had never been in his shoes, with such a major illness.

Not my business, Adam reminded himself. Yet it was difficult not to be concerned and his sympathy for Kevin McClaskey's habit of getting overinvolved with clients was growing by leaps and bounds.

Cassie's lips twitched when she opened his gift—a DVD of *The Court Jester*.

"Do you know the film?" he asked as she examined the cover.

"Yes. I haven't watched it in years, but it has one of the funniest scenes in movie history, at least as far as I'm concerned."

Adam rattled off a few lines of the film's dialogue that rhymed, which he was sure she'd know. He tipped his bottle of all-natural root beer at her and grinned.

The twins blinked in confusion, obviously unfamiliar with the quote, but Cassie smiled her beautiful smile and he was glad he'd come to help celebrate her birthday.

CHAPTER THIRTEEN

FRUSTRATED, ADAM FINALLY found a parking space near the building being leased as a studio by the movie company. He was late for his latest appointment with Cassie to talk about the website, but the afternoon traffic had been appalling. He hurried to the door and showed his pass to the security guard, who waved him inside.

The producer, Preston Davis, saw him and immediately walked over.

"Hey, Adam."

"Hi. How's it going?"

"Those kids are amazing, almost too good to be true."

"Almost?"

Preston shrugged. "They're teenagers, so a few behavioral issues can be expected. I suspected we'd have more, but their aunt keeps them balanced. I've been trying to work up the courage to ask her out. Do you know if she's involved with anyone?"

Adam's muscles tightened unaccountably. "Can't say."

It was true; Cassie liked her privacy and he'd promised that Moonlight Ventures wouldn't reveal personal information about her or the twins.

"Obviously she's devoted to Tiff and Glen," he added.

"No doubt about that."

More than anything, Adam wanted to tell the other man to back off. The irony was hard to miss. This was the second guy that he knew of who'd been attracted to Cassie over the past few weeks. It wasn't a surprise, except for knowing she seemed too reserved to return their interest.

And why wouldn't they want her attention? She was pretty, had beautiful hair and eyes and moved gracefully, qualities he'd always admired in a woman. She was also intelligent, talented, kind and had a nice sense of humor.

Adam suddenly got the oddest feeling that Isabelle would be kicking him in the rear end, though he wasn't entirely sure why. Shaking his head, he told his imagination to cease and desist.

"Is it okay if I meet with Cassie?" he asked Preston.

"Sure. They're rehearsing right now, so we aren't recording."

Cassie was sitting to one side in a comfortable chair, her computer on a folding table in front of her.

"Hi," he said as he walked over. "My apologies for being late. There was an accident on the freeway so the traffic was completely snarled."

"I hope no one was hurt."

"Without rubbernecking, it was impossible to tell. Preston tells me the kids are doing a good job and that a lot of it is due to you."

"The crew members are the ones who've been so nice. They even found a table for me."

It seemed typical that Cassie would refuse to accept credit for the important role she played.

He glanced at the set. "I understand they're going on location next week."

"That's right. It should be interesting. So far, we've mostly had late calls to the studio, but tomorrow and on location we'll need to be there early. *Really* early." She made a face.

"My sympathies," Adam said.

Sitting in a nearby chair, he watched the rehearsal for a few minutes. From what he'd seen, it was a good script. Tiff and Glen were playing the kids of a Seattle police detective whose husband had recently died in the line of duty. Heavy stuff—a cop show, but also a family dealing with grief and survivor guilt.

"What is that expression about?" Cassie asked.

He shouldn't have been surprised she'd noticed something different in his face. For all her technical expertise and loner tendencies, she seemed to pick up on people better than he did. And she didn't even realize how good she was at it.

"I was just thinking about survivor guilt, along with other kinds of guilt. I've been trying to talk to my mom about her surgery, but can't find a tactful way of leading into the subject."

Cassie leaned forward. "Glen is a perceptive kid, but that doesn't mean he's right about your mother feeling guilty."

"But it makes sense," Adam said, thinking about the things his mom had said over the years and how touchy she was when someone asked about her health. "Getting sick was just one of those things that happen. Things changed because of it, but that isn't her fault and nobody blames her."

Cassie nodded. "And while you can tell Elizabeth that she isn't to blame, how do you get her to feel that way?"

"Exactly. A few months after the surgery, her doctor told us she felt guilty, but we figured it didn't make any sense. That she'd get over it quickly. I mean, we started being careful about what we said around her—and still are, for that matter—but we never sat down and discussed it as a family. I'm sure Dad's attitude about me becoming a model didn't help."

"Elizabeth mentioned that Dermott's fellow construction workers would often joke about his son, the swimsuit guy."

Adam winced. "I know, he's grumbled about it often enough."

Cassie's eyes were warmly sympathetic, easy to read for once, and he wanted to kiss her more than ever. "Dermott has held on to his disappointment longer than some men would. I've been thinking about it ever since he looked so pleased about being able to fix my barbecue. Maybe he wonders if his life has made a difference."

"Of course his life makes a difference," Adam said indignantly. "He's a great guy."

"I'm talking about your success. Maybe he longs to feel as if he's contributed, not to take credit, but to feel as if he's been of use. Look at it this way—he worked and planned and saved to get you through school. But instead, you ended up paying your own way and helped cover his wife's medical bills."

Adam groaned. "Maybe my dad and I are just too stubborn."

"It's ironic that I've gotten to know your parents better than my own. Did you know that Dermott keeps coming over and fixing things for me? At first I tried to pay him, but Elizabeth said not to because it makes him feel useful."

It was true that his father had seemed happier lately, with more energy.

"I think they've been good for you, too," Adam said slowly. "Having them around broadens your social circle, doesn't it? You've mostly had Orville and the twins, and now you have my parents, too."

Cassie frowned. "You've already suggested reclusiveness is a family trait. But I *do* have friends. One is working for me as a subcontractor and another may be starting soon, another college friend, Heather McDonald. And there are others."

"Still, solitude seems to run in your family. Your brother gets a divorce and disappears into the Mount Rainier backcountry. Your father goes through a spate of ill health, and your parents turn into hermits as a result." He forced a laugh. "See? You don't have to apologize for offering an opinion, because I just did the same thing."

Cassie bit her lip. Guilt struck him as he wondered if his "opinion" might have hurt her somehow.

"Hey, don't pay attention to my meanderings."

She shrugged. "You could be right. I've been frustrated with how my parents are acting, but maybe I've been following their pattern ever since I broke up with Michael."

A lock of Cassie's hair curled around her arm and Adam longed to reach out and touch it, the way he had the night he'd told Glen and Tiff they'd been cast in the television movie. Instead, he forced a smile. "You know what? Our lives need better comedy writers."

"Okay. You catch 'em, I'll clean 'em." Her own smile faltered. "That's what my dad used to say when we went fishing together. But he hasn't touched a rod or gone out in his boat for years."

"Who's missing a sense of humor now?" Adam asked lightly.

"You're right. Maybe instead of giving each other advice, we should look at the preliminary design I've done on the website."

He moved his chair closer so he could see the computer screen, and her scent drifted around him again. Peach with a hint of vanilla seemed like an old-fashioned scent for an information technology specialist, but he loved it.

GLEN WAVED AT Aunt Cassie when the director gave them a break. It had been great when the crew hunted up a desk so she could work better.

Everyone was pretty nice, even the leads in the show. Not that they were megastars, but he'd found them on the internet.

Jeez. He suddenly wondered if he'd show up on the internet after a while. Maybe Adam could tell him what that felt like—he was even on Wikipedia.

Doing the movie was fun, but he hoped Adam could get him into a science fiction movie or series. That would be cool.

Elizabeth had finally sent him one of her novels. The story was good, but she acted as if it wasn't worth much and didn't want to send it to a publisher. It seemed so weird that he'd talked to Aunt Cassie about it. She'd asked him to imagine how scary it would be to let a stranger make a decision on something he really, *really* cared about. What if they said it wasn't any good?

Okay. He kind of understood.

There were lots of things it was hard to let people see or know about, like stuff about his mom.

Sometimes he was able to pretend everything was normal. But other times he still had nightmares about those horrible last months in San Diego. Elizabeth kept saying he should tell Aunt Cassie, but it wasn't as if telling her would change anything. And it would be lousy if Tiff found out and got mad because he'd turned Mom in—while she hadn't gone to jail, the police and judges had gotten involved and there'd even been a kind of trial.

"Attention, everyone," the director called. "We'll run the lines one more time and then roll the cameras."

It was incredible to him how real a fake kitchen or living room seemed on film. On the first day, one of the cameramen had let him look through the camera and see how he could move the focus close and farther back, making sure that only the set was in the shot.

Glen almost wished life could be like that... If something was wrong or bad, cut it out of the picture. Except it only worked that way for an hour or so, minus time for commercials.

CASSIE SIPPED FROM her cup and watched Adam as he looked again at the samples she'd shown him for the Moonlight Ventures website.

"Our biggest problem will be deciding between the layouts," he said finally. "Do you usually come up with several different options?"

"Not this extensive." She laughed ruefully. "I'm afraid this particular job has gotten personal—you know, with the twins being connected to the agency and all."

He laughed as well. "I understand. Tiff and Glen are the first clients that I'm representing from the start of their careers and I'm finding it impossible to stay detached. I've finally decided there's no point in fighting the impulse. It's like the tide coming in or out, a force beyond your power to change."

That was exactly what Cassie was afraid of, forces beyond her control.

"Maybe that's what I enjoy about website design. It's something I can manage and direct," she murmured.

"Until someone hacks your code and wreaks havoc."

She shook her head. "So far that hasn't happened. One of my specialties is security, so I'm hopeful it won't be a big problem."

"Nice to know." Adam glanced at her computer. "I'm still in awe of how good these are. I know they're mock-ups, but they capture exactly what we wanted."

"It helped that I was able to consult with Nicole and Rachel and also do a video chat with Logan."

"I didn't know you'd been into the agency."

"Last Thursday. I think you were out." In fact, Cassie had deliberately set the appointments for a time when Nicole had mentioned Adam had other commitments.

He gestured toward the set. "I'm glad Glen was willing to share what he was worried about. It seems to have relaxed him enough that he emailed, saying he hopes to audition for science fiction roles."

"No surprise there—he loves sci-fi. He even talked your mother into sending him one of her novels."

Adam jerked and spilled coffee on his jeans. "Really? Nobody has read Mom's stuff in years. She usually clams up tight if somebody asks. It's always bugged me to think she worked at another job instead of being the writer she should have been. Literary success is never a guarantee, but at least she should have tried. Instead, she was too busy helping Dad build a bank account."

"Guilt must be a Wilding family trait. Think about it. Why did she stay at that job?"

"Because she and Dad were saving money for my sister and me to go to college."

"Right." Cassie cocked her head. "And you feel guilty about *that*, even though you were a kid and didn't have a say about what they were doing."

Adam's eyebrows rose. "Is it fun always being right about people?"

"Are you kidding? I'm hardly ever right."

"Not from where I sit."

"Then move your chair."

A laugh burst from his throat. "You're sharp, Cassie Bryant."

"Yeah, you should see me cut tomatoes."

He stretched. "As much as I'd love to stay and swap one-liners for the rest of the afternoon, I shouldn't interfere with your work any longer."

"You don't have work to do yourself?" she asked.

"I didn't say that. I started at five this morning, so if I was on an hourly wage, I'd be on overtime by now."

"I'm familiar with the feeling." She rolled her eyes. "That's the downside of working for yourself—the boss can be a royal pain in the neck."

"And if you throw yourself a Boss's Appreciation Day, it just looks egotistical."

Cassie focused on the set to avoid looking at him. A man as attractive as Adam could easily become egotistical. Yet somehow he'd avoided that trap. He had used his fame to do public service and as an agent he clearly worked hard to help his clients succeed. He wasn't a noble knight, but he was the kind of man a woman could love forever.

Drawing a swift breath, she decided to pretend the idea had never occurred to her.

"I was wondering something," she said, desperate to think about something else. "Have you ever thought of helping your mom get published?"

His eyes crinkled, perhaps in confusion at the change of subject. "What do you mean?"

"You said you were interested in being a literary agent so there might be things you could do."

He snorted. "I doubt a manuscript being marketed by the author's brand-new agent son would be considered."

"Possibly. But aren't there other aspects to getting published? While I don't know much about it, surely it isn't as simple as sending in some typed pages."

Adam's brow creased. "You mean helping Mom put a manuscript into a professional format, writing query letters and synopses. That kind of thing."

"Sure. You might even do some research and be able to tell her what publishers are the best possibilities."

He sat silent for several seconds before nodding. "It's something to consider. In the meantime, I could use another cup of coffee. Can I get you something?"

"Iced latte. But I thought you needed to leave."

"Maybe I'll stay awhile longer."

He stood and Cassie deliberately didn't watch as his tall figure strode toward the food area. It wasn't a big help since his picture was on the computer screen as part of the website mock-up. Logan Kensington had done photographs for all the partners that emphasized professionalism rather than physical appearance, though there was no denying they were an exceptionally attractive group of people.

They were the kind of people Adam was accustomed to dealing with—beautiful women and handsome men who were sophisticated and dynamic. So it had to be her imagination that he'd looked at her earlier as though he found her attractive… Imagination and wishful thinking.

Okay, she *would* like to fall in love again. Not using Michael's definition of love, but with a guy who wanted the same things as she did. She'd thought that would be with a man who'd share her dream of a house in the mountains and a quiet, peaceful life.

Now she was realizing that she might be copying her parents. Maybe her brother had done the same. It wasn't as if she'd always dreamed of living lost in nature. Someplace out of the city, perhaps, but not a total withdrawal from people in general.

But even if she'd realized her plan wasn't a good idea, that didn't mean Adam could be part of a new plan, so she'd better stop noticing the things she appreciated about him.

ADAM FELT LIKE whistling as he waited for the caterer to make the coffee. Being with Cassie made him feel good, though she'd also made him want to kick himself.

Why hadn't he considered working with his mother to submit her novels to publishers? Only a small percentage of authors could earn their entire living on writing, and Mom had been writing anyway. The only difference between her and other writers was that they were trying to get published and she wasn't.

"I didn't think to ask Cassie how she wanted her latte," he told the caterer.

"Medium sweet with a dash of cinnamon," the man answered. Since this was Seattle, it hadn't been surprising to find that the caterer was also a barista. He did, however, have an ironic nametag—Joe.

"You're good at your job, Joe."

"Cassie is nice. She tried paying me and I told her no, then she still tried to pay me." The caterer put two cups on the counter, one was clear plastic with whipped cream under the domed cover and a straw, the other was paper, with steam rising. "I had to get the producer to explain this is a service for everyone on the set. She's a class act."

"You don't have to tell me."

Carrying the two cups, Adam glanced at Cassie, who was focused on the twins.

"Quiet on the set," a voice called.

He softened his footsteps, aware of how sensitive the microphones were. When he handed Cassie her latte, she mouthed a thank-you, still focused on the unfolding scene.

Adam had never been interested in acting, but now, watching Glen and Tiffany, he felt a jolt of accomplishment to know he'd recognized their talent and hooked them up with the right people. Of course, there was no guarantee that their early success would continue—it didn't for some clients.

It was a concern. He cared about the kids and didn't want them to be disappointed. But while building their careers was part of his job, his concern had become complex and personal because of Cassie. He thought about her too often for comfort.

"Cut," the director called. "Tiffany, you forgot to point at the cat—that's part of what will lighten an intense scene."

"I'm really sorry."

"That's okay, but we'll need to start again at Brent's line."

Mistakes were normal and no one was upset, yet Tiffany looked chagrined. There would be times when the twins received reproofs and rejections, but Cassie would do her best to keep them levelheaded. And she'd probably succeed since her primary interest was their happiness, rather than their acting or modeling success.

"I feel bad for Tiff," Adam murmured when the director called for a short break. Typically, Glen was headed for food while his sister went to talk with the acting coach the studio had hired.

"Me, too," Cassie agreed. "But maybe pretending mistakes away or not having kids deal with the consequences sets them up for a rude awakening in the adult world."

"Do people do that?"

"I've seen it. I'm sure the intent is to build a positive self-image, which is important, but since we all make mistakes, it's also important for children to learn how to deal with them and try to make amends."

"I never thought about it before," Adam acknowledged. "But I guess you've had to consider all sorts of things now that you're raising Tiff and Glen."

Cassie reached back to massage the space between her shoulder blades and he stifled a groan. He wanted to comfort her and help ease her tired muscles.

"If you ever decide to have a family, you'll probably have the advantage of starting out with a baby," she said, shaking him out of his wayward thoughts. "By the time they're teenagers, you'll have had twelve years of on-the-job training."

He chuckled. "Sure, start me off with a baby I'm afraid of breaking."

"You have to begin somewhere."

WHILE ADAM HAD always wanted a family, the realities of parenting had never entirely seemed real. He'd seen his sister frazzled at handling two babies together, but his closest friends had yet to start families of their own. Nicole might be the closest to making it a reality—she'd said her fiancé wanted to become a father, but it was still a theoretical in-the-future sort of thing.

When there was a break in filming, Adam stood and told Cassie he was actually leaving this time. He tossed his cup in a recycling can and left, suddenly anxious to get going.

He didn't want to waste any more time, or rather, he didn't want his mother to waste any more time. In the car, he called her cell phone.

"Hello, Adam."

"Hey, Mom, are you free this evening? I'd like to take you and Dad out to dinner. You've wanted to try sushi and I know a great place."

"Let me fix something instead. I talked your father into having Thai food last night and I don't think he's ready for another culinary adventure."

Adam rolled his eyes. "He's *never* ready for culinary adventure."

"He tries. Come over when you're free," Elizabeth urged.

Adam stopped at his office to do research and print information off the internet, ordered several books for prospective authors, then drove to the cottage his parents were renting. By the time he got there, his mom had salad and enchiladas ready, stuffed with carne adovada and swimming in melted cheese.

After they ate, his dad read a newspaper while Adam helped with the dishes.

"I don't think you enjoyed the enchiladas as much as usual," Elizabeth said when the last fork was in the drawer. "Was the sauce too spicy?"

"It can never be too spicy, you know that. The food was wonderful, but I have something on my mind. I saw Cassie today and she mentioned Glen loves the story you sent him." Adam assumed a mock hurt expression. "You haven't let me read your stuff since I was kid. What does Glen have that I don't?"

Her cheeks turned pink. "Nothing. But he asked several times and I decided to go ahead and send it to him. He's just being generous to say it's good."

"Maybe not. You should submit your work to publishers and see what they think. I brought general material that talks about formatting a manuscript and writing query letters and have ordered some books on publishing."

She shook her head. "That's kind, but writing is just a hobby. Anyway, I'm too old to make it in sci-fi or fantasy. My work is outdated."

Adam tried not to get frustrated. "Mom, it's never too late, and you can't know your stories are outdated unless you submit to a publisher. I hate thinking that you and Dad gave up your dreams trying to help Sophie and me."

Dermott dropped his newspaper and both his parents stared at him in shock.

"What do you mean?"

"I mean that Dad wouldn't take the risk of starting his own business because of us, and you put all your time and energy into working at that dull teleservice job so you could save for our college expenses."

His mother carefully hung up the dish towels. "That was a choice we made together. It wasn't your responsibility."

"I still feel bad about it."

Her chin firmed. "You shouldn't. I'm the one who feels bad for the pressure we put on you to become something you didn't want to be."

Dermott scowled and leaned forward. "It was cruel to hope our son and daughter would become lawyers? *No.* Son, you could have been the first brother and sister on the US Supreme Court."

Elizabeth's face grew more strained. "Dermott, listen to me. We made a mistake when we pushed them the way we thought they should go. They had a right to decide for themselves."

"Dad, I know you want the best for us," Adam added firmly, "but you wanted us to achieve 'the best' in one particular way. We chose our own paths. It's okay. You both did a great job raising your kids. We're fine."

"Don't argue about this anymore," Elizabeth pleaded. "Sometimes I think if I just hadn't gotten sick, we would have worked everything out better."

His father looked appalled. "Lizzie, none

of this is your fault. You're the glue that holds this family together."

"The surgery took over our lives for a long time and cost us our savings."

Dermott slapped his hand down on the table for emphasis. "I'd sell my soul to keep you with me. I just regret the pain you went through and failing to see you weren't feeling well," he added. "I regret it more than I can say."

The tenderness in his father's voice made Adam's throat tighten. His parents had been together for over thirty-six years and it was nice to be reminded that they still loved each other deeply. He might have wondered sometimes how two such disparate people had made a marriage work, but that was the answer.

Her husband's declaration may have been what Elizabeth needed most, because her expression eased and her eyes shone.

"Well, then," she said, clearly pleased and embarrassed at the same time, "as long as we're being honest, I want all of you to stop treating me as if I'm about to break. I'm perfectly healthy and don't want to be handled with kid gloves."

"We don't do that," Dermott said.

"Sometimes it feels that way. The doctor

wants me to stay away from *too* much stress, but it's also stressful if I can't really be there for my family. Besides, I'm tougher than any of you think."

Adam grinned. "Then you can prove it by sending your stories to an editor."

"Absolutely," Dermott agreed quickly. "If I'm willing to start that handyman business, you can get serious about being published."

"Oh."

Adam saw a range of emotions on his mother's face and hoped he'd done the right thing. Getting rejected by an editor could happen no matter how good the writing might be. And it could be painful. He had to discuss the possibility with his mother. It's what a proper agent would do.

"You'll do it?" Adam pushed, knowing he couldn't backtrack now. They would have to deal with whatever happened, when it happened. Besides, trying to protect her from disappointment might fall under the stop-treating-me-as-if-I'm-about-to-break order she'd given them.

His mother suddenly looked excited. "I suppose I could try. It would be nice to know what someone in the field thinks about my work.

Anyhow, don't a lot of books get turned down a bunch of times before they get published?"

"That's what they say. Anyway, I'd better get going. Dad, do we have time to give my bumper a quick check? I was tapped in the parking lot a few days ago and I'm not sure if it's loose."

Dermott followed him out, probably knowing the bumper was just an excuse, though he gave it a cursory shake. "It's fine. What's up?"

"Uh, well, Cassie also mentioned you might wonder if your life makes a difference," Adam said slowly. "It does. In a thousand ways, every single day. That hasn't changed because Sophie and I didn't become lawyers. I've never known a man I admire more."

Dermott's tanned skin turned ruddy. "Thanks, son," he muttered. "Maybe I needed to hear that from you."

They hugged, hard, and Adam wasn't surprised when his father abruptly turned and headed away, gruffly saying he needed to walk off his dinner.

Mom was at the window, so Adam gave her a reassuring wink before getting into his car.

Problems remained, but things had been said that were long overdue. He'd had an amazing evening, in large part because of Cassie.

Adam grinned and started the engine. Maybe he should let her know how much he appreciated it.

A turn stripped and slapped the original file hp's he should let her know how much he appreciated it.

CHAPTER FOURTEEN

CASSIE WAS CURLED up on her comfortable couch, the television turned low so it wouldn't wake Tiffany and Glen, though once they were asleep, little seemed to rouse them. They had an early call the next morning so she'd insisted on a reasonable bedtime.

She'd just started *The Court Jester* when she heard a light tapping at the front door. For a minute, she considered not answering, but didn't want the kids to be disturbed. She got up and peeked through the curtain to see Adam.

She opened the door. "Hi. The twins are in bed already," she said softly. "Is something wrong?"

"Nope. Just thought I'd stop by."

He grinned as he came into the living room and saw the movie on the screen. "A woman after my own heart. Can I hang out and watch with you?" he asked in the same low tone she'd used.

A woman after my own heart…

Cassie's pulse skipped, though surely his comment hadn't meant anything. "Uh, sure."

"How about popcorn?" He looked like a little boy asking for a treat. "I know you probably don't approve of the microwavable kind, but I stopped at the store and found one that's organic in case you were in the mood for a snack."

Cassie fought an irrational flash of feminine satisfaction. Of all the women Adam must know, he'd come over to her house. The kids might be his clients, but there was no question that the relationship was skidding over normal business boundaries.

"The kids mostly eat air-popped popcorn," she explained. "But the machine is noisy and might wake them up, so we can make the microwavable kind. Come on back to the kitchen."

Within minutes, the tantalizing odor of buttery popcorn rose in the air. They filled a bowl and returned to the living room.

Adam settled close to her on the couch while she restarted the film. Midway through, they put the player on pause, made more popcorn and cups of decaf coffee and chuckled their way through the jousting scene.

"It's a great old film," he said as it ended.

"Were you hoping to watch *The Court Jester* when you came over?" Somehow she'd ended with her feet tucked under her and leaning against him while they jeered at the bad guys. It was a lovely, cozy sensation. She could never have imagined an evening like this the day they'd met.

Adam yawned lazily. "Not exactly. I had something to tell you."

Swinging her legs down, Cassie brushed a few stray crumbs of popcorn into the empty bowl. "So…what is it? You saw me only a few hours ago at the studio."

"I took your advice and talked to my mom this evening about getting her writing going."

Since his mood still seemed positive, Cassie hoped it meant that the conversation had gone well. "What did she say?"

"With prodding from Dad as well, she's going to give it a shot. Of course, then I silently stressed over whether I got her hopes up for nothing. Getting published isn't easy."

"Trying always means the possibility of failure. But it's sad not to go for your dreams."

"Is that why you let Tiffany send her picture to the agency?" His posture was no longer as relaxed as it had been during the film.

Cassie nodded. "I worried about it and I still

worry. But it makes me crazy when I saw how some people seem to write Glen and Tiffany off because of their background. I want them to dream whatever they want to dream."

"You'd probably make a good talent agent."

"Me?" She snickered. "Hardly. I like my orderly career in web programming. It makes the rest of life's messiness easier to face."

"You're great with computers, but you also have good instincts for people."

The compliment was sincere, but it was the look in his eyes that made her pulse jump. When he leaned closer and kissed her, it was everything it should have been. His lips were firm and warm, his arms strong and gentle. But it was so brief, it left her aching for more.

He pulled away and stood. "I shouldn't keep you up any longer. I know the kids have an early call in the morning."

Cassie tried to copy his nonchalance, though she noticed his breathing was faster than normal…just like hers. "Besides, your day began even earlier than mine."

"Right. I originally planned to be in bed by now, but decided to come over and say thanks."

"I didn't do anything, but it's nice of you."

"You did a lot, so let's not argue about it.

Thanks also for letting me stay. I haven't relaxed this much in ages."

She walked him to the door, wondering if he planned to kiss her again, but he just squeezed her hand and left.

While Cassie put the bowl and cups into the dishwasher, she tried not to overthink the evening. It was a simple kiss. He definitely hadn't been inviting her to fall in love. So as long as she kept her good sense, she'd be fine.

Still…she couldn't help recalling the way he'd breathed faster, just from that brief, innocent touch. The memory alone would be enough to keep her awake.

THE NEXT MORNING, Elizabeth read Glen's text.

OMG OMG Go4it

She frowned. "Dermott, I just got the strangest message from Glen."

"That's probably because I emailed him to say you were working on something to send to a publisher."

She tried not to be exasperated. "You aren't giving me a chance to back out, are you? Now you've enlisted Glen to pressure me."

"Well, I've been thinking. Instead of pushing the kids to be lawyers, I should have been pushing you as a writer."

"And I should have pushed you to start your own business," she retorted.

"Which I'm going to do. A couple of days ago, Cassie showed me a sample webpage she's designed for Wilding Handyman Services. I didn't ask her to do it, but you know her."

He seemed more like the old Dermott, the man who'd courted her and played with their kids when they were little.

"Yes, I do," Elizabeth told him. "Adam and the Bryants are right, we aren't too old to have dreams and make them happen."

"Agreed. Now I'm going to leave so you can concentrate on your novel," he told her. "I want to fix Cassie's deck. The guy who built the thing must be incompetent. It needs twice the support or it won't hold up much longer, especially under two active teenagers."

"Cassie is really special. Could Adam be interested?" Elizabeth asked wistfully. "I didn't think it was possible at first, but they seem to have become friends. After all, we began as friends."

Dermott kissed her. "We can hope, but it's up to them. It's too bad they're so different from one another."

"So are we. Maybe we could encourage them... Find a way to show them how good they'd be together."

He waved an admonishing finger. "Honey, I thought you said pushing our kids the way we think they should go was a mistake."

She made a face at him. "I hate a man who throws my words back in my face."

"Too late, we're already married. You know, I'd love having Cassie and the kids as part of the family, but it isn't up to us."

Elizabeth smiled. They'd talked more in the past few days than they had in months. "I'm a mother and can't help wishing I could help them just a little."

"And I'm a father, but we'll have to help each other stop poking our noses in their business." He was chuckling as he went out the door.

THE MORNING AFTER watching the movie with Cassie, Adam had awakened feeling peaceful and happy. Then he'd gone into the office and seen his picture of Isabelle. Tension had immediately gathered in his gut and had stayed with him for the following week.

"Something wrong?" Nicole asked one day as they sat in her office.

"No."

"That's a very short answer from a very grim face."

"It's nothing."

"Hmm." She didn't push, but turned to the large television screen where they were evaluating which shots of their clients to give to Cassie for the website. Unable to choose between her mock-ups, they'd asked her to decide.

Adam noticed Nicole playing with the engagement ring on her left hand. Isabelle had done that, too, when the ring was new and she was getting accustomed to wearing it.

When their meeting was over and he'd worked several hours, he glanced at his phone, wondering what his father was doing. Now that they were talking more openly, there was something he'd like to ask.

He dialed his dad's cell number.

"Hi, son," Dermott answered, sounding breathless.

"What have you been up to?"

"I've reinforced the foundation on Cassie's deck and now I'm fixing the drain on a neighbor's bungalow. It's mostly an excuse to keep out of your mom's way. She's working on her novel." His father sounded smug and Adam restrained a laugh.

"Want another excuse? If you haven't eaten, we could get lunch."

"I'd love to. But regular food, not anything unusual," Dermott said emphatically. "How about the steak house where we ate a couple of weeks ago?"

"Sounds good. See you at one."

At the restaurant, Adam hugged his dad but didn't say much as they studied the menu and ordered.

"Is there something on your mind?" Dermott finally asked.

"Uh, yeah. Ever since the other night when you talked about Mom being sick, I've been wondering what you would have done if…if she hadn't made it. Would you have fallen in love with someone else eventually?"

His father's eyebrows drew together as he thought. "Hard to say," he admitted. "Back then my reaction might have been 'when hell freezes over.' But I'm older now. It isn't as if you're born with a certain amount of love to give away and once it's gone, that's it. Maybe being able to love somebody else is a powerful compliment to the one you've lost."

"Compliment? But doesn't it mean you're moving on, not needing them anymore?"

Dermott looked uncomfortable; he wasn't

a man who spoke easily about his emotions. "Not for people who feel deeply. I think it means their love made you a better person for loving and being loved." He paused as the waitress refilled their coffee cups, then he looked at Adam. "Are you thinking about letting go of the past and finding someone to share your life with?"

"I thought I had let go, but maybe not as well as I'd hoped. A while back, I had the strangest feeling that if Isabelle was here, she'd be kicking me in the backside."

Dermott chuckled. "Probably, and she'd be telling you to get on with it. Isabelle had a big heart and wouldn't approve of you being alone."

Adam knew it was true—he'd known from the beginning. And it wasn't as if he'd buried himself in grief. He'd had fun exploring the world and getting to know new people. There had been a multitude of things to make life full. His friendships had been satisfying as well, especially with Logan, Nicole and Rachel.

"You're right," he said. "But when it comes to love and having a family, I put them into a comfortable category of 'someday.' It was going to happen when the time was right and I'd met somebody great. After my friends and

I decided to buy an agency, I figured it would be after we were all here and things were running well."

Their steaks were delivered and they started eating. For once, it was a comfortable silence between them. It was only as they finished that Dermott wiped his mouth with a napkin and looked at Adam.

"Son, you must know that love rarely shows up when it's convenient. It comes when it comes and you need to hang on when it does. I know, because my granddad married the woman his folks wanted him to, instead of the one he loved."

Adam was shocked. "I didn't know he and Great-Grandma weren't happy. They always seemed so comfortable together."

"They weren't unhappy and they cared about each other, even though they were both in love with someone else. But after your great-grandma was gone, Granddad told me so I'd understand. I hope you'll never have the regrets they did."

It was an unexpected insight into the Wilding family history.

CASSIE WAS ACCUSTOMED to long periods of solitude on her computer and had expected the daily film schedule to be nerve-wracking with all the distractions. But she was adjusting. Even now that they were on location most days, the crew was making sure she had a good space to set up where she could also keep track of the twins.

Oddly, she was doing better work than ever.

And now she had something else to think about… Preston, the producer, had asked her for a date.

He was a nice guy and she'd almost agreed, mostly to convince herself that she wasn't getting loopy about a certain tall, handsome former model. But she didn't want Tiffany and Glen to be reminded of their mother's revolving boyfriends. It also wasn't fair to Preston to use him as an emotional shield. So she'd made an excuse about needing to wait while she figured things out with the kids' acting and modeling careers.

The twins worked more limited hours than the adults in the cast because they were minors, so they'd be finished by two for the day. At noon, a break was called and everyone headed for the food. Cassie wasn't hungry, so she just watched the twins mingle with their fellow actors.

Everyone seemed happy to have them around.

They were adept people-pleasers, probably from growing up as they had. Being socially skilled was fine as long as it was for the right reasons—she just didn't want them doing the wrong things to fit in with their friends.

Adam's voice startled her. "You look as if the weight of the world is on your shoulders."

He dropped into a nearby chair. She hadn't seen him since the evening they'd watched *The Court Jester* together and had assured herself that things were just reaching a new normal.

"Not at all," she said lightly. "What are you doing here?"

"I wanted you to know I've had three inquiries about Tiffany's availability as a model and two for Glen."

Cassie frowned. "That's nice, but they can't work more hours than they already are."

"Yes, but according to the production schedule, they'll have a week off soon. Is the pace getting to be too much? I know it must be wearing for a recluse."

"How many times do I have to say I'm not a recluse," she returned sharply. "You make it sound as if I'm… I don't know, emotionally damaged and need to hide like a hermit."

"I'm just aware that you seem to enjoy being alone."

He was partly right. She was naturally an introvert and it took energy to be with people. Being alone helped recharge her, which would probably be incomprehensible to Adam, who seemed to be the opposite.

"I like people," she said at length. "But you're an extrovert and I'm not. I doubt you can understand the differences between us. That's okay, maybe I can't understand you, either."

Adam seemed strangely disappointed, but Tiffany was coming toward them, so he sat back and smiled at her.

"Here, Aunt Cassie." Tiff handed her a bowl filled with salad and a separate container of dressing. "Joe said to tell you..." Her brow wrinkled in concentration. "He said you need to eat healthy or he'll call your mother, whatever that means. Grandma doesn't bug you about food, does she? You eat, like, *super* healthy."

"He was just teasing." Cassie noted the salad contained a wide variety of vegetables. Joe was an excellent caterer, and while he teased about her usually vegetarian choices, he made sure there were plenty on hand.

Tiffany flashed a grin at Adam. "I got you

a sandwich on a French roll." She handed him a plate.

"Thanks, Tiff."

Suddenly Tiffany looked shy. "Uh, I don't know if you know, but Preston asked Aunt Cassie out."

Cassie sat straight upright, nearly tipping the salad into her lap.

"Oh?" Adam said.

"Yeah. We think she put him off because she worries about us. I know you aren't her agent or anything, but could you tell her it's okay?" Tiff shifted from one foot to the other as she looked at Cassie. "Glen and I talked about it and he didn't want me to say something in front of you, but I thought it would be okay. Are you upset?"

"Of course not. I just didn't realize you knew," Cassie said.

"I heard him asking. He's really nice."

Cassie's insides were curling into a tight ball, but she smiled at her niece. "Yes, he is."

"Anyhow," Tiffany said, "that's what I wanted to say. I'm gonna go eat. Joe made me a special salad, too."

"Sorry about that," Cassie muttered when she was alone with Adam again.

"No worries. So, Preston got around to asking you out. He asked if you were involved with someone. I didn't tell him anything to protect your privacy, but he must have guessed you weren't."

A strange calm settled over her. If Preston Davis had asked Adam something like that, then they were plainly being seen as simply friends or business associates. It was depressing, but it was also a category she understood.

"Do you want to go out with him?" Adam asked.

She shrugged. "He's nice, though it's hard to believe a computer nerd and a movie producer have much in common. But the biggest consideration is that my sister hung around with a lot of different men. I want the twins' lives to be more stable, so I've ruled out dating for a while."

"Then Tiffany is right that you refused because of them. Is that any better for the kids— all or nothing? Surely it would be healthy for them to see how normal people act."

Cassie stared at Adam in exasperation, but resisted telling him to mind his own business. After all, she'd offered her own share of opinions about *his* family.

"I've only had the twins for a year and I'm

still figuring out the best course," she said, keeping her tone even.

"At one time you planned to marry. Did your bad experience convince you to live a solitary life forever?"

She poured dressing on her salad in an attempt to look nonchalant. "I have nothing against marriage. Besides, you're a fine one to talk. You're four years older than me and still single." Aghast, she suddenly realized how horrible that must have sounded. "Wow. That was extraordinarily insensitive. You lost the person you loved."

ADAM LOOKED AT Cassie's contrite face and chuckled. "Don't apologize, I prefer it when people don't tiptoe around about Isabelle. She was an important part of my life. I thought it was great when you said real love ought to be remembered."

"It still isn't my business."

"We've discussed almost everything else in our lives, why not that? Not all the women I've known have been as generous as you were about Isabelle."

In fact, some of the women he'd dated had resented seeing Isabelle's picture in his home.

Who knows how they would have reacted to know he still had the engagement ring her parents had returned to him. He didn't talk about it, mostly because some people felt keeping the ring was morbid.

He began unwrapping his sandwich as Cassie dug a fork into her salad.

"At first I felt guilty," he admitted. "I was alive and she wasn't. It was an aneurism and I couldn't help thinking if I'd been there, I might have recognized something was wrong sooner, or gotten help in time to save her. Instead, I was in Japan on a photo shoot."

"I'm sure we all ask that kind of question of ourselves."

"Probably. It just seemed so unbelievable that she could be playing tennis one minute, vital and healthy, and be gone the next. I don't want to stop loving her in order to start loving someone else, so what you said that day at the wildlife center meant a lot. My dad said something yesterday that helped, too."

She glanced up. "Being asked for input must have made him feel useful."

"That's partly why I did it. And, as it turns out, a guy can always use the benefit of his father's experience."

Her face shadowed and went blank.

"Now I should apologize," Adam told her hastily. "Your folks don't choose to be available, do they?"

"Not really." Cassie smiled sadly. "Sometimes I'd like to ask their advice about doing the best thing for Tiff and Glen, but when I call, they're just not...not completely there. It's as if they're living in a bubble. I'm glad Dad is alive, but I wish..."

Adam suspected few people would understand the uniqueness of her loss—her parents were alive and not estranged, yet they weren't really there, either. "Feel free to draw on my folks for their opinions. They'd love it."

That prompted a more cheerful expression and she ate another bite of salad while he bit into his sandwich.

Spending time with Cassie could easily become a happy habit, but Adam wasn't sure she wanted to share that habit with *him*. The contrast in their life goals was glaring with her desire to retreat into near solitude and his career being all about working with people. Still, he'd be grateful if they could be friends. Cassie was caring and aware, and she thought things through on a deep level; it challenged him to do the same.

Yet suddenly he felt a chill, which made no sense at all…unless he wanted more than friendship.

CHAPTER FIFTEEN

GLEN TRIED TO concentrate on his lines, but he kept thinking about Aunt Cassie turning Preston down for a date. At first he'd been glad when Tiff told him about it... He *liked* how they were with just the three of them. Then he'd felt bad, knowing Aunt Cassie must have done it because of him and Tiffany.

"Duh," Tiff had said when he told her. "Of course it was. She might have other reasons, too, but I bet it was mostly us."

So they'd talked about how they could get Aunt Cassie to feel it was okay to go on dates and do the normal stuff she'd do if they weren't living with her. Tiff had suggested talking to Adam, and then she'd done it right in front of Aunt Cassie.

The cameras started rolling and he had to concentrate on playing his part. At least they were doing short scenes and it was easier to remember what he was supposed to say. The script was serious, but once in a while there

was a funny section and he had to stay focused. The acting coach had helped and he
was doing better than in the beginning.

"Cut," called the director.

Sometimes Glen wondered how a movie got
finished when they filmed such little bits at a
time. And they did some of it over and over,
and then again for close-ups.

It was a surprise when two o'clock came. He
wouldn't mind staying longer, but everyone
said there were laws about how many hours
he and Tiff could work during a week.

Adam was still sitting with Aunt Cassie, and
Glen went over with Tiffany.

"I hear you guys are doing well," Adam
said.

Tiff grinned, but Glen hunched his shoulders. "I guess. Is everything okay?"

"I came with good news. If you're interested, there are modeling jobs for each of you
on your week off—the photographers aren't
even asking for go-sees. But I'll understand
if you'd prefer just having fun."

"I'll do them," Tiffany said instantly.

Glen hesitated. When they worked, Aunt
Cassie had to work. "Maybe." He nudged his
sister. "We should talk first."

Aunt Cassie nailed him with a look. "What's up, Glen?"

"You have to come, too, that's what."

"We've talked about that. It's fine."

"I still don't know."

Adam's forehead creased, then he said something into Aunt Cassie's ear and she nodded.

"Glen, how about going with me for a chat?" he asked.

"Uh, okay." They went to an area of the set that wasn't as busy. "Yeah?"

"As your agent, I need you to tell me if something isn't working for you. Do you want to stop modeling? It's okay if you do. And I understand not wanting to discuss it in front of your sister or even your aunt, though I don't want to keep secrets from her."

"I don't mind the modeling. The problem is what I said…about Aunt Cassie having to work so much."

"Except she already told you it's okay, so something else must be bothering you. I'm just guessing, but are you afraid she won't want you to live with her if it's too much trouble?" Adam asked softly. "Because that isn't going to happen."

"Uh…" Glen focused on the ground, misery twisting his stomach. Maybe he was worried about that. He worried about a lot of things, like maybe he was a rotten, no-good kid. Some of his teachers in San Diego had figured he wasn't worth much, and he'd heard one of the social workers saying he'd never amount to anything. The other social worker had gotten mad at her for it, but still, he'd heard it.

"Glen?"

"I'm not sure why she took me and Tiff in the first place," he finally said. "I know she loves us, but if our mom couldn't hack having two kids, why should Aunt Cassie?"

"I don't know why your mother has so many problems and turned out the way she did, but I'm absolutely certain that Cassie wants you. She's a very strong person."

"But she doesn't know—" Glen stopped. It was bad enough that he'd told Elizabeth about calling the social worker and Adam had already said he didn't like keeping secrets.

Adam put a hand on his shoulder. "Glen, I get you're worried there's something so bad, it could change everything. But I don't think it will. In fact, I believe everyone will feel better if you're honest with them."

"That's what Elizabeth said. Sort of."

"My mom is pretty sharp. Maybe you should pay attention."

Glen scrunched his nose. "I know it isn't your job as an agent, but will you be there if I tell Aunt Cassie about it?" He would have asked Elizabeth, but she was working on her novel and it didn't seem fair. Besides, Adam seemed…right.

"We've all become friends, so I'm not just your agent," Adam told him. "I'll be there if it's okay with your aunt."

CASSIE WAS CONCERNED about the intense way Adam and Glen seemed to be talking. She'd known something was still bothering her nephew and hoped he was finally opening up about it.

"What bug is in his brain now?" Tiffany asked, sounding completely normal.

"I don't know. Do you have bugs in your brain?"

Tiff giggled. "Most of the time, but boys are weird and Glen is the weirdest of the weird."

"I used to say stuff like that about your Uncle Devlin."

"Guys are strange."

Glen and Adam were returning and maybe it was her imagination, but they looked like two guys who'd joined shoulders in solidarity.

She ought to know, she'd seen it often enough with her dad and brother.

Adam looked at her. "Can I invite myself to dinner tonight? If you don't mind takeout, I'll bring the food."

With the look of pained anticipation on Glen's face, she could only agree. "That would be nice."

"Great. Cassie, I'll email to see whether my cuisine choices are acceptable." The significant look he gave her suggested the email wouldn't be entirely about food.

Back at the house, Cassie sent the kids upstairs and went straight to her desktop computer. The promised email had already arrived.

Cassie, Glen wants to discuss something with you. It seems to be a big deal for him and he asked if I could be there, too. I said okay if you're all right with it, so I'll make an excuse if you'd prefer I don't come. I'm not sure what it's all about, but don't worry, I know you'll handle it as well as you do everything.
Adam

Her eyes pricked and she blinked rapidly. Adam's kindness to Glen hit her hard enough, but there was also his thoughtfulness in trying to ease her concerns.

She was failing at guarding her heart against him. If he found out, then he'd really feel sorry for her.

Cassie sat back in her chair and stared at the computer screen. For three years, she'd tried to fit into Michael's world where she always came up wanting. It would be just as miserable trying to do the same for Adam, except it would matter more, because he was a better man and deserved more.

At least she had one consolation—her taste had significantly improved when it came to the other half of the human race.

Taking a deep breath, she typed out an answer.

Adam, you're welcome to come. I've known something was bothering Glen. Hopefully he'll feel better once everything is out in the open. Thanks, Cassie

Another email arrived three minutes later.

How about 6:30? I was thinking about Chinese food. I know you told my mom that none of you had allergies, but are there any major dislikes? Also, do you like spicy?

A simple inquiry about food preferences shouldn't make her eyes sting again. She wasn't an emotional crybaby; she was a computer nerd, for heaven's sake. She solved programming programs and made it difficult for hackers to access the websites she'd designed. So she ought to be able to figure out this problem without tears or an aching heart.

Her fingers typed rapidly.

6:30 works. We love Chinese food and it's a great way to sneak veggies into the kids, especially Glen. We like a mix of mild and spicy, just nothing very hot.

Cassie waited a few minutes, but no more messages arrived. After all, there was nothing more to be said.

For the next hour, Cassie worked on the Moonlight Ventures website, which wasn't the best antidote for an aching heart. But no matter what, she wouldn't be able to stop thinking about Adam, so she might as well get it done.

Dinner was strained. Only Tiffany was cheerful and it didn't take long before she spoke up.

"What's wrong with everyone?" she finally demanded.

Cassie realized she should have asked Glen ahead of time if he wanted Tiffany around for his talk. Though they were unusually close, that didn't mean they were always a unit, or should be required to act as if they were.

"Don't be a pain," Glen ordered his sister. "I just asked Adam to come so I could talk with him and Aunt Cassie."

"Without me? What am I, stale bread?" She stuck her bottom lip out in a mock pout.

"Tiff, it's okay for Glen to have things he wants to discuss alone," Cassie warned, keeping her tone light, "and that goes the same for you."

"She can stay," Glen said unexpectedly. "She'll just bug me until I tell her, so I'd rather get it over with now."

"You're doing good at school, have friends and you're acting and modeling," his sister groused. "There can't be anything that awful going on."

"We'll see," Glen muttered.

They went into the living room and some-how Cassie ended up next to Adam on the couch, almost the same as when they'd watched the movie. Tiffany perched on the other arm of the sofa while Glen drew up a straight chair, which told Cassie quite a bit about his frame of mind.

There was a long silence, while Tiffany rolled her eyes and bobbed her foot back and forth.

"Okay," Glen finally mumbled. "Here goes. The thing is, it's my fault we're here."

Confused, Cassie frowned. "What are you talking about?"

"I'm the one who called social services and told them about Mom. If I hadn't, you wouldn't be stuck with us. It just had gotten so bad and I didn't like her boyfriends. A couple were…" He stopped and glanced at his sister. "Some of them were real jerks."

Cassie felt sick at the thought of what could have happened to her niece if Glen hadn't been brave enough to speak up.

"You're a dope," Tiff said immediately. "What's the big deal? Mom is lousy at being a mom and if you hadn't called, then somebody else would have. Maybe me."

"Glen, I don't agree with the dope part," Cassie interjected, "but I'm glad you stopped what was happening. And I don't feel stuck. Far from it. Asking for custody was my choice. I've told you how much I love having you and Tiff here and I hope you'll start to believe me."

"But you have to do all kinds of stuff for us and you had to get rid of your cool car. You won't even take money from our modeling."

Adam leaned forward. "Glen, Cassie and I have talked a lot about you and Tiffany. I'd know if she wasn't happy having you live with her. Nothing could be further from the truth. She loves you both."

His calm, authoritative declaration seemed to help and Cassie couldn't help thinking what a difference a man could make for a boy of Glen's age. Her nephew had never experienced a positive, strong male influence, so it wasn't a surprise that he responded to Adam as the most sympathetic man he'd ever known.

"I still say you're a dope," Tiffany contributed.

Glen glared at his sister. "You can call me that tonight, but I'll put snakes in your bed if you keep it up tomorrow."

"Dope."

"Was there anything else you wanted to talk about?" Cassie asked quickly. Normal squabbling was one thing, but she wanted to be sure Glen had said what he needed to say.

Her nephew gave her a weak grin. "I guess not. Gee, I feel kind of—"

"Like a dope?" Tiffany inquired. She smiled sweetly and Cassie flashed back to when she was a kid herself, giving her brother a hard time. She and Devlin needed to talk more. Their parents may have retreated from the world, but she didn't want to lose her big brother, too.

"You really love this, don't you, Tiff?" Glen asked.

"Come on, dope, let's go watch a movie. Dibs on the squashy chair."

"Not if I get there first." Within seconds, both of them had scrambled up the stairs.

ADAM GAZED AT where Glen had been sitting and shook his head. Poor kid. Some things seemed insurmountable when you were thirteen. To think he'd been carrying his secret around for a year, believing it was a huge deal and that his family would hate him for it.

A soft sound caught his attention and he turned to look at Cassie. Her beautiful eyes were filling with tears, though she was obviously trying to control her emotions.

"Hey, it's going to be okay," he murmured. He tugged her close and held her while she cried. And as bad as he felt for the pain she was suffering, it was wonderful to support her so closely.

After a while, her sobs quieted and she pulled herself upright. "If I'd known how bad things had gotten with Marie, I would have called social services myself. If anyone is to blame, it's me."

"Stop that," Adam admonished. "Glen spent a year feeling ridiculously guilty and you aren't allowed to pick up where he left off."

At that, she laughed, drew a deep breath and let it go. "It was nice of you to share the Bryant family's dramatic performance night."

"Hmm." He pretended to examine her carefully. "You know, I might be able to find you a gig somewhere."

"Maybe at Melodramatics Anonymous."

With sudden clarity, Adam knew exactly what part he wanted Cassie to take, but didn't have a clue whether she'd be interested in a lifetime run.

"I brought a box of my favorite cookies," he said, lifting a grocery bag she hadn't noticed before. "How about indulging before we let the kids eat the rest?"

We?

He restrained a groan. Cassie wouldn't play a "role" in his life, she'd be his life. His father was right. Love didn't come in limited quantities, and the more someone gave, the more they had.

Cassie shook her head. "You're almost as

bad as Tiffany and Glen. I don't know how you stay so trim."

"Shall I sneak them out of the house unseen?"

"No. Maybe a few extra treats are good for the spirit. Would you like yours with coffee?"

"Sure."

While she made the coffee, he put several cookies on a plate. "Shall I take the rest upstairs?"

"Go ahead. Just follow the noise."

It felt like a triumph that she'd let him go on his own, or at least he hoped it meant something. At the top of the stairs, he did as Cassie had suggested, following the noise past two bedrooms to a third one converted into a comfortable teen hangout.

Tiffany put the DVD player on pause when she saw him.

"I brought cookies," Adam said, handing the package to Glen. "What are you watching?"

"Tiff wanted a girlie movie, but we agreed on *Star Trek Beyond*."

"Because sometimes dopes get their way," Tiffany said sagely, "as long as they admit they're dopes."

"Only for tonight," Glen warned.

"Whatever you say, dope."

Adam's heart pumped harder. He'd only just

recognized how much he loved Cassie; now he realized that Tiffany and Glen had also taken up residence in his heart.

Maybe it was his imagination, but he felt as if Isabelle was saying, "*You're* the dope. What took you so long to figure it out?"

Adam would have found it amusing if he had more confidence in the eventual outcome with Cassie. How many times had she pointed out their differences?

"See you," he told the kids and they waved, engrossed once again in the *Star Trek* world and the battle between good and evil.

"Uh, thanks for the cookies," Glen said absently, already munching one.

Adam trotted down to the living room where Cassie had the plate of cookies and cups of coffee waiting. He sat next to her and wished they could put on a movie while he held her and they contemplated the marvelous possibilities of a future together.

"Tiffany says she let Glen put on the movie he wanted because dopes get their way. I was tempted to remind her that men are often dopes, but then she added that it was only because he'd *admitted* to the condition. So I think she's safe."

Cassie laughed. "That's Tiff." She leaned

back, looking exhausted. "I feel like a limp washrag now that the adrenaline has run out."

"Understandable." Adam wanted to confess how much he loved her, and ask if she could possibly love him for the rest of forever, but she was tired and had gone through an emotional ringer with her nephew. Besides, he needed a better lead-up to eternal declarations of devotion. After all, he'd never actually courted Cassie, asked her on a date, sent flowers or… Well, he'd kissed her twice.

"This was good," Adam said, finishing his coffee and last bite of cookie, "but you've had a long day. I'm going to leave so you can crawl into bed or work on your computer or do whatever helps you recharge."

"Thanks for coming."

"Anytime. I mean that."

Cassie's eyes seemed puzzled at the intent way he'd spoken, but she just smiled and walked him to the door.

Back in his sedan, Adam studied the house and saw a crack of light at the window next to the door. Was Cassie watching him leave?

Adam waved and the curtain dropped into place.

Feeling more hopeful, he started the car and left. He needed a plan.

CASSIE WAS EMBARRASSED that Adam must have seen her at the window. Not that there was something wrong with it. A person had every right to look out and see if all was well. It didn't have to mean anything. Adam was sensible. Unlike her, he probably didn't imagine something out of nothing in seconds.

Tired as she was, she wasn't sure she'd be able to sleep, so she went into her office. It was her safe place, the spot where she was needed and valued for her skills and creativity. Yet despite the framed fantasy art pieces on the walls, it also seemed sterile and lonely... or perhaps not, provided it wasn't a substitute for real living, she reminded herself.

Stop.

Cassie shook her head to clear the thought. She was glad Tiff and Glen were part of her life for many reasons, one of them being they'd forced her to become more connected to other people. That was best, even if it meant an aching heart over Adam.

CHAPTER SIXTEEN

CASSIE SAT AND watched as the cameraman ensured the Space Needle would be in the background of the scene being shot. She'd decided not to bring her computer that day but to just enjoy the pleasure of fresh air and open space.

It was a luxury she could afford because she'd accepted Shane Wolcott's offer to do consulting work for his game company. He'd promised she wouldn't be disappointed by his offer and he was right. The money was eye-popping and she still wasn't entirely sure how she was supposed to earn it, but in the meantime she was going to enjoy being in demand.

Adam's voice startled her. "How's it going?"

She glanced up at him. "To be honest, I don't know enough about moviemaking to tell."

Why did he keep showing up? It couldn't be that he had nothing else to do; from her discussions with the agency partners regarding the website, it was clear that Moonlight Ventures was getting plenty of business. But she'd seen Adam every single day since Glen had revealed his call to social services.

Adam pulled a chair up and sat next to her. "I couldn't resist coming over on a break. It isn't that far. Glad to see me?" he asked.

It was an odd question that made her stomach turn over. She could almost believe it was personal, and that scared her as much as it gave her hope.

"Of course," she lied, or it was sort of a lie. "You're always welcome, as I'm sure you know."

"That's good."

She was glad to see him, yet it also hurt. But since Adam was a semipermanent fixture in her life as long as he was the twins' agent, she'd better get used to mixed emotions.

"Did you get my email?" she asked. "I put the website up last night."

"Yeah, it looks terrific. Say, my folks told me they're taking the kids to the Gingko Petrified Forest on Saturday. Are you going with them?"

She shook her head. "I have an appointment in the morning. A new fashion house in Italy is interested in me designing their website."

"That's great. Then how about early afternoon, around one? There's something I want to discuss."

"Can't we talk here?"

"I'd rather do it then, if you don't mind?"

"It's fine with me. I just thought you'd prefer time off from being an agent." She smiled. "Don't you guys get any free weekends?"

A strange expression crossed Adam's face. "Yes, of course. Unless a problem crops up."

That made sense, though she couldn't imagine what sort of business he wanted to discuss, unless he was hoping to get his relationship with her and the twins onto a more strictly professional foundation.

Was that the reason he stayed—to watch the scene being filmed?

It was a challenging scene for the kids, because their characters' mother was trying to talk with them about her choice to remain a cop, even after their father's death in the line of duty. The emotional range went from fear and frustration to love and support.

"No doubt I'm biased," Adam murmured during a break, "but I think Tiffany and Glen are doing great. Did you work with them on it?"

She shook her head. "I don't know anything about acting, though we talked about how they'd feel if something like this happened to them. The acting coach suggested it since playing this kind of part can get to their emotions. Everyone has been nice and they seem to be careful about not doing anything that might disturb the kids."

"Good. I don't want any client to work for jerks, but I admit to being extra protective of Glen and Tiff. I also don't want you in a situation where you have to leap in and protect them."

He kept saying that sort of thing, as if he cared about her and the kids more than the average client. It was really messing with her emotions.

"That's nice," she tried to respond lightly.

"You understand," he added with a wink, "it's mostly, but not entirely, for your sake. Knowing what a fierce mother bear you are, I'd probably have to hire a defense lawyer after you got finished with them."

His glance was admiring and full of warmth. Cassie reminded herself that his sincere good-guy looks had been part of his stock-in-trade. Advertisers had known that other men could see him as a buddy and women would envision him as the hero of their dreams who'd never let them down. Makers of everything from jeans to cars to wine had wanted his face to enhance and sell merchandise.

"Did you ever have to model for a product you thought was terrible?" she asked curiously.

"I turned down jobs for something I didn't like, or if I had questions about the company's dealings."

"That's nice to know."

His eyebrows rose. "What brought that up?"

"I was just thinking that advertisers must have loved the sincerity you project."

Adam's brow furrowed. "Cassie, I've never put on an act with you, and I never will. Everything should always be honest between us."

"I'm glad." Yet she squirmed, knowing if she was really honest with Adam, she would have to admit that she'd stupidly fallen head-over-heels-in-love with the guy. Except she wasn't about to reveal her foolishness to anyone, and especially not to him.

Unable to meet his gaze for more than a few seconds for fear of betraying herself, she turned back to where cameras were about ready to roll again.

After a few minutes, she saw Adam glance at his watch, sigh and stand. Bending, he kissed her quickly on her forehead. "Wish I could stay," he whispered, "but I've got an appointment."

She nodded, her throat so tight she was nearly choking.

ADAM DROVE BACK to the agency. He'd stayed longer than he'd originally intended, but how did a man court a woman like Cassie? She put up so many barriers he didn't know where else to start.

Once, she'd obviously expected to get married and have everything that became possible when two people loved each other. He couldn't believe she'd abandoned the idea altogether, yet she'd turned Preston Davis down—a successful and a genuinely nice guy. Plenty of women would be thrilled to attract his interest.

Adam pulled into the Moonlight Ventures parking lot and got out, only to lean against his sedan and gaze toward Lake Washington.

Okay, Cassie said she wanted to keep things stable for Tiff and Glen. Maybe he could suggest that he'd make a good partner because they were both committed to giving the twins a good life.

As soon as the idea formed, he dismissed it. He wanted a marriage based on what they felt for each other. Besides, Cassie was too bright to think it was a good basis for marriage.

All the same, he was trying to show he cared about Tiffany and Glen, because even if Cassie wouldn't marry a guy just for them, he was equally certain she wouldn't tolerate one who didn't have their best interests at heart.

Sighing, Adam went inside for his appointment with a potential client. The little girl was engaging and the mother was a single mom who seemed sensible. He decided to offer them a representation agreement. Since Rachel had started full time at the agency, he would be able to transfer some clients to her, which would give him more time for the rest of his client list…hopefully also for a honeymoon and starting a whole new life.

"You obviously have something on your mind," Nicole observed as they chatted at the end of the afternoon. "I can't quite put my finger on it, but something is different."

"You're right, but it isn't a subject I can discuss now."

She looked at him speculatively and Adam wondered if she suspected. After all, she was in love herself and probably had her radar out for romance. Still, the first person he wanted to declare himself to was Cassie, so he simply showed Nicole the file for the agency's new client.

Saturday couldn't come soon enough.

It was the day he'd decided to make sure Cassie knew his intentions toward her had nothing to do with agency business.

ELIZABETH STOOD BY the car, running over her mental list. Lunch was in the cooler, plenty of things to drink had been loaded along with snacks, and she had a sunhat, sunscreen and a cloth to put on the picnic table. It seemed complete.

Her husband's hand slipped into hers.

"I'm not much with words," he said, "but I want you to know I'm glad you pushed me to come to Seattle."

"Are you still unhappy Adam didn't become a lawyer?" she asked. Lately they'd been more open with the subjects they discussed.

Dermott sighed heavily. "I hung on to the dream far too long. I should have been satisfied Adam was achieving what he wanted. He's tried to tell me, over and over, but I have a thick skull. I'm still worried about Sophie, though."

"I understand, but she's a good mom. Her business is flourishing and it appeals to her artistic side. I don't want to put pressure on her or our grandchildren. There shouldn't be any 'why doesn't she become a doctor' or 'maybe he should be a lawyer.' Passion for something needs to come from inside, not from us."

His smile turned wry. "I'll try to restrain myself."

Elizabeth breathed a little easier. Now that Dermott was accepting Adam's choices better, she'd been afraid he'd lay a double helping of his ambition onto Sophie. Not that she was certain their daughter was living up to her potential. Sophie was intelligent and talented, but she'd had too much responsibility early in life.

"What's the matter?" her husband asked.

"I'm torn. I love my grandchildren, but Sophie might not have become a mother so young if she hadn't needed to deal with my illness when she was still a kid."

"It isn't your fault and no one knows what might have happened. Sophie is happy and I suppose that's the most any parent can hope for their child."

He pulled her close and Elizabeth sighed. It felt the same as when they'd first fallen in love.

"We'd better go," she said, leaning her head back and smiling at him. "Glen and Tiffany will be waiting."

"Yep." He grinned. "I hope you packed a lot of food."

"Naturally."

Elizabeth suddenly realized she didn't feel old any longer. Even if she never got published, it was good to be seriously writing and dreaming about the future. In Albuquerque, she'd mostly thought about how she could get Dermott doing something besides just sitting around, while *she* could have been the one looking for something meaningful to do.

Life had plenty of possibilities ahead.

CASSIE HUGGED ELIZABETH when the Wildings arrived and took a chance on hugging Dermott as well, who gruffly returned the embrace.

"Are you sure you can't go with us?" he asked. "We'd enjoy your company."

"Thanks, but I've got a Skype meeting with a client," she explained. "He's in Italy and this is the only time he has for us to talk."

She waved as the car drove down the quiet residential street and returned to her office, waiting for the scheduled meeting time.

Not long ago she would have been dreaming about a row of windows looking into a forest or over a lake, secluded and private. She might not have run from life physically, but she'd tried to do it every other way. There was no denying that Adam was right about that.

At 8:00 a.m. she made the connection with her potential client. It was a productive half hour and when she signed off, it was nice knowing she now had her first international contract. Once she would have avoided doing a website for a fashion house, thinking it was far outside her area of expertise, but it didn't worry her any longer.

Working hard, she finished the projects she'd set for herself just in time to answer Adam's knock at the front door.

"Hi," she said brightly, as if her heart wasn't beating so hard it hurt. "Want to talk on the deck?"

"Sure."

She'd put a pitcher of iced tea on the picnic table and Adam absently poured them each a tumbler before pulling her down to sit with him on the wicker love seat.

"There are some things I've been wanting to tell you," he said softly.

She smiled and nodded, then was astounded when he began talking about his fiancée and how hard it had been to let go, feeling almost as if doing so would negate how much he'd loved Isabelle.

Cassie didn't know what to think, especially when Adam put his glass down and threaded their fingers together.

"You know how much I appreciate what you said about remembering love," he murmured. "But I've since realized that part of me didn't want to risk getting hurt again. I thought I was ready to move on, but I really hadn't dealt with those feelings yet."

Cassie wasn't sure if Adam was telling her as a gentle way of letting her down, or if there was another reason. After all, she'd swear he didn't know how she felt about him. "I understand." She tried to keep her voice steady.

"Anyway, I'm also wondering if that's part of your problem, too?"

The bald question startled her. "What do you mean?"

"You got hurt, and from what I can tell, you haven't gotten involved with anyone since then. Not even casual dating, of which I admit to doing my share."

"I, um…don't think I want to discuss this."

Adam looked at her intently, his eyes more serious than she'd ever seen them. "I have to talk about it, Cassie, because I'm in love with you, and I'm praying you love me, too. I want us to have a future together and we need to banish any ghosts that could get in the way."

Cassie stared, feeling as if her brain had frozen. She'd hoped and done her share of daydreaming, but a declaration of forever was almost beyond comprehension.

"Cassie?" Adam prompted. "I just told you I love you. Is there any chance that you feel the same in return?"

She drew a shuddering breath, telling herself to be sensible. Even supposing he truly loved her, could they make a life together work?

"Adam, think about it," she finally managed to say. "You're a peacock and I'm an everyday robin. Two such different birds might become friends, but they can't make anything else work."

Proud of herself for her steadiness, Cassie didn't know what she hoped for next.

ADAM RECOGNIZED THE panic in Cassie's eyes and understood it thoroughly. Loving someone was a terrible risk.

"In the first place, I'm just a guy, in love with a very special woman," he said. "If things had gone a little different, I might be an accountant or work in a bank. I might even have gotten my father to start that construction company he dreamed about. Becoming a model just happened and now I'm a talent agent."

"Maybe it just happened, but women go breathless when they see you, while I couldn't even satisfy an average guy at a corporation."

"Your ex was a fool. I think he recognized how special you are and tried to drag you down with him because he couldn't deal with having a woman he didn't deserve," Adam said, annoyed. "But I don't want you to change."

"Except you're Adam Wilding, international model. Your picture is still taped on the doors of half the girls' lockers at Tiffany's school. I'm just a computer geek."

"I can't let you compare those things as if one is wonderful and the other lacking. Modeling was a job, creating websites is a job. We're two people who are fortunate to have met and connected."

Adam was sure now that Cassie loved him, but was afraid to say so. Why else would she come up with excuses, instead of saying *I don't love you*, the one thing that would send him away?

"I know you wouldn't marry me just for the twins," he continued, "but I want to help raise them and be the best dad-like uncle possible.

I'm going to ask one of my colleagues to be their agent though, because it's no longer possible for me to be objective. Even if I didn't care about Tiff and Glen, no man could be objective when it comes to the woman he loves and the children she holds in her heart."

TEARS STUNG CASSIE'S EYES. "Your world is high fashion and sophisticated people. What do I know about either one?"

Adam chuckled. "In the first place, sophistication isn't all it's cracked up to be, and I'm uncomfortable in high fashion clothes. I don't need you to adorn my professional world like a trophy wife, though in my opinion, you'd fit anywhere. What I want is a wife to love and make a life together."

His sincerity was impossible to miss. He was strong and confident and it was his strength reaching out, not his weakness.

"It still seems as if we come from such different worlds," she said.

"Not that different." He leaned closer. "I'm proud to be the son of a construction worker and I'd rather drink iced tea with you than go to a cocktail party. Since you're making excuses, can I assume it isn't because you don't love me?"

Cassie's face went hot. "Assume anything you want."

"Good, then I'm going to assume the best. Look, Cassie, I know we'd have to make compromises, but that's true whenever two people get married. It's part of making a relationship work. There are lots of things we need to discuss, such as having children. Is parenting Tiffany and Glen as much as you want to take on, or would you like to add to our family?"

"I'd want more children...if..."

"That suits me as well. Now, I can't pretend I want to live in the mountains in isolation, but I'm willing to buy a house up there or at the beach so we can escape on weekends and vacations. That's a bribe, by the way. We should also get a bigger place, but not in the city if that's what you want," Adam said quickly. "I can compromise on that."

Cassie cleared her throat. "I don't want to run away any longer. You were right. It's become a family trait and I don't want to pass it on."

"Then we'll get a cabin where we can build good memories with our family, and a home that's close enough to take advantage of the city, but doesn't have the traffic problems."

It was a wonderful portrait he was building, and she wanted to believe in it.

"You make it sound terrific, but—"

"I'm not pretending there aren't risks or pitfalls ahead," he interrupted, almost sounding desperate.

Desperate?

To love her and have a life together?

Hope began to curl inside Cassie's heart and she smiled encouragingly. "Yes?"

"Well, that's why marriage vows are for better or worse. We'll have our share of problems. For one, we'll be an instant family. Tiffany and Glen had a rough start in life and they'll have issues that resurface. We'll do our best to help them, along with our other kids, and we'll make mistakes. That's life."

"Anything else?" she asked in a wry tone.

"Well, I won't claim to be a tough guy. Nobody is eager for pain—I already know what can happen when you love someone."

Cassie gulped as she thought of Isabelle. What if she lost Adam the same way?

"Hey." He pulled her close and kept talking. "I'm not trying to scare you. But if we let go of each other, we'll hurt anyway, so we might as well take the risk together."

Being held so tight made her feel as if she'd

come home and was flying to the moon, all at the same time. Then she laughed, because under her ear, his cell phone was vibrating.

"Ignore it," he said.

"No." Cassie pulled back and stood. "I need a minute anyway."

She would have headed for her office, but that would seem too much like she running to a safe lair, so she went into the kitchen, where it was more about waking up and facing reality.

She stood and thought about Adam's proposal. The gulf between their worlds seemed vast, but maybe that was just surface stuff, because the things they valued were the same. He was honest, practical, hardworking, strong, sincere and loving. Those were the things that mattered.

ADAM LISTENED TO his father explain that Tiffany had tripped and banged herself up a little.

"We're taking her to the emergency room," Dermott explained, "but it's just as a precaution since she seems okay. Aside from everything else, she's worried how this will affect filming. That's why she wanted me to call you first." A chuckle came over the line. "Glen just told her not to be such a drama queen."

"Okay, Dad. Tell her not to be upset. We'll figure everything out. You don't need to call Cassie. I'll talk to her."

"Thanks, son."

Adam got the name of the hospital from his father, thanked him and got off to hurry inside the house. He found Cassie in the kitchen and when she turned at the sound of his footsteps, her smile made his heart leap.

"I hate to interrupt your thoughts," he said, returning her smile. "But that was my dad. He said Tiffany tripped. She isn't badly hurt, though they're taking her to the ER as a precaution. We can head over there right now. Mostly Tiff is worried about the movie and Glen is calling her a drama queen."

Humor glinted in Cassie's beautiful, changeable eyes. "In other words, they're acting like themselves, which tells me she's okay."

"Right. Now, shall we go take care of our kids?" he asked, holding his breath as he held out his hand.

Her shoulders straightened and she joined fingers with his. "You bet." Then she gave him a short sweet kiss that sent his senses reeling. "By the way," she said, "I guess it's time I told you outright. I love you, Adam Wilding, with all my heart."

"Great to hear it," he replied, his heart thumping hard with joy. "The feeling is completely mutual."

* * * * *

Other Emerald City romances from Callie Endicott are available today from www.Harlequin.com!

Get 4 FREE REWARDS!

We'll send you 2 FREE Books
plus 2 FREE Mystery Gifts.

Love Inspired® books feature contemporary inspirational romances with Christian characters facing the challenges of life and love.

FREE Value Over **$20**

Get 4 FREE REWARDS!

We'll send you 2 FREE Books plus 2 FREE Mystery Gifts.

Love Inspired® Suspense books feature Christian characters facing challenges to their faith... and lives.

FREE
Value Over
$20

HOME *on the* RANCH

YES! Please send me the **Home on the Ranch Collection** in Larger Print. This collection begins with 3 FREE books and 2 FREE gifts in the first shipment. Along with my 3 free books, I'll also get the next 4 books from the Home on the Ranch Collection, in LARGER PRINT, which I may either return and owe nothing, or keep for the low price of $5.24 U.S./ $5.89 CDN each plus $2.99 for shipping and handling per shipment*. If I decide to continue, about once a month for 8 months I will get 6 or 7 more books, but will only need to pay for 4. That means 2 or 3 books in every shipment will be FREE! If I decide to keep the entire collection, I'll have paid for only 32 books because 19 books are FREE! I understand that accepting the 3 free books and gifts places me under no obligation to buy anything. I can always return a shipment and cancel at any time. My free books and gifts are mine to keep no matter what I decide.

268 HCN 3760 468 HCN 3760

Name	(PLEASE PRINT)	
Address		Apt. #
City	State/Prov.	Zip/Postal Code

Signature (if under 18, a parent or guardian must sign)

Mail to the **Reader Service**:
IN U.S.A.: P.O. Box 1867, Buffalo, NY. 14240-1867
IN CANADA: P.O. Box 609, Fort Erie, Ontario L2A 5X3

* Terms and prices subject to change without notice. Prices do not include applicable taxes. Sales tax applicable in NY. Canadian residents will be charged applicable taxes. This offer is limited to one order per household. All orders subject to approval. Credit or debit balances in a customer's account(s) may be offset by any other outstanding balance owed by or to the customer. Please allow 3 to 4 weeks for delivery. Offer available while quantities last. Offer not available to Quebec residents.

Your Privacy—The Reader Service is committed to protecting your privacy. Our Privacy Policy is available online at www.ReaderService.com or upon request from the Reader Service.

We make a portion of our mailing list available to reputable third parties that offer products we believe may interest you. If you prefer that we not exchange your name with third parties, or if you wish to clarify or modify your communication preferences, please visit us at www.ReaderService.com/consumerschoice or write to us at Reader Service Preference Service, P.O. Box 9062, Buffalo, NY. 14240-9062. Include your complete name and address.

Get 4 FREE REWARDS!

We'll send you 2 FREE Books plus 2 FREE Mystery Gifts.

FREE Value Over **$20**

Both the **Romance** and **Suspense** collections feature compelling novels written by many of today's best-selling authors.

YES! Please send me 2 FREE novels from the Essential Romance or Essential Suspense Collection and my 2 FREE gifts (gifts are worth about $10 retail). After receiving them, if I don't wish to receive any more books, I can return the shipping statement marked "cancel." If I don't cancel, I will receive 4 brand-new novels every month and be billed just $6.74 each in the U.S. or $7.24 each in Canada. That's a savings of at least 16% off the cover price. It's quite a bargain! Shipping and handling is just 50¢ per book in the U.S. and 75¢ per book in Canada*. I understand that accepting the 2 free books and gifts places me under no obligation to buy anything. I can always return a shipment and cancel at any time. The free books and gifts are mine to keep no matter what I decide.

Choose one: ☐ **Essential Romance**   ☐ **Essential Suspense**
                    (194/394 MDN GMY7)   (191/391 MDN GMY7)

Name (please print)

Address   Apt. #

City   State/Province   Zip/Postal Code

Mail to the **Reader Service:**
IN U.S.A.: P.O. Box 1341, Buffalo, NY 14240-8531
IN CANADA: P.O. Box 603, Fort Erie, Ontario L2A 5X3

Want to try two free books from another series! Call 1-800-873-8635 or visit www.ReaderService.com.

*Terms and prices subject to change without notice. Prices do not include applicable taxes. Sales tax applicable in NY. Canadian residents will be charged applicable taxes. Offer not valid in Quebec. This offer is limited to one order per household. Books received may not be as shown. Not valid for current subscribers to the Essential Romance or Essential Suspense Collection. All orders subject to approval. Credit or debit balances in a customer's account(s) may be offset by any other outstanding balance owed by or to the customer. Please allow 4 to 6 weeks for delivery. Offer available while quantities last.

Your Privacy—The Reader Service is committed to protecting your privacy. Our Privacy Policy is available online at www.ReaderService.com or upon request from the Reader Service. We make a portion of our mailing list available to reputable third parties that offer products we believe may interest you. If you prefer that we not exchange your name with third parties, or if you wish to clarify or modify your communication preferences, please visit us at www.ReaderService.com/consumerchoice or write to us at Reader Service Preference Service, P.O. Box 9062, Buffalo, NY 14240-9062. Include your complete name and address.

STRS18